HYDRO

G.H. LUSBY

For Emma

CHAPTER 1

We bury Isabella, and the dust rises from her grave like an escaping spirit.

Then I too try to escape, slipping away and stumbling through the banyan grove, down to the sacred river.

There, the pilgrims are burning their dead.

Behind me, I hear shouts as the other mourners notice my absence and start the pursuit. They follow through the trees, but their voices trail off in the direction of the residence. They'd never come down here. No Englishman comes down to the riverbank when the fires are lit.

The smell gets in one's clothes.

I keep a respectful distance, hovering at the tree line, not daring to emerge onto the broad rocky slope that descends to the water's edge. I don't want to be disturbed in my grief, or disturb the pilgrims in theirs.

I feel disconnected from the world, as though staring at it through a dusty window. My heart beats somewhere in my rib cage, muffled by a thick layer of aspic jelly.

Hoisting my trouser legs, I sit on a rock in the overarching shade of an ancient banyan and watch the men (for they are all men) busy themselves with sticks and bundles of dry scrub. Even at a distance, I can make out the swaddled body on its pyre, supported by a lattice of thicker logs, doll-like and garlanded with chrysanthemums. The men take longer branches and stack them, bivouac-like, around the corpse, padding the frame with thick faggots of kindling.

I admire their dispassionate, practised industry and I wonder, with the entitlement and naivety of the colonial, if they feel as I do.

Further down the shoreline, a pyre from an earlier cere-mony is reaching its final stages of collapse. It could be a campfire, it's so small. I wonder if it ever contained a human body. Perhaps a child? Even further down the riverbank, almost lost in the haze of smoke, a few men are raking the last embers and ashes of yet another into the river. Black and grey remnants fizz in the sluggish water, sending up shim-mering clouds of steam to merge with the smoke.

On the opposite bank, squatting groups of women wash clothes, rolling and slapping red, blue and white fabric against the rocks. Children and dogs play in and out of the water to keep cool.

Isabella is in a hole in the neat, meagre churchyard of St Joseph's, just behind me through the trees. Natives are likely shovelling dirt onto her as I sit here. Her coffin scraped and bumped as we lowered her into the dry pit. The curate, a dipsomaniac Welshman, had to lift his voice during the committal against the cicadas. His cassock was sweat-soaked and his bald head was red in the afternoon sun.

My friends stood around me, almost in a protective cordon, trying not to swipe away the flies that buzzed and zipped around their faces. All wore expressions of stoic blankness.

I wonder how many of them blame me for her death.

I wonder how many of them are secretly employed by my father.

THE MEN FINISH BUILDING THE PYRE AND ONE OF THEM takes a long, straggling torch of bundled grasses and lights it. Then he busies himself around the pile of wood, pushing the flames into its cage, seeding orange flowers. The other men stand back and watch as the whole thing catches and crackles into life. Billowing clouds rise and extend like outstretched arms across the broad river towards the women on the opposite bank.

A pariah dog, denuded by mange, comes hobbling up, tongue lolling, looking for food. Its scrawny legs can barely support a body that's all ribs and swollen teats. I flap at it to go away and it looks at me with wild, blank eyes. Then it limps off in the direction of the mounds of ashes that litter the shoreline. I wonder with a shudder what morsels it will find there.

Isabella's eulogy in the sweltering clapboard church was brief and heavily censored. The congregation didn't want to know the details of her life. In their minds, all of it was incidental to the moment she met me and caused my disgrace.

I suspect they know more than they let on, anyway. I have found since arriving in India that in the boredom of the tropics, the true economy is gossip, the currency spite.

There were words of condolence, of course; hollow, comforting platitudes. But I shrugged them off, all of them.

When I broke for the trees, leaving them all staring after me, they likely thought I'd gone mad. I knew they smirked and glanced at each other.

India was not where she would want to be remembered. She hated it, and it hated her back. Rumour pursued us from

London, travelling far and fast. There was no escape, not even half a world away.

The wind changes and smoke from the pyre and its hissing, rendering cargo wafts like a spectre towards me. My eyes water and the scented, fatty smoke clogs the back of my throat with bitter residue. I pull her handkerchief to smother my mouth and I breathe in her perfume, mingled with the taste of the burning cadaver. Through my tears as I stand, I see the group of men around the fire watching me, their faces unreadable.

I stumble over the rocks back into the trees.

The broiling sun is setting, ripened red by the smoke haze.

This was my doing. I could have saved her. I could have turned her from herself. I could have defended her, done something to stop the tragic flow of events. I had thought we could escape it all by coming here, but the accusations followed and pinned us like butterflies to be gawped at.

I am certain, at this moment, that half the people I count as friends here are in the employ of my father. I feel his talons stretching out across the surface of the earth towards me, drawing me back to set me right, to put me back on the track he has built for me.

I am sure when he catches news of my wife's death, if it hasn't already coursed its way through the telegraph wires, he will give one of those short, humourless barking laughs of his.

I draw myself up and swear that I will not let myself be ground down by his machinations.

I failed Isabella but I will not fail myself.

I hear a branch snap behind me.

Simpson emerges, irritated, hunting. When he locates his quarry, a look of sympathy smears across his face.

"John, what are you doing down here, old boy? Are you alright? Come on back to the residence, there's a good chap."

It's over.

"We should have a chat about you going home. There's nothing for you here now."

I consider having it out with him, accusing him, but there is no point. There will be another, and another, until I am brought home to face my father, and my appalling inheritance.

Knowing it's useless, I hang my head and set off back with him.

Then I glance behind me.

Down by the river, the pyre, hollowed out, falls in on itself, sending a swarm of sparks spiralling into the sky like fireflies.

I watch them spin and fly, and for a moment I am with them, ascending, weightless.

Then Simpson calls me.

I'm pulled back.

CHAPTER 2

The morning I arrive in London, I go straight to ask Isabella's mother for her forgiveness.

We'd met once before, while Isabella and I were courting, and before either of them had found out exactly whose son I was. I haven't seen Mrs Smith since. She was not privy to our elopement.

I have the address to her house, which stands on a side street in the one respectable sliver of Bermondsey. After disembarking from the Southampton train at Waterloo, I take steps to avoid being followed, sending my bags on to my own house in Bloomsbury. Then I hail a Hansom and take the quick ride southeast.

London hasn't changed, but I have. There is a surge of returning memories. The scale and noise of the capital overwhelms me and I sit back in the clattering cab, peeking out at the world through the mud-spattered window. I'm as vulnerable as a peeled prawn before the whirl of towering stone walls and throngs of drab, threatening people. Compared to India, London is monochrome. All colour has been leached from the city and it's been veiled in mist.

We finally arrive at our destination just off Monnow Road, on a small, neat terrace of stone-fronted houses. I pay the driver and stand shivering and exposed in the cold, wet air. The damp seeps beneath the folds of my clothes. Children play in the street. Thick-armed women defend their doorsteps, gossiping with their neighbours and staring at me.

Number seventeen has a freshly painted door, in stark contrast to the generally tatty appearance of the rest of the street. Mrs Smith is respectable working class and wants everyone to know it.

I take a breath and knock.

There is a twitch at the window as the net curtains stir. Then, after a moment, the door opens to reveal a little thin-lipped woman. Her face is pulled tight by a screwed-down bun in her grey hair. She squints out through round glasses, looking me up and down. Then, with sudden recognition, she raises her hand to her mouth and cries, backing into the shadows.

I follow her without waiting for an invitation, stepping over the threshold and taking off my hat.

"Mrs Smith. May I come in?"

I close the door behind me, glad to be out of sight.

"I'm so sorry. I've come straight from the station to see you."

Mrs Smith, trembling, eyes filling, suddenly breaks into racking sobs and hides her face in her hands. Unsure of what to do, I move to place a comforting hand on her shoulder. To my surprise, she readily accepts it and then throws her arms around me. I hold her frail body against mine, her face pressed into my chest as she cries, saying again and again, "My poor little girl."

Finally, she releases me and I'm free to wipe tears from my own eyes with the back of my sleeve.

"I'm so sorry, Sir," she says, "you must be tired after your long journey. Can I make you a cup of tea?"

We sit in her cramped parlour. It has two elderly armchairs draped with antimacassars. A cheap print of the Queen hangs on one wall. Other little pictures in frames litter the room, cramming the side tables and the bureau, stuffing the place with memories. I wonder how a family of five can have lived in such a small house.

The afternoon light filters in through heavy net curtains at the window. On the windowsill sits a huge bowl of glistening waxed fruit.

A large part of the room is given over to an ornate gilded bird cage containing a noisy mynah bird.

She goes to make tea and I look at the pictures. They are all of family, sons, daughters. I spy a portrait of Isabella that I had commissioned, a miniature as a keepsake for her mother, to remember her by while we were away. It seems a slightly cruel gift in retrospect.

I can barely stand to look at it.

The bird whistles.

I go to the window and edge back the net curtain. I don't seem to have been followed. It's always a possibility with my father.

She re-enters with a tray on which judder two china cups on saucers, the tea swaying dangerously. I take it from her with a smile and ask her to sit.

"I've got biscuits?" she says. "You must be hungry."

"Thank you, Mrs Smith, I'm fine."

"Don't you mind Nelson," she says, "he's excited because we don't get many visitors, do we, my darling?" She runs her fingers over the bars, plucking them like a harp.

Then she lowers herself into the chair and smooths down her dress, preparing for the worst.

Over the whistles and clattering as Nelson flaps from

perch to perch, we talk about the news and finally settle on Isabella.

"I got your telegram," she says. "The rest of the street was agog. No one here had ever got one. Of course, when I read the news..."

I sip my hot tea. I've rehearsed this many times on the journey home, but still, the words come out hard and sharp. "I'm sorry that you had to find out that way, but I felt you needed to know as soon as possible."

She slurps her tea, the steam misting her glasses for a second.

"Can you... can you tell me what happened to her?"

The question plunges my stomach down to my feet. I know that I will have to lie, that's partly why I've come here.

"She was taken badly. There are many diseases in India, Mrs Smith. They seem to thrive in the heat. She wasn't ill for long. There was a doctor, an Englishman. She had the best care while it lasted."

"Did she suffer?"

"A little, but not for long. She had a fever. I don't know how much of it she would have truly felt. She slept a lot."

"That's a mercy," she says. "Were you with her when she... passed?"

"Yes." That, at least, is true.

She bites her lip and dabs her eyes with an embroidered handkerchief.

"I wanted to save her," I say. "I tried, but in the end, the place was too much for her. I came here to ask for your forgiveness. We should never have gone. It was my doing. I'm very sorry, Mrs Smith. I'm so sorry."

I feel hot tears running down my face and my voice breaks.

"If it hadn't been for me..."

She hands me a clean handkerchief and puts a gnarled hand on my knee.

It tightens beyond the point of comfort.

"Yes," she says, biting out the words, "if it hadn't been for you, she would have still been here with me. But you came along, didn't you, with your money and your promises, and you took her from me. You used her. You used her to get back at your father."

I look up in shock at hearing my own thoughts issue through her puckered mouth. My heart goes cold and chilled blood pumps into my limbs. I can't argue with the truth.

"She would have been here now, on the same street she'd been raised on, looking after me. But you took her, Mr Edgeland, you took my daughter away from me."

"I wish... I wish I could have saved her."

"Yes, I'm sure you do."

She releases me and pats my sleeve.

I feel my rotten core of guilt. I want to confess everything, how Isabella really died, but I know that would break her heart.

Then the old lady stands and takes down a daguerreotype in a frame from the side table. It's of a man in uniform.

"My husband, Bill. He died in Africa, you know, fighting the Zulus in seventy-nine. They gave him a medal after he died. Stood alone surrounded by them, defending a poor injured boy on a scrap of dirt somewhere. Noble self-sacrifice, they said. A hero."

"I'm sorry, Mrs Smith," I say, for what feels like the eighth time.

The mynah bird flaps and whistles at the bars of its cage.

She eases herself back into her chair and looks at me over the rims of her glasses. "The world is full of dead heroes, Mr Edgeland. Battlefields are full of them. It takes a real man to face his responsibilities. To make his mistakes, to accept them and carry on with life and try to be a better man than he has been. My husband didn't come back from Africa. My daughter didn't come back from India, Mr Edgeland, but you did. Don't waste the life you've been given."

I CURL UP INSIDE WITH GUILT AND SHAME.

I want to make this right, but know that I can't.

I should see her right financially at least, but to raise that now feels cruel, and vulgar. As if I am trying to buy her off.

On the surface of the storm, we chat about India and I tell her about our sea voyage there, how Isabella marvelled at her first sight of Bombay, the rigours of the heat and our travels around the country. I tell her about the position I took, under an assumed name, with a newspaper. How we had native servants.

She listens, her eyes holding me, neither impressed nor angry anymore. Just listening.

I wonder how to broach the subject of money.

"And what are your plans now?" she says.

I look out of the window. Through the netting, I can see children outside, running around like ghosts, chasing each other. Their cries are muffled by the glass.

"I don't know."

"Will you be going back into the family business?" she asks.

That is the question I knew I would have to answer on my return. I no more know the answer now than when I was mulling it over in my cabin, all the way from Bombay.

"We shall see," I say.

"I'm sure they'll be glad to see you when you return. I've read that your father is not a well man these days."

I doubt that anyone in my family will be glad to see me.

It's time to ask the question.

"Are you taken care of? Do you for need anything?"

She sits back, stiff and proud. "I am very comfortable, thank you."

"But, if you don't mind my asking, how do you live?"

She looks over at the wax fruit. "Not that it's your business, but I have some means. Bill's army pension and some savings."

She seems a little evasive.

I look again around the room. The ornate bird cage, the wax fruit. The silver picture frames. These things cost money, and more money than a widow in Bermondsey could afford on a soldier's pension.

I know then that my father's men have paid for her silence. There are plenty of newspapers that would have been interested in my wife and her background.

I wonder if she was paid a visit by my father's men when they heard about my imminent return. I wonder whether she's going to be filling them in on my movements and intentions after I'm gone. That would explain the questioning.

I decide to draw my false confession to a close.

I take my hat, stand and bow. She shows me to the door.

"Thank you, Mr Edgeland," she says, stiff and formal. "Thank you for coming to see me. It was very thoughtful of you."

She pauses.

"I never believed the papers, by the way, some of the things they said about my Isabella. I know she loved you, poor girl. It wasn't about the money. I'm old enough to know what love looks like."

I allow myself a thin smile. It's all I can manage without letting my face collapse back into grief. Then I reset it hard to face the world.

Out on the street, the gossips are still there, leaning in

their doorways, eyeing me with suspicion. There's a nip in the late afternoon air and from the clouds gathering above, it looks like rain.

I stride down the street, dragging my burden of guilt behind me like cans on a string.

CHAPTER 3

I expect them to be waiting for me when I arrive home, but there is only my valet, Bell. He is nervous and unsettled that I am suddenly back with him after all this time. My luggage has arrived ahead of me and stands piled in the tiled hallway, dusty and battered.

The modest townhouse I keep in Bloomsbury has been closed up, the furniture probably covered over with dust sheets. Word has reached him that I was coming home. I'm not surprised.

The hollow house echoes in the twilight. Bell has done his best to brighten it for me, but the fresh beeswax polish can't cover the smell of stale absence. Everything, the portraits, the damask wallpaper, and the Persian rugs, seem very dark and dense after the space and light of India.

He doesn't seem thrilled. I get the sense that I've interrupted quite a nice stretch of holiday for him. He has probably been living quite happily at my expense with very little to do but dust and check for mice.

I never even considered taking him to India with me. The

fact that I kept him on at all suggests that somewhere, some-how, I'd known that I'd return.

"Mr Edgeland," he says, clearing his throat as if for a long-rehearsed speech, "I'm so sorry about your dear wife, if you'll permit me to say. She was a bonny thing."

Underneath his fussy crust, I suspect he is a good soul. He seemed able to look past my wife's former profession.

"Was it the heat?"

I nod, vague, feigning tiredness. Then a great racking cough doubles me up. I wave away his help.

"It did for my cousin, Fred, Sir. Terrible place. Full of heathens too. Well, you're home and safe now and here you can stay for a while. You must be exhausted after all the strain. Look at you, thin as a rake, and if those aren't streaks of grey in your hair?"

I draw back myself up. "Bell," I say, "I appreciate your care, but I am rather tired and I'd like to bathe, eat and retire in quick succession, if that is at all possible?"

He nods and backs away. "I'm sorry, Sir, but we've all been worried about you."

"All?"

He looks sheepish. "Well, it did cause something of a stink, Sir, if I may be so bold. With your father's men. They were round here the day after you'd gone, couldn't stop them. They were asking where you'd both headed. I had to tell them about the wedding, although I reckon they knew already."

I speak gently. "I'm sure they did, Bell. There isn't much that escapes their notice."

"Indeed not, Sir. But we were so worried about you both. I expect you will receive a call shortly. They were here yester-day, asking after you. That's how I knew you was coming."

"I imagine they have been following my progress since I left Bombay. My father has representatives in just about every port between Southampton and India."

That isn't all. I'm fairly sure that one of my fellow passengers, on the SS *Abyssinia* from Aden to Southampton, was following me. I was convinced that I'd seen his face before, perhaps in Calcutta. It isn't beneath my father to hire retired police officers, or the like, to follow his wayward son. It's happened before.

Bell helps me unpack and draws me a bath, then, with a silent nod and a flicker of a smile, leaves me to it.

I slump in an armchair. I am shaken to the root by my visit to Isabella's mother.

Nothing is forgiven.

But in a way, seeing her first was the easier option.

I know I must now face my father.

But not tonight.

I set Isabella's picture frame next to my bed, but don't dare look too closely at her picture. There is a resistance still, a kind of magnetic pressure that keeps me from facing her memory face on.

Sober, at least.

There is a place in my heart I dare not look, something that cannot see the light. I carry her memory within me. If I carry it carefully enough, like a baby bird cradled in my hands, then she will not be gone after all. I can carry her all the days of my life and no one will know. She will be my secret companion, perfect, pure and just for me.

But I can only see her out of my peripheral vision, if I dare turn to look at her direct then, like Eurydice, she will be dragged to Hades for eternity.

I strip and bathe, a necessity, not a pleasure. I try to be vigorous in the tub, not daring to sink back and relax in case it brings back memories of that night.

Then I'm out, dried off and pulling on softer clothes.

I descend the stairs, craving a simple, plain meal. Bell brings my favourite, lamb chops.

As I chew, I decide to see my father in the morning, and, in preparation, ask Bell to bring a bottle of Claret. I drain it to its sandy dregs.

Then I take her picture and go to sit alone with it in the parlour, listening to the grandfather clock slice away the seconds.

The edges of the room are blurred by the wine and the candlelight. The ticking of the clock reminds me of the mechanisms in my father's mills. As I drift, I feel myself part of some enormous machine, the teeth on the cogs drawing me ever closer to my inevitable destiny as heir apparent to his sprawling empire.

In the interplay of shadow across the walls and ceiling, I fancy I bear witness to the eternal struggle of light and dark. The forces of the dark are the terrible mills and factories of my father, the forces of light are poetry, love and the freedom of the human spirit. And between them, there I am, feeling the inexorable tide of the shadow as the night deepens and eats everything before it.

Still, for now I am safe, cocooned in the silk of the wine until what little time is sliced away by that pendulum. There is still a portion of seconds allotted to my soul between now and dawn.

She stares at me from within her silver frame, always in the corner of my eye.

I am weary but anxious, too dulled to move my limbs. The only solace is nullification.

I call for Bell and ask him to bring me brandy.

I drink alone until the candle beside me has guttered out, leaving only the glowing ashes of the fire to hint at the lineaments of the room.

I take her picture from the frame, taking care to not look at it directly, and cast it into the embers, watching it catch and curl in a final death flare.

In the swirling spark-lit vortex that follows, I allow myself to peek between my cradled fingers, try to remember her and try to weep, but can't find either her face or my tears in the darkness.

I crawl up to bed in the early hours.

❧

THE NEXT MORNING, I RISE LATE, IRRITABLE, ACHING AND head-fogged. I pace the house, wondering when I should abandon its defences and face the world.

I'm certain they are coming for me. Perhaps they've given me an evening's grace just to settle back in. I didn't expect that much.

The cold light of the morning fuses with the fumes of the brandy in my brain to give everything a stark sharpness. The very furniture looks threatening.

I wash and dress, noting that my still-brown face is puffy and red-eyed. I sit waiting for the inevitable in the parlour, unable to settle into anything.

Where are they?

Finally, I can stand it no longer and tell Bell that I'm heading out.

Perhaps they will give me another day's grace? Well, perhaps if I'm not here when they arrive.

I grab my coat, hat, and a stick, and hurry to the front door. Opening it a crack, I glance out to scan the street.

There they are, approaching.

Three of them, striding in synchronisation, almost comical, down the street.

Crows, I called them as a child. Black silk top hats and starched collars. Serious men of business who surround my father like courtiers. Always stern, always dressed in black. Men whose eyes view you not with affection but as an asset to be manipulated, or as a potential threat to their livelihoods.

My first instinct is to close the front door and lock it against them, but I know it's futile. They know I'm at home. Besides, they probably have a key.

Instead, I take a deep breath and open the door wide. I step out and wait for them on the top step, hoping through some advantage of height to gain a semblance of authority.

They see me and stop at the bottom step. The central crow, who I know to be my father's lawyer, a Mr Herbert Mire, removes his hat and looks up at me with a joyless smile just visible through his black, greasy beard.

"Mr Edgeland. So good to see you safe at home again, although under such sad circumstances." The false smile rearranges itself into false sadness. "May I offer my condolences?"

"Thank you," I say. "What can I do for you gentlemen?" I offer no hand of friendship, nor do I invite them to come in.

"Your father has requested your presence, are you able to come with us?" It is not a request.

"Sadly, gentlemen, I have already made my plans for the morning. I am, however, able to come later this afternoon if that suits you?"

Mire looks mildly put out, but not surprised. He glances around him. "Sir, if we may come in," he speaks in a low voice, "I think it is important that we speak in private. It concerns your father's health."

I consider for a moment, then reluctantly nod. What can I do?

They stalk up the steps and cross my threshold.

I lead them into the parlour, but I don't ask them to sit. Instead, I stand by the fireplace, my coat still on, my hat clutched at my side, trying not to look nervous. I am sure now we are indoors they can smell the brandy on my breath.

The crows arrange themselves around me as if to block off routes of escape.

"Well?" I say at last. "Is my father very sick?"

Mire looks at me intently. "He has not been himself since you left for India. There are physicians in attendance, of course, several over the last few months. They come and go, what with his temper. If one gives a prognosis he doesn't like, he dismisses him and replaces him with one who seems more hopeful. The hope, however, never lasts for long."

"What is the nature of his illness?"

"Cancer. His current doctor reckons, privately, that he will not last the month. However, you know how indomitable his spirit is. He could go on for a year yet. You will understand that it is causing some challenges for the running of the business. He is continuing to manage as best he can but the question of what is to come after is paramount and the other shareholders are becoming jittery."

"I am sorry to hear it," I say, "about his illness, I mean." I am surprised to find that I mean it. I do not love my father, but besides a few idle fantasies, I have no great wish to see him suffer.

Mire shifts, uncomfortable. "He is very keen to see you, Mr Edgeland. He was quite firm on that. A Brougham is waiting for us at the end of the street."

"I'm sure," I say, "but as I say, I have a commitment this morning. I will call this afternoon at around three?"

One of the other men steps forward. He is larger than most of my father's associates. I seem to remember him from an incident somewhere in my drunken youth. An incident involving restraint and a certain amount of carrying.

"We have instructions to bring you now, Sir," he says.

CHAPTER 4

My father's Kensington mansion, Ingram House, is officially his second home, but the practicalities of business mean that he spends most of his time there. As a child, I visited whenever we were up in town, of course, but I was raised at the family estate in Buckinghamshire. My mother and I tended to avoid Ingram. My father was in his element there, whereas whenever he came back to Buckinghamshire, he was distracted and irritable. At Ingram, he is another person entirely, a machine. Surrounded by his flunkies, he holds court. He spends his days meeting a constant parade of businessmen, processing people like cattle in a market. He pulls the strings of his vast empire from dawn until late into the night. We were not welcome there.

Ingram is more an office than a home, filled not with family but with crows.

They are there now: the lawyers, the accountants, the outer layer of the family, circling, salivating and pre-emptively dressed in mourning. They cluster in the halls and lounges, gossiping, biding their time, waiting for the inevitable moment when a doctor (whoever is employed today) will emerge and finally announce his death. There is a hushed atmosphere of expectation across the mansion. Plans are being drawn and redrawn.

Somewhere at the centre of the web of intrigue, in a shaded bedroom, in a massive four-poster lies great Jacob Edgeland, reduced to a wheezing woodlouse under his coverlet. Everyone else bides their time, waiting for the moment he departs from this world, leaving only a desiccated corpse and an industrial empire to be divided and plundered.

They know there will be no one to stop them once the old miser is gone, certainly not me, his only son. How I haven't been written out of the will is a miracle, but here I am, a sole benefactor in waiting. Heir to the Edgeland fortune.

Not to worry, I will be easy pickings, especially in the tender grieving period when my judgement will be cloudy and my generosity ripened by loss.

Except that I hate the old bastard, and I hate the crows almost as much. But most of all, I hate my father's businesses and all the horrors they have brought into the world.

"The price of cotton has fallen almost by half," says Mire, eyes straight ahead as we march through the halls. "It's like a contagion spreading across Europe. There's nothing that can be done. It needs to run its course until confidence is restored. Import tariffs in America, France and now Germany. We have done everything we can, of course, to shore up profitability. We've managed to reduce our workforce by ten per cent, and cut wages on the remainder. Somehow we are managing to keep the thing afloat."

I look around at the marble statues and velvet curtains as we stride through yet another echoing gallery. It doesn't look like an enterprise in terminal decline. I wonder how the poor workers who have been turned away are faring. To say nothing of their families.

"Of course, our shipping businesses are doing better, and

we are moving into armaments. Artillery production at our steel mills, taking on the Germans at their own game. We have secured some lucrative contracts from the army. Still, it's touch and go as to whether we'll make our planned revenue for this year. We've made some investments in mills in the north, buying out some family-owned firms that were struggling. It should put us in a stronger position when this all blows over. Of course, all this is presuming we have strong leadership at the top. That's the biggest worry the minor shareholders have. A potential unknown on the board with a controlling share."

He's talking about me. I listen, only taking in around half of what he is saying. My mind cringes away from all talk of my father's business, even though I know with a grim certainty that soon I will need to face it head on.

We reach the door to my father's private rooms.

Outside stand a queue of nervous-looking businessmen, some frantically reading documents, preparing for their five minutes with the great man, perhaps after months of waiting and rescheduling.

Every so often, the door opens and a frazzled-looking individual emerges, scurrying away, to allow the next to be ordered in.

As we approach, the queue shuffles and looks momentarily distracted. There are some signs of surprise and recognition. Word passes down the line in hushed tones.

"The prodigal son."

"Won't be long now, then."

"This should be interesting."

I ignore the stares and try to swallow my fear. It doesn't go down, but lodges in my throat like a fishbone.

Mire opens the door a crack and says something to the attendant within. The door swings open and we are admitted to the inner sanctum.

"I don't think he has long to go," Mire murmurs as we enter. "You should go and say some final words to him, John. Try to find..." and he places a hairy, soft hand on my arm, "try to find some reconciliation."

I nod, shrug off the tarantula as politely as I can and approach the bed. The gauntlet of crows part as I approach, all turning to look at me with eyes that betray their amusement.

The irony is that at that moment I desperately want to be a good son, to put all the years of bitterness and shame behind me and create at least one memory of my father and me together with something approaching actual love. We have had our differences, but the final journey brings a great levelling. Time is up and it is our last chance together.

But my father is obscured by the crowd. He is seemingly occupied with a balding, flustered man who stands turning his hat round and round in his hands like a naughty child.

My father's voice rises through the throng and it shocks me. It is like the feeble scraping of a sharpened fingernail on a blackboard, mean, shrill and weak.

"Put them out, Mr Stone, we cannot afford to carry any more dead weight. We have committed to reducing our operating costs at the mill by thirty per cent, with no corresponding reduction in production. You need to put them out, Sir. We cannot afford to carry the burden of excess workers. The remainder will thank you for it. The price of wool is at its lowest in eight years. The mill is not sustainable. They must be put out. Those left must strive harder, Sir. As must you. There are plenty of keen, younger managers in my other businesses who would like to cut their teeth at a mill such as yours."

"But that mill has been in my family for generations, it was founded by my grandfather, Mr Edgeland."

"That is an irrelevance, Stone. I am the controlling shareholder and I am perfectly within my capacity to replace the management if I deem it's not doing what's necessary to maintain our interests. Difficult decisions, and the strength of will to make them quickly. We are not a charity, Sir. I don't hold with this pious philanthropy which infects other enterprises. We are men of commerce, and commerce is the way to improve society. The creation of wealth. And you, Sir, are frittering away that wealth on sentiment. Do it, or I will find someone who will do it in your place. Now go!"

The man turns, and barrels past.

The crowd notices me and parts around me like iron filings suddenly repelled by a magnet.

The way is clear. My father is visible, as am I.

"Jacob, your son is here," says my Aunt Edith, who stands by his side. Her tired face is pinched from her vigil. She appraises me with cool eyes and places her little dry hand inside my own as I approach and squeezes as if to say, "Remember your Auntie after this. Remember her share, boy."

I look down at him. He seems so small, so wizened, his bald parchment skull buried deep in the pillow, gnarled hands resting neatly on his chest as if already placed there by the undertaker. His eyes, though, are narrow and piercing.

I stand, respectful, at his side.

"You came, my son. Thank you," he says. His once commanding, dismissive voice is drained of its power, but not its venom. That bile is reduced to a nasal wheeze, a mere shaping of the breath through the flaccid tongue and dry lips. "Thank you for making the effort."

I bow my head. The watching crows probably think that I'm too choked with emotion to speak, but the truth is I simply don't know what to say. There is too much to go over, and I can't make small talk with a dying man.

"You are still brown from India, I see," he says. "How long

have you been back in the country?"

"I arrived in London yesterday, Father."

"And it's taken you two days to come and see me, despite the fact that, as you can see, I'm not long for this world. I hear you found time to go to Bermondsey, though..."

I hang my head, not in shame, but in an attempt to control my temper. The world is watching and I'm not about to start an argument. Let him have his say, I think. He deserves his last moment.

"Your mother would have been very proud of you, John."

I look up in surprise.

"Look how handsome you are. She would have loved your independent spirit and your artistic leanings. She was always romantic like that. I am sorry that she didn't live long enough to see you grow up."

"As am I, Father," I say, tears rising unbidden to my eyes, "and I am sorry that you didn't get more time with her."

He nods and I feel smiles of relief blossom in the crowd around me. Aunt Edith again slips her hand into mine. This is going better than anyone expected.

"She was a beautiful, kind woman," says my father, his own eyes misting. "I suppose I will be with her soon enough. Of course, I lay much of the blame for how you turned out on her. She pandered to you, encouraged you in play, but never in work, never taught you the hard realities of the world. She ruined you and after she went, there was nothing to stop you from running off and living your little fantasy life. I can never forgive her for that."

I feel my heart quicken, my jaw muscles bunch. Here it comes.

"That is why I am leaving everything to you, John. I know how you despise my work, the fruit of all my labours. I have invested and built and slaved to make something in this world. I have built mills and factories. I have brought work and prosperity to hundreds, thousands of people. I have strived to bring progress to this country and wealth to this family, and all you have done is reject it all. Well, now you will have no choice. You will have to learn the business as I always intended. It will make a man of you."

The expectant eyes of the crows turn for my response as if they are watching a tennis match.

"I... I will do my best, Father," I say.

He lets out a wheezing cackle. "It will break you utterly, boy! Then, with luck and hard work, you will be remade as something more substantial and worthy. You can put all your former mistakes behind you."

"Mistakes?"

He gives an evil leer from the depths of his pillow. I wonder if he will say it out loud, in front of this audience.

Of course he will.

He takes a deep, rasping inhalation and lets it out in an explosion of venom. "What mistakes? Running off to India with that whore, that actress, that's what. Marrying without my blessing, that's what. Jeopardising my whole enterprise with slander and innuendo. The embarrassment of it all. Well, that worked out beautifully for you, boy, didn't it? She couldn't stand it in the heat and the filth, could she? Fragile little thing. I'm glad she could never bring my grandchild into the world. I wouldn't want her half-wit progeny sullying my legacy. Well, now she's dead and buried in some Indian field. Good! Perhaps now you can get on with living a real life in the real world!"

I fling myself at him, swinging my fists, wanting to smash that taunting, snide face once and for all. I land two or three punches before the crows drag me off him, carrying me backwards, flailing, and pulling me out of the room.

Behind me, I can hear his thin, crackling laughter and hear the satisfaction in his blackened heart.

CHAPTER 5

I am not treated too roughly. I'm too important to everyone's future for that. The men deposit me, not into the street, as I had hoped, but onto a chaise in the long gallery, then stand around, unsure of what to do or say.

I scramble to my feet and push through them, looking for the way out.

"We can make this right, Mr Edgeland," says Mire behind me, but I know there is no need. My inheritance is Father's revenge, and I know my little tantrum has only validated that plan in his mind.

I rush from the house, despite the best efforts of Mire and his associates to keep me there.

I stand, panting and dishevelled, before the wrought-iron gates and think about my next move. I decide it will be, if nothing else, in the direction of a pub. Hailing a cab, I head back towards Trafalgar Square.

Sitting back, safe in the Hansom, I look at my shaking hands. I have never dared raise my temper to meet my father's before. All my rebellions have been passive, covert or indirect. I remember his admonishment of me when I began courting Isabella, ridiculing my endless vigils at the stage door. His shame. I just stood there, head bowed, and took it like a boxer hoping to tire his opponent.

I wonder how much of my adoration for her was a reaction against him. Did she grow in my heart because it caused him so much anxiety?

Oh, that had been a sweet day, when I had announced my intention to marry. His dismissive tone, his guidance that I should sow my oats and enjoy it while it lasted because he had altogether different intentions for me. I knew he sought to use me as a bargaining chip in some great future business alliance. I knew it would not be for me to say with whom, or when that alliance would be.

He had tried to pay her off. Mire had visited her, and visited her mother, had gone to that little house in Bermondsey and made an offer.

I'd known that if that offer had been refused, it would be replaced with threats and that those threats would be followed through.

I'd seen great men toppled for less. My father had no moral boundaries that I was aware of. I'm not sure he even understood the concept. There was, of course, the risk of public approbation (that was a concern as it influenced share price), but as long as what needed to happen got done in the shadows, and was sufficiently distanced from him, then all was fair.

I remember the case of the Reverend Samuel Leith, a campaigner for workers' rights. He had singled out Jacob Edgeland as a prime example of cruel practice in industrial production. His use of children in mills, using them to scurry under the clattering machines to gather stray bits of cotton. He had used the death of some poor motherless girl, Margaret Yeadon, her seven-year-old hands mangled in the jaws of a weaving machine, bleeding to death on the factory floor, as the subject of a campaigning pamphlet that had gained some notoriety.

Rumour was that the Reverend Leith had been approached by Mire with offers to desist. There followed the presentation of some evidence that shone a light on the good Reverend's own, quite different sins. A testimony from a former chorister who had doubtless been paid handsomely for his tale. The Reverend Leith had hanged himself in his vestry shortly afterwards. Discovered by the verger before the evening service.

There was even some suspicion that it had not been suicide.

That was the thing that decided it for me. I knew I would have to take action to remove that power from him, to stand up for my right to love. To protect Isabella and her mother from the infection that was my birthright. At the same time, I wanted to strike my father in that tender place where it would hurt him the most.

I could only imagine his reaction when we eloped. We left on a late train to Southampton, and from there a ship to India, newly married. The telegram I sent to *The Times* to give them notice of our wedding had been the coup de grace.

He first heard about it over breakfast, at the same time as the rest of the world.

That still feels satisfying. A half smile spreads on my face.

I bring myself up short. No. I cannot let that cynical memory sully hers.

I did love her. Adored her.

There's no question of that.

A plan forms in my mind, quite clear. I am going to get wretchedly drunk.

Instead of going to my old club on Berkeley Square, I disembark at the door of an at least partly respectable gin palace off Holborn, check around for any evidence of pursuit, and go inside to seek anonymity and oblivion.

I TAKE UP A POSITION IN A CORNER, WHERE I CAN WATCH the door, and pay the barmaid to bring me my drinks. She does so with great regularity, sensing my mission to obliterate. She makes a little conversation with me, but I cannot face the thought of flirting with a stranger. Although a free man, I can't countenance anything like that with the memory of my beloved still coating me like vernix.

The place gets busy.

A gentleman travelling alone approaches me and asks if he might take a seat at my table. He is an older, sallow-faced man, who looks as if he has been hastily assembled from twigs. He is clearly from out of town. He has that look of overwhelmed uncertainty, his hollow eyes surveying the room on a slow constant watch for metropolitan danger.

"Dr Sebastien Strangler," he says, handing over his business card.

I introduce myself and I see that he has no recognition of my famous name, or if he does is kind enough not to show it.

"I am in town for a seminar on nervous conditions at the Royal College, staying at the Coutances Hotel over the road," he says with a flicker of a smile. "Truth be told, I'll be glad to head back to Yorkshire on Saturday."

"I wish I'd never returned to this damned place," I say, already drunk.

He studies me with dark, dispassionate eyes.

We make fleeting further small talk, but it is clear that I want to be left alone and so, at the first opportunity, he flees.

I DRINK AND BECOME DRUNK. IT DOESN'T BRING THE RELIEF I seek, but instead a terrible self-consciousness. I sit, numbed, but not content, in the shadowed corner of the bustling pub as the afternoon wears on. Finally, darkness descends outside. I watch the swirling demimonde of London emerge and begin their nightly dance around me. It is so long since I've been in this world that its facile pantomime fascinates. I watch the comings and goings with almost scientific disinterest. The painted faces of the women, the extravagant whiskers of the men. The hollow laughter and one-upmanship of the conversations. There is so little that is real, or truthful in any of it.

Eventually, the noise and rising chaos of the scene drive me to stand, swaying, and lurch for the exit. I fall and stumble into a party of swells. They manhandle me, dragging me to the door, and throw me out into the street, planting at least one foot in my backside to help me on my way. I stagger forwards, not bothering to berate them, instead righting myself well as I can. I fling one leg in front of the other and launch off in what I assume is the general direction of Bloomsbury.

I wander, bracing myself against the unpredictable and surprisingly unsteady streets of Holborn. The world is a tipping maelstrom of sudden threat – carriages clatter by, piles of manure lie waiting to pounce, and pedestrians throw themselves into my path. My inner compass is broken and I need refuge from the onslaught.

I think about my father's reptilian face, crumpling beneath my fists.

I think about the burning pyres by the river in India.

At one point on that strange walk home, I think I see her ahead of me, walking arm in arm with another man. I give chase, crying out, then seeing her turn with another woman's face, I fall to my knees.

I seek rest on a bench in a little park, thinking that I might stay there for the night. I curl up, shivering in the night breeze, and glance up at the stars rotating above the branches which seem to pulse in and out of focus. I am a single point beneath the spiralling cosmos, alone and fixed.

I feel the organism of the world reject me, as a host might reject an unwanted parasite. The very earth seems to be repelled. I dare not put my feet back onto the turf for fear it will sting and bite and push me away. I should be sucked up into the universe, away from the earth, to be lost in its vast oblivion.

Then the night breeze stirs my bladder to sudden, urgent attention.

I haul my heavy body up off the bench and shuffle up to a tree, unfasten myself and let rip against the trunk, hoping that the noisy spattering can't be heard from the street where families are strolling.

Then, blissfully relieved, my great odyssey continues.

Finally, that strange homing instinct that is common to pigeons and drunks guides me back to my quiet side street and I fall against my door, using it like a raft to stabilise the bucking city.

The world becomes still and the churning migrates to my stomach.

My knees turn to water. My guts turn over. I vomit over my front door, collapsing, palms slapping into that hot vinegar slurry. The smell brings more bile to my gorge and I heave again.

With weak fists, still bruised from my father's face, I batter the door, calling out for help.

Finally, it opens and light falls on me and my disgrace.

I feel hands on my shoulders, under my armpits and I am dragged inside.

Once I make it to sanctuary, I black out.

33

❖

WHEN I WAKE, AT AROUND FOUR IN THE MORNING, I HAVE a brief moment of elation as I find myself in a comfortable bed. I seem to have escaped the rigours of a hangover.

Then it comes down on me like a war hammer.

I groan, feeling my emptied stomach clench and unclench, searing, pulsing pain behind my eyes. The room rotates like a carousel. I lie, unable to escape myself. Finally, I swing my itching legs out of bed and shuffle to the nightstand to get a glass of water.

I fumble for some matches and light the lamp with shaky hands.

The world coalesces around me and I see the reassuring forms of my room take shape.

Bell must have dressed me in my nightgown and cleaned me up. Stray fragments of memory begin to come back to me, the park, my doorstep.

I am enveloped in shame.

A shaving mirror sits on the nightstand. I tilt it up to look at myself in the lamplight. The face that looks back is puffy, blotched and rancid with drink. My eyes are bleared to the point of opacity, deep black pouches slung beneath them.

I sip the water, feeling it gurgle down into my volatile stomach and reawaken the griping there.

God, what a wreck of a man. Worthless. Shameful. A disgrace to everyone.

I remember punching my father and wince.

I calmly put the glass back down on the nightstand and stare at myself again. Then I slap myself across the cheek. The pain is numbed by the alcohol but there is something there, cutting through the haze. I do it again, harder, and again with the other hand. Then I ball my fist and punch myself in the eye.

Again. Harder. And again.

Then comes a flurry, slaps around the head, tweaks of the nose, punches to the ear and side of the head, trying to jar some kind of feeling, some satisfaction of meted punishment.

I look down at the razor, folded neatly next to the basin. I take it, opening it out and looking at the glint of steel in the lamp light. I touch my thumb to the blade, gently, and test it with the slightest pressure.

Bell has done his work well: a bead of glistening blood balloons on my thumb and a second later I felt a sting. I look at the tiny droplet and transfer it onto the blade edge where it thins and trickles. I toy with an idea, then with sudden fear fold the razor and place it back on the stand, leaving a crimson stain on the towel next to it.

I don't have the courage for that.

I stare at my reflection and let out a silent, yawing scream, the distant part of me studying the contortions of my face, the stretching of the skin over my cheekbones, the alien hollows beneath my eyes and the blackened lips.

I fall back, shaking my head, then tumble into bed and let myself be swallowed by the sheets.

CHAPTER 6

"Sir!"

I feel a hand shake me awake. I open my gummy eyes and Bell swims into focus, standing over me with a look of horror on his face.

The pain returns, less intense but like a ringing inside my head.

"What happened?" Bell says.

I pull the sheet up around my face, wishing he would go away, and find that it is wet and sticky. I hold it out in front of my face and see that it's stained with blood.

Sitting up sharp, I examine the stain, not huge but enough to cause worry, perhaps around a foot in diameter.

I hold up the first finger of my right hand, and see the wound across its tip. Dried blood has stained my hand brown, hair-thin coagulations in the whorls of the print.

"I cut myself, Bell. No need for alarm," I grunt.

He takes the bed sheet and pulls it away to reveal a larger stain on my nightshirt and under-sheet. My leg is bleeding, and lying next to me, open, is the razor.

"How did that get there?" I wonder aloud, then pull up

my nightshirt to reveal a slash in my thigh. It is not serious, a scratch really, probably an accident, but enough to have caused a mess.

How is razor in the bed with me? I distinctly remember putting it back on the nightstand.

Did I rise again in the night? I was probably drunk enough. God, I could have accidentally killed myself.

The sting of both wounds emerges through the fog and I wince. "Do you have bandages?"

Bell takes the sheet off the bed and says, "Would you try and stand, Sir? I'll need to strip the bed."

Gingerly I climb out of bed, leg stinging, wet nightshirt clinging to my legs. I pull it over my head and stand there, shivering and naked as Bell bundles it with the stained sheets.

"We need to get you cleaned up, Sir. I'll get some hot water and a cloth. Sir, you were in a bad way last night."

I shiver, head pounding. "I don't feel very good, Bell," I say. "I think I need to sit down."

I fall into the chair by the window. My stomach is in turmoil still, gnawing and mashing on the dregs of acid that slosh within.

"I'll get you some liver salts and some tea. Perhaps some toast?"

I feel drained of all strength. "That would be appreciated, thank you."

In the cold light, I look down at my skinny naked body, plastered in its own blood. God, what has become of me? I wish I could crawl out of my skin and hide in a sewer until I'm forgotten.

The two razor wounds hurt like the devil.

I feel weak. I don't know if it is the loss of blood or the hangover.

Why would I have brought that thing into the bed? If I can't trust myself...

I'm frightened.

"I think, also, I should see a doctor."

"I'm sure it's just the after-effects of last night, Sir. And those wounds aren't serious. We'll have those patched up in no time."

"No, Bell. I'd like to see someone."

"Dr Wheeler?"

I consider for a moment. "No. He is one of the family physicians. If I see him, word will get back to my father."

"Understood, Sir."

"Anyone else? I need someone discreet. But decent, this isn't just a patch job, I want to talk to someone."

"I'll do my best, Sir." He places a clean woollen blanket over my trembling naked body and leaves, taking the sheets.

I wash, scrubbing the blood off me, and pull on a clean nightshirt. Then I lie on the bare bed.

Bell returns.

"There is no one," says Bell as he places the toast and tea next to me on a tray, "not that I know of, anyway. I'm afraid you are too well known. I don't see the harm in using one of the family's physicians."

"No," I say. "That simply can't happen."

Then I remember the man from the previous night, the sallow gentleman from the pub.

"In my breast pocket, Bell. There is a business card."

Bell retrieves it and peers at it before handing it over.

"I think he was staying at the Coutances Hotel on Wilmot Street," I say. "He should still be there, I think he said he was in town till Saturday. Do you think you could arrange for him to come and visit? He will be well compensated."

It's perfect. A stranger that my father has no connection with.

I stare at the wall for a while, force down the tea and toast, and then hobble to the clothes that Bell has left out.

D R STRANGLER ARRIVES AT AROUND ELEVEN O'CLOCK.

I have made myself respectable again, at least on the outside, and receive him in the parlour.

He enters, looking nervous and confused. My memory of him is blurred by alcohol. I hardly recognise the man.

He is around fifty, and sallow of complexion, thin with a looseness to his joints that reminds me of a marionette. His narrow skull stretches up high, and he has lost the hair down the centre of his head, but there is a thin growth on either side, along with somewhat limp sideburns that drape down over his cheekbones. His eyes are sunken and dark, with a calm, studious gaze that doesn't hurry, just moves from object to object, analysing, not judging, then moves on again.

He steps into the parlour, hat in hand, and gives a slightly old-fashioned bow.

"Mr Edgeland." His voice is deep, the words slow and careful.

I struggle up out of my chair. "Dr Strangler. I'm so grateful you were able to come. I apologise for dragging you away from your seminar."

There is a heavy waft of cologne.

He raises a placatory hand. "Think nothing of it, Sir. I am due to speak later this afternoon. This morning is given over to some lectures that are of little interest to me. I was happy to come. I assume, Sir, that you want my opinion as a medical man?"

"Indeed, please take a seat. Bell, can you fetch tea?"

Strangler arranges himself in the chair opposite and I

lower myself back down into mine, flinching as the dried razor cut in my thigh splits.

He seems to look into my soul with his heavy-lidded yellow eyes. When he smiles, just the corners of his mouth tilt up in an efficient, soulless kink, creasing his papyrus skin into a hundred striations. I imagine that facial hair has never grown on his face, such is its preternatural smoothness, but I note that his long neck hangs in dangling folds of wrinkles, not unlike a turkey.

"What ails you, Sir? How may I be of service?"

I compose myself, feeling skittery and liable to break down. "I am not myself, Doctor. I find myself behaving in ways that I wouldn't normally consider acceptable. I drink, to excess, regularly. I am finding my sleep disturbed. I am short with people when normally I pride myself on being an accepting, genial fellow. I am..."

At this, I collapse into a flurry of sobs. I cover my face with my hands so he should not see my shame. I gather myself and, through the blur of tears, I see his face has not changed in expression, the same calm, non-judgemental gaze. I take out my handkerchief and dab my eyes.

"I'm so sorry, Doctor. Whatever must you think of me?"

"Not at all. Mr Edgeland, has something happened in your life that has caused this sudden change of feeling and behaviour?" His neck cranes forwards, his head bobbing on the end.

"Yes, I..." I steel myself. "I lost my wife. It was in India. I am only back in the country this week. I understand that there is grief, of course there is, but there have been other aspects to it that I had not expected."

"I see. And you have found it difficult to adjust?"

"Yes... yes."

"Have you been drinking to excess since your wife's sad demise, or had it started before?"

"Since..." I lie. "In the main."

He nods. "And these 'other aspects', what has prompted you to seek medical advice? Have you been tempted to commit other, more serious, solitary sins? Why today? Why me?"

"Last night, after you left the public house, I drank very heavily. I mean, when you saw me, I fear I was already inebriated, but I continued. I made my way home eventually, but in the night, I did something I have no memory of. I cut myself with a razor."

He nods, never blinking.

"I am not, by nature, a morose person, Doctor. You have to understand. This is very uncharacteristic."

"Are you injured, physically? Other than your finger, I mean."

"My thigh. I have bound the wound, it's just a scratch, really, but I was sufficiently worried. I don't feel that I can trust myself. It's not the first time that I have had lapses of memory."

He takes a sudden breath and rearranges his long legs, crossing them and sitting back. He brings his fingers together before him as if in prayer.

I hope for some kind of medicine. A pill, perhaps.

"I think, Sir, you have been through an ordeal, terrible grief, and are still going through it. It sounds like this has been exacerbated by your return to London, which, as I can personally attest, is an assault on the senses for those not used to it. Your drinking needs to be moderated, but in the short term, I would advise abstinence. That may not be easy."

I nod. I had feared that.

"However, that will not help you right yourself. By good fortune, I am something of a specialist in nervous conditions. I work at a hospital in the north, a place of refuge for troubled souls who have degraded far from where you are right now."

"An asylum?" That hadn't even occurred to me.

He is not going to lock me up.

He winces. "It is not a word that I favour, Sir. We are doctors, not jailers. Our aim is the treatment and rehabilitation of unfortunates."

"I am not mad, Sir. I am not going to be your patient there."

He holds out a placatory hand. "No. No, of course not, and I would not suggest that you are. Our patients are many steps further down that path and I do not think for a moment that I should treat you. But I can offer an alternative."

He looks me in the eye. "You are grieving, Mr Edgeland, and have in all likelihood polluted your organs with excess. The two factors are likely working together to create a spiral of misery. This is all perfectly normal. In my work, I see cases like yours. You are not mad, Sir. You just need rest and healthy living to cleanse your system. That is not, however, an inducement to apathy. It is important that this rest is structured and that you receive some appropriate treatment. But not from me."

"What treatment?"

He smiles. "My hospital, as I say, is in Yorkshire, near the moors around the town of Whitmoor. There is a proliferation of hydropathic hotels around that village. I think a stay in one of those would be highly beneficial to you."

"A water cure?"

"It is wonderful for the body and the soul. And a pleasurable rest. It does not feel like medical care, but more a supported programme of cleansing. The waters around Whitmoor are highly beneficial, being pure, coming straight, as they do, from the hills themselves. They are also infused with vital minerals that help purge the body of effete material. They help restore vigour to the body and calm to the troubled mind. I have a particular recommendation as to the establishment. Its proprietor is one of the leading exponents of the treatment in the world. You won't find a better selection of treatments in Europe."

He pulls out a pad of paper and a pen and jots some details down.

"If you'll permit me, Mr Edgeland, I would like to contact the hydro myself with details of your case, in strict confidence, of course, and make you a priority booking. You are a risk to yourself in your current condition. This needs to be addressed, and quickly before you do more harm."

"I do not need a rest. I have too many responsibilities here."

"Then," he says, rising and suddenly stern, "I fear you will continue to suffer as you are now. There is no other way, Sir. I see it all the time at my 'asylum', as you call it. Take the cure now, Sir, or face the consequences later. I do not think you would look well in a straitjacket."

I waver. "What is the name of the hydro?"

"Cragside."

CHAPTER 7

In the afternoon, Mire returns, bearing news.

I let him in, embarrassed about my behaviour the previous day. The hangover clouds have receded a little, but my hoarse voice and pale skin betray me.

Mire, however, gives no recriminations. He is calm and subdued. He enters quietly and I let him take a seat in the parlour.

"Your father has taken a turn for the worse, I'm afraid," he begins. "After you... left yesterday, he was fine for some time, a little worn out, perhaps."

"Was he injured?"

"I don't believe so. A little bruised, perhaps, but nothing serious. His illness, however, has been becoming more serious in recent weeks and last night he declined quite significantly. He is not able to function or stay awake for longer than a few minutes. It will not be long now, I fear."

I sink my face into my hands. So I am a parricide.

"I should go and see him," I say. "Apologise and pay my last respects."

"He has expressly asked that you don't, John."

I look up. "My father and I... we have never enjoyed a close relationship, but..."

"I think that is quite obvious to anyone who was in the room yesterday," he says, without a hint of a smile, "but what I came about today is to discuss what comes next. Your father's instructions in his will are quite clear. If you wanted him to change his wishes with that little outburst yesterday, then I fear you have only strengthened his resolve."

I shake my head.

"There are many that would envy you, Mr Edgeland," he snaps, "and many that would seek to take advantage of you. You have been raised knowing that this is your birthright. I want to finish your schooling before they seek to take advantage of you. You saw for yourself yesterday that the vultures are gathering. Let me help you."

With his greasy beard, bald head and formal black clothes, he looks ready for the funeral already.

"You will need to get working straight away, there will be no time for grief. There are pressing matters and your father, for all his diligence, has not been able to address everything. The depression deepens and we are taking on water. I have drawn up an agenda for the next few weeks. I see no harm in you assuming some responsibilities now, meeting some of our main customers and shareholders and assuring them that the Edgeland empire is in safe hands during this interregnum."

It's finally caught up with me.

Exhausted and dissipated as I am, I see that I am boxed in. I take the list from Mire without looking at him and glance down the names and times. It is very long.

"Is my life not my own then?"

"Every man has responsibilities, John. Yours are here. Many, many people depend on you now for their wealth. In time, perhaps you will come to understand that. There is a grand tradition for you to maintain. I have every faith that you will rise to this."

He sounds like he is trying to convince himself.

"I... I can't."

"Don't be pathetic, boy. This is your duty. To your father, your family, to the shareholders." He stands. "There is a line of people still outside your father's bed chamber waiting for an audience. While he is on his very deathbed. Will you not do your duty? All that is needed is your presence and some reassuring words. They just need putting off until this is over."

I sigh and rise.

"I'll come, I suppose."

He stands next to me, too close, and claps his hairy hands together. "Good boy. You'll make him proud yet, I'm sure."

I glance at the mantlepiece and see a scrap of paper with the details of the hydropathic hotel. There is no time for that nonsense now. I'll need to let Strangler know to hold off on his arrangements.

The fates have different plans for me.

☙❧

I ALLOW MIRE TO LEAD ME BACK TO INGRAM, ALTHOUGH he is at pains to point out that my father will not be expecting to see me, and has no idea that I am due on the premises.

Instead, we enter via a side entrance and he takes me deep into the bowels of the building to a comparatively modest reception room where stands an oak desk and several wing-backed Chesterfield chairs. He draws two together and we sit. Above us, on the wall, hangs a great oil painting of my father, sitting stern and judgemental, gazing down through the muddy patina.

This is how I remember him from my childhood, impassive, his slight frame somehow made massive through self-belief. I shift, uncomfortable beneath his gaze, feeling inadequate for the task ahead.

I realise that of course this is the desired effect, that the supplicants who come to this antechamber will be similarly cowed.

"The list is long. We are going to be some time, and I will do most of the talking. You must stay detached, but with intent. Speak little. They all need to know that you are in control now. The way to do this is to stay quiet. Don't smile. We are in a vulnerable state at the moment with your father unable to receive. We can't let them know we are weak."

Can't let them know that *I am* weak, I think.

"I will listen and learn," I say.

"Sit straight, keep your gaze on them. Strong and steady."

I nod.

"The first meeting is with Jasper Dyer, he represents one of our suppliers of iron ore. I fully expect he's going to try and negotiate a higher price per tonne, but we are not going to let that happen. Our margins on iron production are under enough pressure at the moment what with the drop in demand for steel. We are expanding into munitions but I don't want him to know that. If we are to get the best contracts from the military, we need to be able to undercut Galton. It's all about owning the supply chain. Dyer doesn't know that we are about to try and buy him out. We need him to get desperate enough to sell to us. When he comes in, don't stand."

I nod, not really listening.

Mire sits back and waves to an attendant, who gives a curt nod and steps out of the room.

A few moments later, the double doors open again and a

fat, red-faced man with enormous white side-whiskers, like fish gills, is escorted in.

Mire rises and shakes his hand. The man is wet and the bitter smell of stale sweat wafts from beneath his straining clothes. He turns to me, his face yanked up into a false smile, betrayed by nervous, swivelling blue eyes.

"May I introduce John Edgeland? Mr Edgeland, this is Mr Dyer of Woodhouse, Dyer & Company, Middlesborough."

He holds out a pudgy hand to me and I stare back at him. Am I to take it? I fight down my instinct to be civil and simply sit there, pretending to study him. I try to appear impressive, rather than insolent, or a half-wit. I fear my flushed face is giving me away.

His face darkens. I can tell that he is not a man used to being treated with disrespect.

"Mr Edgeland, can I just say how sorry I am to hear about your father's decline in health? I trust that he is in the best of care."

"Obviously," I say.

"And I was surprised to see that you are returned from India. I trust you are settling back into London life?"

I stare at him, genuine dislike in my eyes. I do not speak.

Mire glances at me, his eyebrow twitching with amusement.

"Please take a seat, Mr Dyer. I would normally offer you some refreshment, but as you have probably gathered from the queue outside, we do not have the luxury of time today. What is the matter that you wish to discuss with Mr Edgeland?"

The man shuffles and leans forward. I watch a trickle of sweat trace across his temple. "Well, I had hoped to talk to Mr Edgeland Senior."

"Mr Edgeland here is acting as his representative. You can speak freely."

Dyer turns to Mire, effectively cutting me out of the conversation.

"If I can get straight to the heart of the matter, then. May I ask when the contract for this next year going to be signed, Sir? We are in full production and other customers are becoming very demanding. Because your firm is such an old and trusted customer of ours, I have held back on committing to some potentially lucrative contracts. International contracts, Sir, that would greatly benefit our future. At the moment, over fifty percent of our output goes to Edgeland companies: rail, shipping, machine works. We are part of your family. We don't want to just walk away from family, Sir."

"If I may be equally straight to the point, Mr Dyer. We are considering a review of our main supplier contracts for pig iron and steel. We are also considering some international options. There have been overtures from some producers in the United States. And we had a visit from a German producer just last week. I'm afraid we cannot commit to a contract until we have carried out a full review of these options. You understand as a man of business, I'm sure. It is the rational thing to do."

"But you've been a customer of ours for decades! Doesn't that mean anything? Doesn't it mean anything to Mr Edgeland Senior?"

"It is Mr John Edgeland here who has insisted upon it, Sir."

Dyer flashes a nervous look at me, suddenly reappraising my role in the discussion.

"A new broom, so to speak," Mire continues, "a fresh perspective from a younger, better-travelled man. The world is opening up, Sir, and we need to think more broadly than just our traditional suppliers. As you know, the economic situation is particularly unforgiving at the moment. We need to consider all options."

Dyer wipes his face with his hand, then sits back.

"Well, if you won't consider our history as a factor in our relationship, then perhaps I will have to abandon sentiment as well and sign these other contracts."

Mire also sits back, crosses his legs and looks him in the eyes.

"There are no other contracts, Dyer. I know Hilhouse were interested but we advised them to look at a producer in the United States. Do you think anyone with the slightest acumen is going to be looking for Middlesborough steel and iron in twenty years, Dyer? Your production methods are old-fashioned. Your labourers are overpaid and sloppy. Your product is slow to deliver. There are plenty of other options emerging, and the cost of freight is coming down all the time. You haven't adapted to the new world we are in. I'm afraid without significant investment in your operations you are going to become obsolete. I'd heard that Luther Peatfield hasn't renewed his contracts with you. Gone to a Pennsylvanian firm, I'd heard."

"Peatfield!" snaps Dyer, rattled.

"Mr Edgeland, what do you think?" Mire turns to me.

I feel a chill. Dyer looks at me, hope in his eyes.

"Should we renew Mr Dyer's contract on its current terms?"

I pause, uncertain what to do. The man before me is physically trembling, somewhere between anger and fear. I try to hold my gaze steady.

"No," I say, the word sounding foreign in my mouth.

"I am already discounted to the point of penury, Sir!"

"Mr Edgeland here has spoken on the matter, Mr Dyer. Perhaps you should go away and consider your position. We do respect relationships, but only to a point. See what you can come back with. You have a week before we sign with a competitor."

Dyer looks between Mire and me, his mouth flapping. "But... this will finish us."

I look away, at something across the room.

"That is all the time we have today, Mr Dyer." Mire stands and extends his hand to the man who staggers to his feet. Dyer does not take it. Instead, he shakes his head and begins to move towards the door. He stops, turning.

"I know you mean to have us. The company that I built. I know you mean to bleed me to the point where I'll sell to you, but I won't let that happen. I won't. I know what you do to firms you buy. I know what you do to the people. You care for nothing. I won't sell!"

He strides out, pushing past the attendant who opens the door for him.

The door swings shut.

"Yes, he will," says Mire, with a smile.

He glances down at his list to see who is next.

There are dozens more of them. Half of the men who come are cowed and beaten into submission, half of them flattered and cajoled depending on what is best for the great enterprise. The tendrils of my father's interests are baffling. He seems to touch every aspect of commerce. I can't hope to understand it.

I sit there, impassive, listening but barely taking most of it in, seeing only the human cost to all this. The broken dreams, the heartlessness. It seems that the very language used is foreign to me, distancing its speakers on purpose from any culpability in the lives of the workers, the invisible thousands who slave in the mills, steel works and manufacturing factories.

All I see is a succession of fat old men, come cap in hand to pay homage to the spider at the centre of the web. Instead, they find his naïve milksop of a son, his soul ebbing away, chaperoned by a viper.

CHAPTER 8

That evening, I drink again, trying to blot out the day.

Bell disapproves, I am sure. Not that he would ever say it to my face, but I can see the flicker in his eyes, and the twitch in his mouth as he retrieves my empty wine bottle after my dinner of trout. I catch it again in the pause when I ask for brandy.

Still, I don't care. The hangover of the previous night has subsided. The wine speeds it on its way, clearing my mind.

A hydropathic establishment! What self-indulgent fancy. What rot!

I need exercise, perhaps, and the distraction of friends and perhaps a little work if I must. I certainly don't need the ministrations of some quack doctors squirting me with freezing water.

I swill the brandy and admire its amber glow in the fire-light. I get caught up looking at its translucent shadow thrown across the corniced ceiling.

Again, I find myself thinking about the battle between light and dark. My vision from the previous night.

I cross my legs and the wound in my thigh stings a little. The brandy has taken the edge off it. The fire shifts and sinks into itself with a hiss, sending a shower of embers up the chimney.

I peer into the flames, looking for her memory, and see nothing.

Strange.

I drink more. The walls buckle and the folds of the drawn curtains become deep and dark, drawing me into their mysteries. Shadows dance and taunt in the corners, and lurk behind the furniture.

What do I want with the north? Bleak, barren moorland with nothing but the wind and rain.

Bell retires in disgust without looking in on me. I suspect he'll creep downstairs after I've retired to make sure that the fire is safe.

I pour another brandy. Just one more to steel myself for the ascent of the stairs.

Finally, I crawl on my hands and knees up to my bed just as the bells of St George's chime twelve.

As the room spins, I listen to the stray sounds of the city, a clopping dray horse, and a drunken shout from the street. In the darkness, the noises take form around me, expand and repeat. I am in the universe now, able to see across London, able to look into all the houses and see the people.

As my bleared eyes adjust, I glance down across the coverlet and see the folds extend far away like a windswept moorland. The dim light from the gas lamps outside gives the ripples a slight edge, a touch of definition. I think I see the heather blowing in the wind.

I PRAY FOR PEACE. BUT I FALL ASLEEP INTO A VISION OF machines.

It's a nightmare I've had since I was a child, a memory really, of being shown around a woollen mill, somewhere in the Midlands, by my father.

In it, I don't know what he hopes to achieve, perhaps that I will instantly fall in love with industry.

Instead, all I feel is horror. Most of all of the great beetle-like machines that stand around me, silent, and waiting to be brought to life. I'm terrified of the drained, hollow-eyed workers lined up in their grubby pinafores to receive us as my father strides around, passing judgement, barking orders. I follow like a little dog, constantly distracted by strange sights.

In the end, I am separated from the group. There's an argument about something, my father shouts. I edge away, turn a corner and am lost.

There in the great cathedral of industry, running, helter-skelter looking for some sign of familiarity, a friend or someone who can help me, dwarfed by pistons, black, oiled creatures. The smell of hot steel and lanolin.

And then the machines start. The noise freezes me, and crushes all thoughts. I think I'll scream.

All I can do is curl up with my hands over my ears.

That is how he finds me, my father. But there is no comforting hug.

Instead, all I feel is the toe end of his boot.

In my dream, I never get that far. I never get past the feeling of helplessness as I run from room to room, surrounded by child-mincing predators.

I am woken around three by a noise from the bathroom.

My head is still thick and dizzy, but the world has stabilised. My drunkenness has not yet calcified into a headache.

I listen again.

A drip.

I groan and turn over, pressing my face into the pillow and trying to loosen my moorings to the waking world. Just as I am about to slip back into sleep, I hear it again.

There is nothing for it. I will have to go to the adjacent bathroom and address the cause. I pull back my covers, feeling the cool night air brush against my leg hairs, giving me goosebumps. I am surprised at the bitterness of the temperature, it being July.

There is no moon, and the darkness in the room is complete. Its boundaries are removed, and for all I know, I could be on a vast plain at night. Or a moor.

I fumble for the matches on the nightstand and strike one again and again until finally a tiny flame spits into life. I touch it to the wick of the candle by my bedside.

Another drip.

I pick up the candle and stand, swaying a little. As the flame takes hold, the room begins to re-assemble itself out of the darkness into its familiar form, the fireplace with its dead grate, the arched mirror over the mantle catching the reflection of the flame.

I shuffle towards the bathroom. The door is ajar and all is dark inside.

Then there is another noise within, a stirring, lapping noise as if a person is in the bath. I stop. There is a sharp gasp of a woman's breath. It echoes off the tiles.

There is something familiar about all this.

"Hello?" I say. My voice cuts through the dull pounding of my pulse and immediately grounds me again.

There is silence.

I stand and wait, my hand and the flame trembling from what I assure myself is only the cold.

Then I advance again towards the bathroom. There is no more noise. It must have just been the residue of a dream. I reach the door and edge around it, holding the candle high.

The light fills the small, neat room.

There is nothing. Just the bathroom as it had been left, the ceramic washstand, the roll-top bath, which is empty, of course.

I listen for the dripping but there is nothing.

Grumbling, but pleasantly relieved, I go back to bed.

I sleep and dream about her.

I can half see her sad face in the hazy Indian twilight.

She was so sad in those final days.

I should have said something, done something, to save her.

Morning comes and I awaken.

I keep my eyes closed at first, wincing from the light, watching the shapes that float across their lenses.

I am very uncomfortable and shivering. I slowly come to realise that I am not in bed.

I am lying in cool water.

There is a hard surface beneath me, and more hardness rising on each side, like some cruel crib.

I open my eyes, a stabbing headache arriving on cue. I look around and realise that I am lying, still in my nightshirt, in a half-filled bath.

I feel a surge of panic. My hands form into claws, scraping at the side of the tub, looking for purchase as I gasp for air.

I cover my face and let out a silent scream, curling up, tucking my feet up into my heavy floating nightshirt as a child might pull them from the reach of an imagined monster.

The soft remaining barrier of my drunkenness melts, and through that single small breach in my armour, memories and regrets flood in.

I twist, wrapping myself in my floating wet shroud.

CHAPTER 9

I f I can't trust myself, then how can I live?

I sit, soaked, on the edge of the bath, shivering like a dog.

There is a knock at the bedroom door. It's Bell.

In the blue dawn, a messenger has come to the house, to tell me my father has died.

I descend, still wet from the bath, wrapped in a robe, drawn and pale, reality still an inch away from the surface of my skin.

The messenger trembles, hat rotating between his hands, a look of fear and shock on his face, as if the world has flipped over and will never be the same again. I sit, that inner part of me that observes strangely calm. I listen to how he passed, quietly in the early hours. I give a quiet acknowledgement and send him on his way.

I try to feel something about his death, but I have so few happy memories of him I can't muster a tear. I suppose I feel shocked, but it is less grief than a terrible sudden sense of exposure, as if the world has turned to look at me.

Bell treats me with respect and restraint. Retreating with

no pleasantries, as if I need the time for some quiet contemplation of mortality and the changed hierarchy of my universe.

All I am thinking about is the hydro and that letter of reference on the mantelpiece.

My mind churns. What to do?

I have time to think. Mire has given me a day off.

I spend it pacing, checking myself in the mirror to see if I am still there.

The next day, it's back to business, and my ongoing tutelage, which takes on a new urgency. The same routines as before, except everyone wears black.

I think Mire senses a change, and he brings less attention to me in our meetings.

He talks and talks about business, shipping, about finance and the cotton crop. I barely listen. It was as if I am in another room, even though I am sitting in front of him. There is cotton in my ears and wool in my brain. My eyes can't focus. My mind feels greasy and won't hold a single coherent thought.

It is off somewhere, plotting my escape.

I DON'T SLEEP WELL IN THE WEEK LEADING UP TO THE funeral.

I ease off the sauce for a few days, although not completely. I'm sufficiently rattled by my experience of waking in the bath, and of cutting myself, that I want a fighting chance of a clean night's sleep. Instead, I toss and roll in the covers, weaving them around me like a cocoon, scraping a few hours of fractured rest each night. When I wake each morning, I am an exhausted husk, winnowed thinner as the days bleed into each other.

For me, the world is ragged at the edges. Sudden movements startle me. I find that I judge my every action and word, often before I utter it. The safest option seems to be to remain inactive and silent, withdrawing into a safe inner place of observation.

I have only to wait for my moment.

The funeral itself is predictably huge, to my father's detailed specifications.

The service, at St Bartholemew's, is the glittering social event of the month. Everyone, short of the Prime Minister, is there. There is an unusual level of hubbub as everyone files in and seeks the best vantage points to take in the crowd. The ceremony itself seems incidental.

Down the front are the crow rows, the family, all of them trying to catch my eye, looking for some acknowledgement or favour. They have unlocked from the dead man's teat and are now crawling towards me, fighting each other for a chance to latch on and suckle fresher milk.

When proceedings get underway, there are few tears shed. In that vaulted chamber, the words of the presiding curate feel even more hollow than they would have usually. In stentorian tones, he extols how my father was a titan of industry, and how countless people depended upon him for a living. How he helped extend the fortunes of the country and brought economic prosperity to millions.

It feels to me that the ledger of his life is very one-sided. Still, it doesn't seem to matter much to those assembled.

I sit in the front pew, feeling as if I am on stage, grateful for the mask of grief that for the moment I am permitted to wear. I fight down a persistent cough, happy to use the tears that spring to my eyes. I have a building sense of trepidation as to what's going to happen after the funeral.

I'll give them something to chatter about!

❦

WE FILE OUT AFTER THE SERVICE. THERE IS A BLISSFUL, respectful silence and I use it to gather my resolve.

Then it is into the carriages and on to Highgate, the way paced out by the professional mourners.

Along the way, people stop to watch, ordinary folk, unaware of who is in the box. Still, they doff their caps, although I wonder if it's to show respect for the dead, the family, or for their own mortality.

The cortege makes its painful way through the wrought-iron gateway of Highgate and we disembark. The sable horses shake their bridles.

Columns of mourners in black crepe file between the mausoleums and memorials, flowing like ants. We pallbearers hoist the coffin out of the back of the carriage and carry it like a leaf back to the nest.

It is lighter than I had expected, although the height difference between me and some of the other, older pall-bearers makes the thing lopsided. I imagine my father tipping, rolling inside. For some reason, this amuses me.

On either side, I see veiled faces and unreadable gazes.

Any tears shed are purely out of concern for future earnings.

I know that I am under close observation by the family after my performance at his bedside, but feel sure that their contempt for me is now leavened by the fact that I will soon be the holder of the purse strings.

I know that as soon as the old devil is safely laid to rest and the forced silence is over, I will suddenly become the most popular man in Highgate.

Already, while we pallbearers advance at our stately pace, I can see some of them, my oleaginous Uncle Campbell, and Mr Sutcliffe, my father's brusque lawyer, trying to catch my eye, to indicate that they would like a "private word" with me after the ceremony is complete.

Mire marches ahead, the Lord High Protector. Kingmaker.

My heart races.

We near the grave, a great obelisk raised above it, prepared years in advance. It casts a long shadow across the mouth of the grave, which seems very small in comparison. A clumsy hole to plant a seed.

I think about Isabella in some hard-scrabble missionary churchyard in the back end of beyond.

Ashes to ashes, dust to dust.

Man has indeed but a short time upon this earth.

What I need is time alone to gather myself.

The bishop mouths the usual words and the coffin is lowered. I, as only son and heir, have the first option of lobbing some dirt onto the top of the casket. It makes a satisfyingly hollow thud as it lands.

I step back, and, breaking the seal of my inaction, determine to make my escape while everyone is bound by convention to the grave side.

I duck back and stride, ostensibly in the direction of the carriages, setting off an avalanche of surprised looks behind me as I go.

Then, with a sudden change of direction, I head east.

I glance back, and the circle around the pit dissolves and begins to wend its way back to the waiting carriages. Some set off after me, to make sure I am well. But I am gone too far ahead, zig-zagging at a brisk walk through the weeping angels and Egyptian needles, not caring whose grave I stride across.

I feel the crows watching me, and almost hear their inner debates as to whether to give chase. Through that necropolis, I keep half an eye out for pursuit. But I think they trust me to return to the coop. Where else will I go?

Somewhere they'll never guess.

Once through the wrought-iron gates, I hail a cab and speed back to my house, where I see a fresh envelope waiting for me on the mantle, placed there by Bell.

I open it and see a crest of griffons. Below are the reassuring words "Cragside Hydropathic Establishment, Yorkshire".

My bolt-hole is confirmed!

I hastily change out of my mourning clothes and pull my trunk from the closet. It is already packed, but I threw a few more sundries in. Before I close it, I stop and look at the picture frame that stands at the side of my bed. I consider it for a moment, then put it in the trunk, my hands trembling.

I leave a brief note for Bell, telling him that I will return in a few weeks, but not my destination. No one is to know that.

I leave for King's Cross.

The world can wait.

CHAPTER 10

The screech of the whistle wrenches me back.

The now familiar anxiety hits me as I wake, but on opening my eyes, I'm where I should be.

My fellow passengers have already started preparations for arrival. I fumble for my pocket watch. There is going to be ample time for my connection. I rest my head against the window, letting the cool glass knock against my skull.

The train pulls into a vaulted station, brakes screaming. The pistons slow to a clamouring chug, like a mighty army beating its shields. I look out at the crowded platform and suddenly am seized by a need to be out of this compartment and into whatever approximation of fresh air is outside. I heave my battered leather trunk, dust from India still lodged in its cracks, from the baggage rack. I struggle out of the carriage door, dragging and bumping it down the narrow corridor as the train comes to a halt with a final death rattle.

Then, braced, out I go, down the steps and into the chaos of the station. I freeze, foggy with sleep, as the rest of the passengers swirl around me in frantic eddies. Porters haul luggage; crowds of men, women and children disembark and thread their way out of the station.

I anchor myself against their flow, for the first time in my life blissfully anonymous.

I have almost half an hour to wait for the branch-line train to Whitmoor. I check my trunk at the left luggage office and go to explore.

Bradford is unpleasant, even though I'm used to the swollen streets of London. Men, women and children with drawn faces and bony frames lounge in pub doorways. A miasma of coal smoke hangs over everything, coating my tongue and catching in the back of my throat. My cough returns in racking spasms.

I feel the gears of the city turning around me and see the dirty, sick people who are being ground by them.

I retreat quickly back into the station.

The train to Whitmoor makes slow progress out of the city, past regimented rows of dirty workers' houses.

My hands seem to develop an involuntary twitch and I tuck my fingers under my thighs where they can flutter unseen. The only other passenger is a florid gentleman farmer. He battles his way through *The Times* and then offers it to me, but the thought of that dense type makes my head pound. I decline, more brusquely than I intend, and then feel his hard gaze on my downturned eyes for the rest of the journey.

The train rolls through shadowed cuttings and drab wooded gorges till we emerge into open countryside. At that moment, the clouds break and the evening sun pours through the sudden gap like lemonade, brightening the valley to emerald green. Hedges and trees shimmer with their full cargo of leaves. Above everything rises the moor, brown and purple; crowned by crags like the crashing crest of a great tectonic wave.

Then, up ahead, I see the turrets of what seems to be a great fairy-tale castle just at the point where the fields melt into the heather. I squint through the glass and realise that I am looking at the Cragside Hydropathic Hotel.

At the quaint Cragside station, I secure the services of a taciturn cabman whose sole task appears to be ferrying patrons to and from the hotel. The cab trundles through the dull grey village that has crystallised around the station and we set out on a winding road that leads steeply up the side of the hill.

I can smell the difference in the air. It's like drinking great gulps of cool pure water with every breath. I can feel it washing the accumulated filth out of my lungs.

In the distance are the low buildings and spires of the local town, Whitmoor, and beyond that the heathery ocean of moors and dales which I suppose roll all the way north to Scotland. I am at the boundary of all that empty wilderness and the realisation is instantly healing.

The road passes through a gateway surmounted by stone griffons, into a shady beech avenue which snakes around a bend before emerging into the manicured grounds of Cragside itself.

I feel a moment of sudden guilt. What am I doing here?

To hide like this when I have new responsibilities!

I feel self-indulgent and weak. I consider telling the man to turn the cab around, to head back down the hill.

Instead, I sink inside myself, become an observer in my own life, and watch as I am carried up the drive.

The hotel's scale is overwhelming. It is a vast purpose-built building in the Scots baronial style: towers and crenellations surmounted by tourelles spreading out from a central building in two wings. The broad driveway leads up to a faux portcullis entrance.

The sunset through the trees casts dark clawing shadows

across the lawns, its reddening glow turning the stones vermillion. The mullioned windows are a constellation of dazzling embers.

We pull up and I pay the cabman. I let him lift my heavy trunk down onto the gravel and he stands next to it, expectant. I sigh and give him another coin. Without a word, he clambers back into the cab and is off.

Save for a lonely, stalking peacock, the grounds are deserted.

There is no one to meet me or assist and so I plough a hissing furrow in the gravel up the neat driveway as I drag my trunk up to the main entrance.

Pushing open the heavy door, I find myself in a dark reception area, panelled with oak. There is no one behind the impressive mahogany desk and no sound other than the ticking of a great grandfather clock in the corner. An impressive staircase sweeps up to the first floor before splitting off in either direction. Open doorways run off either side of the reception area. I drag my trunk over the carpet and, looking around nervously, tap a brass bell on the desk.

The ping travels out into the corners of the room and then dies into silence. I wait, then hit it again a little harder. A seed of doubt creeping into my heart.

"Hallo!" I call out.

I listen carefully and hear gentle murmuring and the clattering of plates and cutlery off down one of the passages. I decide to follow the noise.

I wander down the high-ceilinged passage, lined with inferior landscapes. Off to one side, I see an empty public drawing room. The noise of dining becomes louder and I catch the tantalising smell of roast beef.

Rounding a doorway, I find myself looking in on a pleasant open dining room with high bay windows. At every table sit guests, tucking quietly into soups, roast dinners and fruit. I feel my stomach growl and I realise I haven't eaten since leaving London. A few of the diners look up in curiosity before rejoining their conversations. I feel self-conscious and turn away to find a slight man with baby-smooth skin and white hair standing behind me.

"May I help you?" He scrolls his eyes up and down and clasps his hands together, for all the world like a little genie.

"I have just arrived, and would like to check in."

The man looks troubled and says, "I see. Of course. If you would follow me back to reception, please?"

He leads me back to the front desk and begins thumbing through a heavy leather ledger, tracing a soft pale finger down the serried ranks of precise handwriting.

"What is your name, Sir?" he says, his eyes not leaving the page.

"Edgeland," I say quietly.

"I'm sorry?" He pauses his finger's motion and looks up.

"John Edgeland," I say, louder, wincing internally at the sound of it.

He becomes concerned as he examines the ledger, then sends his finger back to the start and begins again, and then flips back a page and does the same again. My hands begin to tremble, so I send them behind my back, clasping them to stillness.

"Is there a problem?" I finally say.

"I am sure you are here somewhere," he says.

He continues to read down the lists of reservations and his face takes on a look of genuine concern. His head began almost imperceptibly to shake from side to side.

I look at the doorway and think again that it's not too late to go. This isn't for me.

"No... no, I'm afraid I can't see a reservation in that name. Are you sure of the date, Sir?"

The tension that's been building in me bursts. "Of course I am certain!"

Then I remember. Anonymity. I asked Strangler to book using an assumed name.

What was it?

My stupid mind is blank.

The head shaking grows more pronounced and he looks up at me and takes on an expression of sympathy, as if the matter were completely resolved.

"I am afraid, Sir, that I have no reservation in that name. There seems to have been some sort of error, Sir. Do you have your letter confirming the booking?"

I reach into my pocket and find nothing. I'm sure I picked it up off the mantlepiece at home before leaving. There *was* a letter. Wasn't there? I visualise it, feel its crisp paper in my hand and see the neat writing and the crest... the crest. I am certain that there *was* a letter. In my mind, I turn it over in my hand. I can see it there on the mantlepiece, behind the clock. There *was* a letter.

What name was on it?

"I know I had a letter, and I know I was booked for this date," I say, fighting down the embarrassment of not knowing my own name, trying to bluster through it.

"Sir, are you feeling well?"

This whey-faced man and his simpering tone are starting to annoy me. I sense that he is trying to undermine me and is secretly enjoying my discomfort.

I have no right or need to be here.

I need to go back to London. I have responsibilities.

Still, he looks at me with pale blue eyes, his finger still paused on the ledger as if it were holy scripture. "You have had a long journey, Sir. You must be tired. Perhaps you would like to take a seat in our lounge while I fetch the owner. I am sure we can clear this up in no time."

My nerve breaks and I feel tears rush to my eyes. Ashamed of my unmanning, I turn away, raising my sleeve to my face. I grab my trunk and in a panic head for the doorway and out onto the drive.

The sun has almost set below the distant hills, casting the grounds into crimson shadow. The glare of its dying flame dazzles my wet eyes.

I will find my way to the town, to Whitmoor, and there I will find a hostelry and in the morning return to London. I will say nothing to anyone.

I catch the scent of incense and cardamon.

I drag the trunk down the drive, squinting ahead into that final morsel of sunlight, cursing under my breath. The sun slips below the horizon and I turn and see the tall windows of the dining room and the candlelight within. Faces turn towards me, watching my shameful retreat. I have tears coursing down my face. What must they think of *that*?

I turn back to look down the drive to the stone gateway.

There is a woman ahead of me, waiting between the stone pillars of the gates.

Even at that distance, and with the afterglow of the vanished sun behind her, I recognise her. Her head is hanging down.

"Mr Edgeland!"

I hear crunching footsteps behind me, running.

The voice, in its thick German accent, calls again, "Mr Edgeland, please come back! There has been an error."

I turn, my head singing, my chest strapped tight. A bear-like man with a triumphant bouncing mane of grey hair puffs down the driveway after me. His bristling sideburns frame a rosy face with eager eyes.

He reaches me, gasping, then reaches out a large sweaty paw to take my trunk.

"Come back to the hotel, Mr Edgeland. Or should I say, Mr Weighton?"

He gives a wry smile.

Weighton. Of course. Fool.

"I appreciate your need for privacy, Sir. We are very discreet here at Cragside. May I say how sorry I am for your loss."

My anonymity has been breached.

"Now, I am sure we can clear up this little confusion. You are very welcome here."

He shakes my hand in a welcoming, wet squeeze and I feel my whole being submit to its authority.

I turn to look at the gateway, but the woman has vanished.

CHAPTER 11

The hand belongs to Dr Waltz, the chief doctor, founder and principal shareholder of Cragside. He guides me back up the driveway, hailing a scampering attendant to take my trunk. Once inside, he pilots me into a comfortable candlelit reception room off the lobby and deposits me on a soft chaise. I sit, embarrassed and pale, waiting to find out what's to be done with me. Not one day into my great escape and I'm already exposed.

Waltz vanishes for a moment to speak to the desk clerk and I hear his angry voice through the doorway. Then he returns, all smiles, and busies himself in the corner at a grand Biedermeier cherrywood cabinet.

I peruse the heavy gilt-framed portraits of serious white-bearded men glowering down from the walls. One, in particular, holds my attention: an old vulture, scraggy-necked and craning out of the oily sludge of the canvas. His hungry eyes seem to look at me as if I am carrion. He reminds me of my father.

"Now then, let me see," says Waltz, scanning the contents of the cabinet. "Bitters, bismuth, Condy's Ozonised Water, heroin cough suppressant. Ah, here we are! Sometimes the traditional cures are still the best."

There is a clink of glass and I snap to attention.

The Doctor turns from the cabinet with a balloon of brandy. "Medicinal, of course, my dear Mr Edgeland. Here at Cragside, self-denial is our watch-word." He unleashes a broad smile as he hands it over.

I sip and then, feeling a sudden familiar gnawing hunger take hold, sip again, letting the brandy's gentle burn sink into my stomach. My head begins to right itself.

He studies me. Then, with a flourish, he throws out his hand to the portraits. "Our very dear patrons and investors, without whom we could not do our great and important work."

He takes a seat opposite me. "Mr Weighton, for I shall call you that out of respect for your privacy, this kind of misunderstanding happens from time to time. If you are still willing to stay with us, and I sincerely hope that you are, there is a very pleasant second-floor room that I can have made up immediately. It is south-facing so you will have a grand view of the moors. One of the best in the facility, I can assure you."

"Any mistake is mine, Doctor," I say. "Please do not blame your man on reception."

"In any establishment, even in a place designed expressly for repose, sometimes stress and confusion can raise their worrisome heads. My job here is to smooth over everything and restore the reign of calm."

He looks me over with an intense curiosity, then grins, showing a phalanx of white teeth. My gaze is drawn again to his enormous hands, less the instruments of a doctor than the tools of a stevedore. I wonder how many emotionally fragile guests those hands have restrained.

"I am sure that you will find our facilities most restorative. One of my doctors will give you a full explanation of our various treatments in the morning. But first, you have had a long day, perhaps I could offer you some dinner or perhaps a warm bath while your room is being prepared?"

He waves to a figure in the doorway and a muscular housekeeper enters, hair scraped into a tight bun, her starched black dress matching the grim look on her square face.

"Room 231 to be made up for this gentleman if you please, Mrs Hubbard."

The woman gives a formal nod and strides off.

I relax a little.

"That exhibition, Doctor, it... it was most uncharacteristic of me." I flush. "I must confess that I have been feeling a little more fraught than usual lately. I've not been sleeping well. I'm distracted. I have also given myself over to some unfortunate and unhealthy habits."

The Doctor nods, shrewd eyes glittering in the candle-light. "I fear nervous exhaustion, however slight, is an all-too-common malaise in these modern times. To have it exacerbated by grief as well. Ah! You are in good company, Sir. Many of the souls who come to Cragside are approaching the, how do you say, 'end of their tether' and are desperate for the uniquely healthful cures that we offer. How much better it would be if the benefits of the moor and its waters were used as a preventative rather than a cure?"

He reaches over and places his hand on my knee, gripping firmly. "This is your home now, at least for a little while."

I feel the warm glow of the brandy and his reassurances spread through me and I smile. For the first time in months, I feel my shoulder muscles relax slightly.

The Doctor releases his grip and nods. "I am sure you will find your time here invigorating as long as you exercise *total*," and he emphasises this word, "moderation in your drinking, and eating, and do not under any circumstances attempt to write letters or conduct business – doing so can be most taxing to the tired brain and burst the bubble of calm we strive to create here. Rest is the key!"

༺✦༻

WEARINESS OVERTAKES ME. I SIGN THE REGISTER WITH MY clumsy pseudonym, and agree to the terms of residency, although I do not read them in detail, such is my haste to get to my room and sleep.

The fierce-looking housekeeper returns, and the desk clerk somewhat sheepishly escorts me up the broad staircase.

At the top of the stairs, we take another narrow spiral staircase up to the second floor, and we pass along a long straight corridor that must cut into the south wing of the hotel where, at the very end, stands the door to Room 231.

The room is spotlessly clean. The bed is modest with plain white sheets and a new flame flickers in a grate that is too small for the large bare wall that it occupies. Through the windows, I can just make out the dark shape of the moor before the clerk draws plain yellow curtains across it. The polished boards of the floor are unadorned by any carpet except a patch of kilim by the side of the bed.

"The rooms are intentionally plain, Sir," says the desk clerk, as if reading my thoughts. "We find that a lack of unnecessary adornment is soothing to our clients."

I thank him and try to offer a coin, which he smiles and waves away. As he turns to head back, I notice a stain on the boards. It spreads out like the petals of a dark flower. There is something about it that is strangely familiar.

"What is that?"

The man peers at the stain and a frown creases his fore-head. "I'm not sure, Sir, if I'm honest. It may be that one of the morning baths got spilt. It happens from time to time. Will it be a problem?"

He seems wary of upsetting me.

"No, no! I was merely curious. Thank you."

He leaves, advising me that he will send up some supper.

If anyone comes, I don't hear them, for I kick off my boots, stretch out on the bed and fall fast asleep.

When I wake, the room is pitch black, the candle has guttered out. I am momentarily disoriented as I struggle up through the riptides of sleep. For a second, I think I might still be in India, in a heavy scented night with piercing stars.

Then the sound of the wild moorland wind battering the window brings me back to the present.

I fumble for the matches in the pocket of my coat, which, of course, I am still wearing. It is not cold, but I have the bone-deep chill of one who has slept on top of the covers for too long.

There is a sudden dripping noise and my heart leaps.

It can't be happening again. Not here.

I think about the figure of the woman I saw at the gateway.

I strike a match, sending shadows scurrying.

I touch the flame to a fresh candle on the side table and rub my face, feel the skin moving over my skull, and try to ground myself back in reality.

Where is that infernal noise coming from? I heave myself off the bed and carry the candle to the corners of the room, listening to the echoing noise, but its location is impossible to determine.

I tell myself it's only a drip, nothing more sinister than that.

I sigh and look at my luggage. It feels too late to unpack, but I open my trunk and pull out my nightshirt. I strip, sensitive and naked in that strange room with the night wind tugging at the casement. I carefully take out the silver photograph frame and stand it by the side of the bed.

I check my watch. It's just gone three. I feel an urge to glance out. I pad to the window and pull back the curtains.

I see my candlelit reflection in the glass, hollow-eyed. Beyond, I can just make out the looming silhouette of the moor against the crystalline night sky, and above it, a silvery half-moon fretted with scudding clouds.

The dripping stops.

I draw the curtains before hurrying back to bed, this time snug under the covers.

I close my eyes and return to the nebulous regions of the dark where I float in memories.

At some point in the night, the dripping returns and wakes me again.

I cram the pillow around my ears and lie there with my jaw clenched, basted in sweat, till sleep drags me under.

CHAPTER 12

I'm woken at a quarter to seven by gentle raps on the door.

I don't have time to get completely out of bed before the door opens and a young man with a professional and practised briskness enters, carrying a pile of towels.

"Good morning, Sir. Sorry to wake you, but Dr Waltz has instructed me to give you your first treatment of the day. Please stay in bed and if you would be so good as to lie back down?"

I settle back into the bed, slightly alarmed, wondering what is to come.

"Work away," I say, with a determination to be healed.

He places the towels on the floor, and then proceeds to pack out my bed with them. After the initial shock of having another man fumbling around under the covers, I am delighted to find that the towels are hot. He explains that they have just come from a steam room. The roasting towels clamped around my body are deliciously relaxing. He goes to the window and flings it wide open, letting fresh air tumble into the stale room.

I lie there, the towels slowly cooling under the bedding, taking deep breaths of cool pure air. The attendant leaves, giving a crisp little bow at the doorway.

I am washed back into the shallows of sleep.

When I wake again, I look at my open watch on the nightstand and realise it's time for breakfast.

I ENTER THE DINING ROOM, KEEN TO BE IGNORED.

There is a spartan banquette, the only fare provided being toast and soft-boiled eggs. I am hungry, having missed my supper, so wolf my toast, ravage my eggs and drain my tea, but I'm left half sated, pining for a kipper.

I spy on my fellow guests.

On the whole, they are older than me, most being in late middle age, generally dressed for outdoor activity in tweeds and outdoor dresses.

It's immediately clear to me which of them have been longer at Cragside than others. Some have an ease of movement around the breakfast room and familiarity and confidence in the way they greet their fellow guests. They seek established spots that they, through habit, have claimed as their own by right.

One well-dressed couple dominates the room. The husband is a rangy man with a large, constantly moving mouth and a puffed-up chest. His wife is a hearty, horsey woman with a voice that makes the plates vibrate.

"Of course, Mr Garstang and I have already taken our customary dawn walk up to the top of the gardens to taste the waters of the great fountain! Once the waters were taken and their invigorating effects were felt, we then took a constitutional hike around the grounds before allowing ourselves the luxury of a plain toast breakfast."

I feel my whole body curling into a snarl. I realise I'm going to have to listen to this kind of nonsense for the next two weeks.

I sip a second cup of tea and watch as a plump young vicar with curly blond locks and wind-scoured cheeks bounds in. "Good morning, ladies and gentlemen," he cries, clapping his hands together with a loud slap. "I hope you had restful nights! I trust you will all be joining me in the lounge after breakfast for our customary morning prayers. You will be pleased to know that afterwards, I will do some further scripture readings for those who are available. Mrs Williams, we are reading from Luke, which I know is your favourite! Later this morning, I will be leading a group up to the very top of the moor, so if you have a taste for exercise and adventure, you can still sign up to join us. Simply go to reception and ask for the list. I will be leading us in a few hymns at the top of the moor by the Guardian Angels standing stones. Our elevated height will help us raise our voices to the Lord!"

Having a distaste for clear-eyed evangelising, I ignore him. I pour a third, stewed cup of tea, and steel myself for my induction into the treatments of Cragside.

My appointed guide is a thin, nervous doctor by the name of Locke. He has a perfectly trimmed, waxed moustache and wet eyes that roll around behind his glasses in a never-ending dance, never once seeming to latch their gaze onto anything, least of all my own.

The induction starts with a consultation. He sits me down in his small plain-walled office and reels off a spiel which I imagine he uses on all his patients.

"Cragside prides itself on the regularity of its environment, providing a well-ordered framework for the delicate souls that it cares for. We aim to reduce the amount of surprise to the bare minimum of that afforded by the change-able moorland weather. To that end, and following the advise-ment of Dr Waltz who I believe you met last night, I am to draw you up a tailored regimen which I would advise you adhere to closely."

His prescription, which he talks me through at length, is a course of cold-water treatment, wet towels, needle showers and sitz baths, with air pressure bathing for the racking cough I intermittently suffer, and hot Turkish baths for my nerves.

These treatments are to be combined with frequent doses of the local waters to cleanse my system of any effete matter (whatever that might be). He seems particularly delighted that I have occasionally suffered a sore throat, although I consider this to be secondary to my main ailments.

For my general lack of energy, he orders a daily walk to the top of the moor, or if my nerves will not allow that, a turn around the grounds. This will apparently open up the passages in my lungs and stimulate blood flow.

Finally, he orders a complete abstention from any intoxi-cating beverages.

This is exactly what I had feared on the way north.

Despite the early promise of Waltz's restorative brandy, staff in the establishment treat the evils of drink very seri-ously and there is a general moratorium on alcohol in all its forms. Tobacco is, of course, permitted but only outside so as not to upset some of the more delicate guests' respiratory systems.

I ready myself, determined to get well, preferably through extended periods of lying down.

I AM ESCORTED BY LOCKE TO THE BATHS, HOUSED IN AN annexe to the hotel in a series of chambers leading off from a vaulted corridor. The building is lit by dim gas lamps whose flicking light glistens off walls wet with condensation.

The steam rooms, Locke explains, were an innovation taken from Dr Waltz's experiences of the Hammams of the Orient. Either side are closed chambers which for some reason make me think of the Spanish Inquisition.

He leaves me to disrobe in a side room. I put on a calico shift, which immediately sticks to my sweaty back, and loose wooden pattens for my feet. Locke then leads me, clopping behind like a sacrificial virgin in clogs, into the baths themselves.

They are decorated in a faux Islamic style, with scalloped arches and high windows. Coloured glass casts vivid pools of red, blue and green light across the carvings on the walls and pillars. I could be in Constantinople. There are a series of heated rooms, each progressively hotter than the previous, culminating with the intimidating Calidarium. The population enjoying the baths this particular morning are male (the sexes alternate mornings and afternoons).

He leaves me to experience them alone.

As I move from room to room, enjoying the changes in temperature and humidity, I find myself slipping into a tranquil reverie, and feel no impulse to make even the briefest conversation with the other men sweating it out.

Sitting in the foggiest chamber in blankets of steam, after a while my fellow guests fade from my immediate awareness and become only shapes in the mist. Some of the other men chat, but their muttering voices are shifting notes in the echoes, distorted beyond meaning.

I feel very comfortable, at ease now with the sweat pouring from my body, and with the waft of my rising animal scent.

After a while, I allow myself to slide into a vivid daydream. The steam is so thick that it blinds me, creating a blank canvas for my imaginings. My mind slips into the past. I travel through layers of memory to India again. I see the colours, and the sights, I can smell the heady mix of wood smoke, incense, spice and decay. I see great lumbering elephants, piles of turmeric, garam masala, cumin and chillies laid out in the markets, rich saris and brilliant scarlet turbans piercing the dun palette of the streets. I hear the sound of the chattering marketplace.

I see the riverbank beneath the banyan trees, dotted with funeral pyres, either flaming and fresh or smouldering around their desiccated char-black corpses.

I see her face, obscured by floating hair like the petals of a flower.

A large drop of warm water falls from the ceiling onto my face. I flinch and snap back into the room, my heart pounding.

"THE AIR PRESSURE BATH IS AN EXCELLENT TREATMENT FOR ailments of the lungs and circulatory systems. It also overcomes stiffness of the legs and torpidity of the womb," Locke says, leading me to a door and swinging it open for me.

I feel grateful that for all my other ailments, I do not suffer torpidity of the womb.

This treatment chamber is much bigger than I had expected and relatively plain. What is more surprising is the huge metal tank that dominates the room, fed by pipes that snake along the floor, bound by rivets. On one side of the tank are pressure gauges and a wheel or tap that presumably controls the pressure within. Yet another attendant stands by the machine, who, when he sees Locke and me enter, immediately grabs the wheel and turns it.

Once the tank is depressurised, I enter using a swing door with a porthole. Inside the metal chamber, wooden seating runs around the walls. A vague beige light seeps in through the steamy window. I sit, nodding my good mornings to two other men. They are both bald, paunchy and red-faced. The attendant swings the door closed behind me with a clang. There is the telltale hiss of hot steam as it begins to belch out of the grilled ventilation tubes. I feel the pressure inside slowly build. A gauge on the wall begins to twitch higher.

The weight of compressed air begins to press against my ears and they both pop and crunch as I move my jaw. I wince and see my fellow prisoners also flexing and forcing yawns. We take deep lungfuls of steamy air. The effect is quite pleasant, but my vision begins to swim. I wonder what safety limits are placed on the flow.

For a moment, I experience a flicker of fear. What if the gauge breaks, causing a sudden influx of crushing pressure? Will we be squeezed to death? My breath becomes short. I grip the wooden seat for reassurance.

My rising panic must show as the gentleman next to me leans in and shouts above the noise, "It's best just to give in to the machine. It's more pleasant when you do."

"It's rather a strange experience," I shout back.

"You'll get used to it. It is far from the oddest thing that they have here. Allow me to introduce myself, I'm Charles Sheppey," he says. I shake his sweaty hand.

Give in to the machine. A strange expression.

I feel like Jonah, helpless in the belly of the whale.

I take more deep breaths and force myself to relax the tension in my shoulders, but the knots twist in tighter.

I start to panic, feel it rise like a wild beast.

At the porthole, I see the face of the attendant, silhou-etted and indistinct through the condensation.

The steam and pressure pile on, but it's not enough to crush the mortal panic that flails and kicks inside me. I hang onto the wooden bench and shut my eyes, locking my jaw to stop myself from screaming.

Then everything goes blank.

CHAPTER 13

The waft of ammonium carbonate jerks me awake. Mr Sheppey stands over me, vaguely amused, alongside the attendant, who is stoppering the smelling salts. Both intervene when I try to sit up (I'm lying on the floor of the pressure chamber). They urge me to stay still.

The door of the chamber is open but the steamy fug has not quite dissipated. After a few moments, I'm allowed to crawl back up onto the bench, and then I'm escorted by the attendant to a cooler rest area where I lie on a bed, my heart hammering and my swimmy vision slowly coming to rest.

Locke bustles in, aghast. He apologises profusely and brings me a glass of cold water which I sip until I'm ready to dress. He advises that the afternoon's callisthenic exercises in the hotel's gymnasium are probably not what is needed, and instead advises rest.

I walk back through the treatment rooms, lightheaded, feeling the corridors tilt slightly, and I reach out my hand to steady myself against the wall.

Once outside, I feel fresh air rush into my lungs and my head clears.

Should I lie down, as prescribed? The thought of being trapped in my churning mind for the afternoon is not appealing.

Back in the hotel, the spiral staircase up to the second floor is quite a climb.

On pushing open the heavy door to my room, I stop and stare.

The stain on the burnished wooden floor glitters in the midday light. I realise there is fresh water spreading across my floor, running in rivulets down the grooves between the floorboards and catching the light from the windows. It is fresh.

I look up at the ceiling but can see no sign of a leak coming from the room above. The water is shallow, merely a puddle, but it distinctly follows the flowered pattern of the stain.

I turn, puzzled, intending to head to reception to fetch someone to assist with the mess, but I'm so fatigued from my faint that I slump onto the bed. I take the picture frame from the side of my bed, hold it to my chest and settle back, fully dressed.

I sleep, not for long, but just enough to touch the bottom of the well and take the edge off my exhaustion. Rubbing my eyes, I sit up and remember the water. I stumble, foggy, to the door and open it. Walking down the corridor towards the far door is a red-headed chambermaid.

"Miss!" I call after her.

She turns. "Yes, Sir?"

"I seem to have a leak or something in my room. There is water all over my floor. Would you mind seeing if someone could come and help with it?"

She comes and stands in the doorway, staring at the pool of water in a state of some alarm.

"Was this here when you got in from your treatments, Sir?" she says.

"It was, although the stain was there when I arrived yesterday. Is there a leak somewhere? I heard dripping last night."

She looks at the ceiling and squints. "I don't see one. Perhaps there's a pipe running under the room that's burst. I'll see if I can get someone to have a look at it." She turns and scurries away.

She returns soon with a mop and an elderly caretaker. His bristling whiskers and bearing indicate a military background, and his rheumy eyes betray a drinker.

He pokes at the ceiling, examines the corners of the room and is generally ineffectual and bewildered. I start to lose my patience.

There is an urgent hunger inside me, a twitching need. I want a drink. But there's no chance of that.

I glance out of the window and see the vastness of the moor and feel a sudden urge to be up there, striding in the wind.

I grab my coat and pull it on, desperate to be away from the confining atmosphere of this place.

The dripping noise again.

"There! Can you hear the drips?"

The caretaker cocks his head to listen, then shrugs. The old fool is probably half deaf.

The chambermaid is still in the doorway, clutching her mop, looking as if the world is going to cave in on her at any moment. Why is everyone so on edge around me?

"Excuse me, girl," I say in as kind a voice as I can muster. "Do you think there's something odd about that water? You've been staring at it in quite a peculiar fashion."

She looks abashed. "No, Sir. This room hasn't been used for some months. It's odd that it should choose to leak the moment that someone takes occupancy."

"Why was it left vacant? I thought Cragside was more or less fully booked over the summer?"

She avoids my gaze, mutters something unintelligible and begins a fresh round of mopping, leaving my question hanging in the air. I watch her, quietly fuming at her ignorance, then stalk out.

Bedrest in that room is going to be no rest at all. I need fresh air.

IT IS A DELIGHTFUL SUMMER'S DAY, ALBEIT CUT THROUGH with a cool breeze. I gaze out of the main entrance at the dappled sunlight tracing across the lawn, then up to the folds of purple heather on the moor. I feel a longing to be up there, in nature. I want exercise and clarity.

I borrow a stick from reception and a pamphlet with a crude map highlighting key points of interest. A new enthusiasm energises me.

The grounds are exquisitely maintained, a sea of clipped lawn in which lies an archipelago of rose beds, bordered by great bursts of rhododendron and lines of yew. I stride up a gravel path that winds up through rockeries. The trail ducks between hedges, breaking into rocky steps when the gradient became too steep. Far ahead, it leads up to a high wall that marks the boundary of the hydro's grounds and then threads its way up the hill away from Cragside to the rough gritstone shoulder of the moor.

As I climb higher, I realise how unfit I am. My breath shortens and I feel a definite flush beneath my clothes till I am again sweating, the moisture on my back chilled instantly by the cool breeze as it sneaks beneath the fabric.

I push on, crossing a tiny beck via a neat little wooden bridge, and continue up the path till I reach a patch of lawn surrounded by ornamental pine trees. In the centre of the lawn stands a fountain, carved with incongruous images of cavorting sea nymphs and various other seemingly random mythological figures. From the mouth of a cherub spouts a jet of spring water. As I enter the glade, I spot the hearty couple from breakfast. They take little tin cups from their pockets, fill them from the spewing cherub then sip the water, throwing back their heads enthusiastically to slosh the liquid around their mouths and throats before swallowing in satisfied gasps.

I step forward.

"Hallo! Have you taken the waters yet?" calls the gentleman, his ferocious white sideburns framing his face like an Elizabethan ruff.

"I'm afraid not. Are they good? I did have a treatm..."

The woman interrupts in a voice that could command a battalion. "Young man! There is simply NOTHING better. These chalybeate waters cleanse the system, restore vigour to the limbs and purify the blood. Mr Garstang and I take them three times a day without fail."

"If I may ask, what is it about the composition that gives them such remarkable powers?" I try to keep a creeping note of sarcasm out of my voice.

"No idea!" says Mr Garstang blithely. "Piped down from natural springs up on the moor. Rich in moorland minerals or something. Mind, it does taste a bit foisty."

He receives a withering look from his wife.

I promise to return later with a cup and sample it for myself, bid them a good day and continue at a brisk pace on my walk.

The path leads to the boundary wall. I pass through a squeaking iron gate and find myself on the moor itself. A few minutes of huffing and puffing take me to a new vantage and I survey the valley below.

About two miles away lies the town of Whitmoor, a small neat-looking place, its low buildings clustered like pebbles, except for the piercing stone spires of three churches. I notice larger newer buildings clinging to the skirts of the moor and wonder if these are rival hydrotherapy establishments.

Across the valley rises more high ground, stretching away into the distance. It is a vast rolling sea of purple heather and grass. Titanic shadows of clouds stream in a shifting kaleidoscope of light and dark.

From above me, I can hear the bleating of stray sheep. Their voices sound eerily like human cries for help. I feel a chill.

I climb higher, almost to the gritstone crags that tower over the hotel like gigantic rotten teeth. I pull out my creased pamphlet. These are the 'Devil's Pinnacles' and legend has it that they were constructed as a prison for Satan by a local holy man in ages past.

There is no direct way to the top of the great blocks, but their summit is attained by following a gentler side path that out-flanks them. I use my hands and feet up a narrow gully and emerge with the wind in my face.

I expected to find myself at the top of the world. Instead, I find that I have merely reached the lip of an enormous plateau. Waves of moorland stretch away before me to the south, a vast plain of bog, grass and brittle heather with a single narrow path leading away to the horizon.

I follow it, trying to ignore the haunting cries of the sheep that dot the moor. The world turns beneath my boots as I stride along, as if I am walking on a circus ball.

I am free from all cares until I nearly step on a grouse and it bursts up between my legs in a sudden flurry, causing my heart to skip.

Other birds zip across the plateau, wheatears, their white backsides bobbing, and curlews.

Finally, at the highest point, I rest and smoke a cigarette, free from the prying, pious eyes of the hydro.

Some way to the east I can see a low stone circle, the Guardian Angels, according to my pamphlet, since time immemorial a way marker for travellers lost in the fog and snow. I doubt that the primitive men who arranged the stones were thinking about angels. I wonder at their original purpose.

Great tides of cloud roll above me.

Caught here between moor and sky, I feel suddenly isolated, surrounded by so much space, with only the wind for company. I can't remember ever seeing a scene so lovely.

I wish suddenly, carelessly, that Isabella was alive to see it.

No.

I push the thought of her aside, and walk further, to the south edge of the moor. There, a new vista begins to open up to me.

It could not be more different to the pastoral idyll I have left behind. Far below me are craning chimneys belching black smoke, the furrows of slate roofs and all the usual scars of industry.

I take out my pamphlet.

The town below me is Blackmoor.

A dark cloud passes over the sun, plunging the world into gloom.

My whole body recoils in horror. I turn and hurry back the way I came, trying to blot out the screams of the sheep in the wind.

CHAPTER 14

I walk down the gravel path to the hotel grounds, terror burrowing inside me like a questing termite. A faint, dusty smell of smoke makes me stop.

I look back at the horizon, to the craggy fringes of the moor, and I see an appalling shroud of smoke rising, casting a shadow over the valley. It is vaguely yellow, drifting in sickening waves across the pinnacles and copses. I can't be sure of the source of the smoke. It's far back in the depths of the plateau.

I expect it is a planned burning, but still, the memory of my cigarette from earlier makes me nervous. I'm sure it was out. I crushed it with my heel, after all.

More anxiety. For all its promise of relieving me of tension, Cragside seems to be doing its best to increase it. I begin to seriously wonder if this is the right place for me.

I must continue to give it a chance. Perhaps things will get harder before they get easier.

I fumble for my card for the day, looking for the reassurance of structured activity, and I see that Locke has scheduled one final treatment. It is at three-thirty and I have twenty minutes to get back. I pick up the pace.

At the appointed time, I go to a room, not in the annexe of the hotel housing the baths, but down a narrow flight of stairs to a corridor running beneath the main reception rooms of the hotel. This part of the hotel looks unfrequented and unloved, the plaster on the walls cracked and flaking. There is a musty smell, a faint odour of mice.

I rap on a solid oak door marked "Private" and wait for a response.

"Come!" There is a familiar voice from within.

I turn the heavy handle and swing the door open. The room is bare, with only a table and two chairs set on either side. The only window is mounted high in the wall, affording only the most meagre, dingy light.

Sitting watching me from across the table is Dr Waltz. In the shadows, he seems less genial, instead almost threateningly ursine. He doesn't smile but gestures with a great hand to sit.

On the table is a piece of brass equipment mounted on a stand. It is like an extended teapot spout, wider at one end than the other and curved in a sinuous, upsettingly organic fashion to a narrow aperture. The spout can be raised or lowered on its stand using a series of locks and screws. Halfway up the stand is a little brass platform behind which is a mirror, in front of which is fastened a little circular lens on a pivot.

I take my seat opposite Waltz, staring at him through the equipment.

He speaks in a low voice. "Good afternoon, my dear Mr Edgeland, if I may use your real name here in private. I trust you are enjoying your stay?"

"Very restorative," I lie. He nods slowly and then gestures at the instrument before him.

G.H. LUSBY

"This piece of remarkable equipment is a laryngoscope of my design. It enables the skilled practitioner to detect afflictions of the throat and mouth. As you know, many of the curative properties of the singular water of these parts are purgative – they refresh the body and clear it of..."

"Effete matter?" I say.

He pauses. "Indeed. This equipment allows me to see some of the physical symptoms that might be caused by this build-up of material. However, to use it, I need a better and more focused source of light."

With this, he leans across and places a candle on the brass platform. Then, taking a box of lucifers from his waistcoat pocket, he lights it with a fizz and flare. He adjusts the mirror behind it and the lens in front of it and a beam of light dazzles me. I blink and Waltz is blacked into silhouette.

"Is it painful?"

"No, no, my dear fellow. A little uncomfortable, perhaps. You must relax and allow the probe to do its work. All that is required is tolerance and patience while I carry out my examination. Now, how have you been finding the treatments today? I hear you were a little overcome in the pressure chamber?"

I shift uneasily. "Otherwise it has been very restful. I have to say, I've experienced a few twinges of anxiety as they've been doing their work."

"That is not unusual, it takes time and repeated exposure to the treatments for them to take effect. Rest is important and cannot be rushed. You have hopefully seen some evidence of their effectiveness in the condition of the other guests here?"

"Oh, yes. Everyone seems quite enthused. I hope that I feel as they do after a few more days of rest."

I'm trying to convince myself as much as him.

"You will, I am sure. Well, to get to the heart of the

mystery of your ailments, I just need you to open your mouth for me."

My eyes stream in the light. Waltz's voice is a disembodied boom somewhere in the corona.

"For the examination to be effective, and so that you are not inadvertently injured during it, I will, unfortunately, need to secure your head," says Waltz, and he moves around the table to stand behind me. I hear a clicking sound of some equipment sliding into place onto the back of my chair, and all of a sudden, his giant hands are gently, but firmly gripping my temples.

"There, just lean back please." He pushes the back of my head into a cradle and then winds a leather strap around my forehead. He tightens it and fastens me secure with a buckle.

"Is that comfortable?"

"It's rather tight, is this strictly necessary?"

"Unfortunately, it is essential. When I insert the probe, there is a chance that you will gag and in a muscular reflex, you may jerk your head. There is some potential for damage to the equipment and you. Now," he says, returning to his side of the desk, "I need you to relax."

He loosens two of the brass keys on the framework of the machine and moves the spout towards me. He pauses, lowering it so that it is in line with my mouth, and then says, "Open wide, please."

As I hesitantly open my mouth, he shoots two thick fingers inside and pulls open my jaws, inserting a steel calliper between my teeth. He prises my mouth open to its fullest extent. I am exposed and helpless. I can taste the salt on his fingers.

He returns to the probe and adjusts it again, moving it closer to my mouth, then deep inside. I feel its brass tube graze the top of my palate. I gag.

"Please try and relax. The laryngoscope allows me to see

deep inside your windpipe. It is a remarkable observational tool, but it requires the subject to submit to it, otherwise, all is difficult."

I feel my breathing quicken and think that I am going to panic and start thrashing about. The brass spout is penetrating further into the back of my mouth, I can feel its curves and cold metallic body with my tongue. I try swallowing but the hard end of the spout against the soft back of my palate prevents me. Waltz is leaning in now, I can feel the heat of his face against mine, the stale coffee smell of his breath. I hear the soft rustling of his nostrils as he breathes.

The brass spout goes deeper.

"Submit to the machine. That's it, that's it," Waltz murmurs.

He lowers his face to the wide end of the instrument and stares into it. I grip the side of the chair as he looks, makes adjustments and looks again. I think I'm either going to vomit, choke or scream.

He sniffs as he makes another adjustment. "With my own patented lens design, I can detect foreign materials and influences in the windpipe. I can see through this now that you have an inflamed windpipe, perhaps you have an infection? Or perhaps you have inhaled smoke recently. Do you smoke, Sir?"

I can't respond but make a high-pitched moan as he adjusts the brass aperture still deeper, tickling but not triggering my gag reflex.

"I have not observed you smoking since you have been with us, therefore this is something of a mystery. Have you smoked?"

Again, there is no way that I can answer but still, he adjusts the end of the machine. "Yes, that seems the most likely answer. I think in this case, smoking has left you with irritation."

I swallow painfully and feel the hard metal tip of the instrument graze me.

"I hope you have seen, Mr Edgeland, that we do good work here. Many ill and troubled people come here for rest and wellness. Perhaps it is to do with the progress of industry in this nation that establishments such as ours are so necessary. Unfortunately, all of this progress comes at a cost. Science does not stand still and it is key that we remain modern, bringing the latest in scientific developments to bear for the sake of our guests. All of this requires investment."

I have a sudden sinking feeling in my stomach. I realise now why he pursued me so eagerly down the driveway the previous evening.

"Public tastes change and sadly this establishment is not as popular as it was, say, ten years ago. If we do not keep developing, we die, I fear. You can see for yourself what a terrible sadness that would be for our guests, the poor souls who rely on us for their health and, in some cases, sanity."

He tilts the mirror and I see him clearly, a breath away from my face, looking intently into my eyes.

"We are always on the lookout for more investors. Have you seen the honoured and philanthropic patrons who hang on the walls of my office? They are men of vision. Perhaps you too have that vision? Perhaps you also wish to give something back to your fellow man?"

Waltz pulls the machine back, letting my tongue squirm free. I'm able to swallow.

He reaches in and releases the callipers, and my aching jaw snaps shut.

He blows out the candle, sending the room into gloom, and I am again forced to adjust my vision.

He stares at me from across the desk, silent and massive.

I reach up and rub my jaw muscles to get rid of the ache

and run my tongue around my mouth, trying to scrub off the metallic taste.

"I am not of a disposition to make investments, Sir," I say, "and I do not appreciate being approached in these personal and difficult circumstances."

Waltz holds up his hands. "My dear Mr Edgeland, forgive me. While I have lived in your country for many years, I still sometimes overstep the bounds of your traditional reserve. I shall say no more about it. Perhaps you do not yet see the value in our treatments?"

"Of course I see the value of your work, Dr Waltz. But please allow me to get better. Let us talk no more about it."

"Perhaps another day we can discuss terms?"

"No, Sir. No. And if you persist with this, I shall have to return to London. I came here for rest, not for business propositions."

"Did you smoke today?" he says in an angry snap.

I shift uncomfortably. "I did, Doctor. Whilst on a walk on the moor."

"The instrument does not lie. It was the likeliest cause. Nevertheless, the cure remains the same." He writes something in his leather-bound notebook and then moves behind me to release my fetters.

Before he does, he leans in close, his breath against my ear. I flinch away from it, but my head is strapped tight.

"While you are in my care, I want to make sure that I have all the information that I need to help with your recovery. Let me assure you that I will not pester you any further. Your health is now the only thing that matters to me."

And with that, he releases the buckled strap and I am free.

At that moment, I resolve to leave Cragside at the earliest opportunity.

CHAPTER 15

Once I am safely out of the treatment room and the door has closed on Waltz, I storm back up to reception with fresh purpose.

It's one thing to be subjected to abstention and quackery for the sake of my health, but to be panhandled for my trouble is more than I can stand.

Before I can properly gather my thoughts, I'm intercepted by Locke, his wet eyes darting around as he takes me to one side.

"Sir, is all well? Have you recovered from the incident earlier?"

"Quite well. I took advantage of the weather and went for a walk up to the moor."

He looks immensely relieved and lets out a sigh. "Ah, that is good news. I was concerned that you were unsure about the treatments and their efficacy. Can I assume that you will be resuming the schedule tomorrow?"

"I'm sure," I lie.

His face lights up. "Excellent, excellent, Sir. Enjoy the rest of your afternoon."

He gives a little bow and retreats.

I consider going back to my room but the thought of staying in the hotel much longer agitates me. Instead, I turn on my heel and march out and down the driveway, swinging my borrowed stick as I go. I will go to Whitmoor to examine the train timetable for tomorrow's departures.

I feel eyes on my back as I go.

The pall of smoke hangs still on the horizon.

I notice here and there that some leaves are already touched by autumn's corrosion. I stride, letting my stick mark my progress in the gravel, feeling the heat between my shoulder blades as the late afternoon sun sears my clothing.

I am halfway between the hydro and the main road when I realise that someone is walking a short distance behind me. I turn and squint but don't recognise him. He clings to the edges of the driveway, in the dappled shadows of the mighty beeches.

A black ant of suspicion crawls into my heart. Why on earth would someone wish to follow me? Have they been commissioned by Waltz?

I reach the road to Whitmoor, which is only a mile distant.

I pass a wagon heading down the valley and exchange a nod with the driver, a craggy, meaty man, taking goods perhaps up to the hotel, and as I do, I glance behind me. The figure continues to follow.

The town of Whitmoor is prettier than I expected. It blossoms like an alpine resort across the valley bottom. Church spires reach up to greet the mighty wave of rock and heather cresting above. There is parkland at the edge of town which steepens and blends into the tamed hem of the moor, dotted with elegant pagodas and drinking fountains. The town is bisected by a wide boulevard lined with cherry trees and fronted by pretty canopied shops stocked with goods far beyond those of a normal market town.

But in my initial surge of excitement at being out of the hydro, I find that I have fully explored it in less than half an hour.

Of my companion on the road, I see nothing.

Who I do see, as I look longingly in the windows of a bakery, is the red-haired chambermaid from the hotel. Her reflection passes behind mine and I turn to greet her.

She is hurrying on an errand and doesn't notice me. She's not dressed in the livery of the hotel, but instead in a tatty green dress, her boots tapping on the stone flags. She is struggling with a heavy basket of shopping.

I consider for a moment. I really should go to the train station.

Instead, I follow her.

"Good afternoon!" I say as I catch up.

She starts and snaps her head around, her eyes flashing. Then, on seeing me, her lips thin.

"Good afternoon, Sir. Is there anything I can help you with?"

"No need for formality. I am just wondering if I might help you with your basket? It seems rather heavy."

She looks troubled and backs away.

"I don't mean to put you in an uncomfortable situation. If it's improper for me to converse with you outside the hotel, then I apologise."

"Well, it's not encouraged by Dr Waltz," she says, "and to be honest, Sir, this is the only time off I have off this week."

"My apologies, I should have thought, I should respect your privacy. Forgive me."

I too back away, and am about to go when she says, "Mind you, it does weigh a ton."

I smile and take the basket. It nearly pulls my arm from its socket.

We walk along and I get the feeling that she is embarrassed to be in my presence.

"Do you live in Whitmoor?" I say.

She nods. "A lot of the staff live at the hotel, but my family are in Whitmoor. My father's not so well these days. I need to care for him and my brother."

"I am sorry to hear that. Do you like your work?"

"Oh, yes, Sir. Well, it's work. It could be worse." The poor girl looks terribly self-conscious.

We proceed in silence, and I notice that occasional locals exchange brief nods with her and cast curious glances at me.

"Are you enjoying your visit, Sir?"

"If I'm honest, I don't think I'm going to stay the course. I had some of the treatments today, but I don't think it's for me, I'm afraid. I very much like the country round here, the moor in particular, but I think I will be heading back to London tomorrow."

She looks straight ahead and doesn't acknowledge this.

"I hope I haven't offended?"

She turns, her eyes hard. "I think you should give the treatments a chance, Sir. What harm could there be in them?"

Then she takes back her basket.

"Besides," she says, "tomorrow is Sunday. No trains are running back to Bradford. The earliest you'll be able to get away is Monday. Maybe you'll have changed your mind by then."

Without another word, she stamps off down the street.

CHAPTER 16

I can't believe I have to wait a whole extra day. I resolve to try to just get through it.

That night, with no wish to make conversation, I take care to enter the dining room late. As a result, I have my pick of the empty tables. I dine alone, making eye contact with no one.

I force down an unpleasant, grainy consommé followed by stringy guinea fowl and then slip out, unnoticed.

To my embarrassment, I see the chambermaid again coming along the corridor from the kitchen. I thank her for her company earlier but feel her recoil from me with something like revulsion. I wonder again if I've jeopardised her reputation or position by being seen with her in public. She scurries off through one of the "Staff Only" doors deep into the labyrinth of the hotel.

I withdraw to my room. My trunk stands in the corner, lid still open, clothes neatly folded and stacked within. I dress for bed and read Henry James for a while, but get lost as usual among his endless sentences. My brain tries to follow their twisting threads, clauses and sub-clauses. Finding no purchase, my gaze slips off the page.

Everything feels strange and distant. I look out at the sunset, burnished through the yellowing smoke on the horizon.

I lie back on the bed, then with a sudden chill realise that the faint dripping noise has returned. I examine the stain on the floor, but there is no fresh water there. The noise continues, echoing around the room. I fold the pillow around my head to block it out and squeeze my eyes tight shut.

I plummet into a deep sleep. I dream about the hotel. I am a disembodied consciousness floating through endless flooded corridors, everything reflecting and swirling, the dripping noise echoing around me.

❧

MORNING. I SWIM UPWARDS THROUGH THE RIPTIDES AND gradually come to, groggy, staring up at the now familiar ceiling.

I sit up in bed and look at the open trunk in the corner. I have not announced my intention to leave to anyone other than the chambermaid, and so I make a silent resolution to keep quiet about it. I have no wish for another "chat" with Dr Waltz or his cronies. I just need to endure one more day.

With newly galvanised resolve, I dress briskly and head out for a morning walk to clear my head. I stride manfully out of the lobby, across the grounds and up the winding path that leads up the side of the moor, puffing and enjoying the beating of my heart, the pumping of the blood through my limbs and the morning breeze on my freshly shaven cheeks.

I note that the fire on the moor is still burning, and has spread in the night. I wonder what efforts, if any, the locals are making to beat the thing out. For now, I am glad the wind is carrying the smoke away from me.

At the fountain, I look back at the hotel and realise with some satisfaction that I'm the first person up and about. I go so far as to do some basic callisthenic exercises in the morning air to stretch life into my limbs, secure in the knowledge that I can't be observed.

As I am stretching, I notice something lying on the ground by the fountain. I squint at it and with a start realise it's my sleeping cap. I recognise the distinctive burgundy stripe.

What is it doing here? Have I unwittingly carried it up with me tucked in the folds of my coat? It's the only possible explanation. But it's muddy and wet through, having been lying on the dewy grass for some time. Perhaps it isn't mine at all? I tuck it into my coat pocket and mentally file the mystery for later.

I see with some satisfaction the Garstangs emerge from the main doors on their morning constitutional. How amusing, I think, they are going look up any moment and see that I have already claimed the first quaff of their damned water.

As I approach, I tip my hat to them and exclaim, "Good morning!"

To my surprise, they back away from me, startled and nervous. They mutter, "Morning," evading eye contact.

Once past them, I shake my head. Their noses have been put out of joint by my morning vigour. I marvel at the pettiness of some people.

As I reach the lawn, more guests are emerging on their morning strolls. Again, I adopt a smile and what I imagine is the worldly look an explorer might have on returning to civilisation after months up the Limpopo. I nod and greet each person I pass.

Yet again there is something out of place. Some are over-friendly and forced, others look at me with an active expression of distaste, and others ignore me altogether.

I look myself over to see if I have some issue with my appearance that might cause such a remarkable array of reactions. Nothing seems out of place.

I begin to wonder if this feeling of paranoia is some manifestation of my nervous condition; if my fellow guests' reactions are perfectly civil but I am experiencing some heightened sensitivity.

As I enter the lobby, I notice the chambermaid again, carrying a stack of sheets. I'm pleasantly surprised when she smiles and wishes a kind, "Good morning, Sir." I smile back and climb the stairs, confused.

As I ascend the broad first-floor staircase, I notice that she is following me, and continues to follow me as I head up the spiral stairs to my corridor on the second floor. I find her suddenly at my side.

"How are you feeling this morning, Sir?" she says.

Surprised by such familiarity, and somewhat perplexed by her change in tone, I say, "Very well, thank you. It's beautiful out there."

She looks worried.

"Is anything the matter?" I say. "I've noticed that people are acting rather strangely this morning. Has something happened that I've not heard about?"

She looks me in the eyes and says, "I'm probably not supposed to be the one to tell you, Sir, but seeing as I found you... Better from me than one of the other guests."

"What do you mean? Has there been an incident? Has someone died?"

"I shouldn't tell you out here. Perhaps in your room."

I'm confident it's not appropriate to take a chambermaid into one's room but there is no one about and I'm sufficiently intrigued.

We enter and I gesture to her to take a seat. She casts an eye at my trunk in the corner and sits on the chair while I sit on the bed.

"Now, what is it?"

She looks at me with compassionate blue eyes and says in her matter-of-fact Yorkshire accent, "Do you remember what happened last night?"

"To me? I dined alone and went to bed early. Got up this morning, and went for a walk. Why, whatever is the matter?"

She takes a deep breath. "This may be a bit of a shock, Sir, but it's not the only walk you've been on since you went to bed."

"I don't understand."

She leans forward and lowers her voice. "I'd finished for the night and was headed home. Probably around ten. As I was walking around the side of the hotel, I saw someone come down the main stairs and out the front door. It isn't that unusual for guests to take the air before they go to bed, but they don't generally do it in their nightshirts and dressing gowns. I followed and saw the figure walk across the lawn and up the path leading to the moor."

I feel a creeping sense of dread.

"I followed, afraid at first, and called out to see if anything was the matter. I hurried as fast as I could, but the figure was walking quickly and this," she points at her dress, "isn't designed for running."

"Go on," I say, bracing myself.

"It was you, Sir. I think you must have been sleepwalking. I caught up with you at the fountain. You seemed intent on going up the moor. I tried to reason with you but was nervous about waking you because I've heard that it can be a terrible, perhaps dangerous shock. You stumbled at one point and I caught you."

I take the muddy nightcap out of my coat pocket, unroll it and place it on the bed beside me. "Did I drop this?"

She glances at it and nods. "Possibly, Sir. I finally convinced you to return with me to the hotel, it took some time and you weren't very coherent."

"Oh, Lord, what was I saying? I hope nothing offensive." My skin prickles. I am plunged into shame. I can see no reason why the girl would lie about this. It all seems perfectly consistent with the cap and the reactions of my fellow guests.

"Nothing that I could understand, Sir. A little about India, and you kept saying a woman's name."

I lose control and hide my face in my hands.

She sits next to me, on the bed.

"We walked back to the hotel," she says in a low voice. "It took some time because you were disoriented. It was when we arrived back that you began shouting."

"Oh, God..."

"I don't know quite what it was about, you weren't making sense, but it caused enough alarm for some of the other guests to come out of the lounge, where Mr Jackson was finishing off his rotten piano recital. I'm afraid there were several witnesses, Sir. It took some time for the manager and me to calm you and walk you back to your room. In all that time, you weren't yourself."

My dressing gown is hanging on the back of the door. The hem is stained with mud.

"Oh, God, what am I going to do? I need to leave at once."

She stands up and cups my chin, lifting my face. I'm surprised at the firmness of her grip.

"You're going to go down for breakfast, Sir. You're going to look them all in the eye and smile and eat. Then you're going to go about your day, and you're bloody well going to get better."

CHAPTER 17

The chambermaid's name is Polly. I thank her and think about what she has said.

With no trains, there's nothing I can do now anyway. Besides, I'm hungry.

The breakfast room feels like a pool full of sharks. I'm desperate to avoid eye contact. The clattering cutlery ceases. All eyes turn to me.

I feel naked. My shame is complete.

A few guests are brazen enough to stare or whisper to their neighbours as I take a seat by the window. I force myself to look up. I wonder if they think I am mad, or a drunk. I smile and nod at a couple of people and they give flickering acknowledgements before their eyes dart back to the safety of their plates.

I chew some soggy toast and I push some scrambled egg around my plate as the thrum of breakfast noise returns.

One more day. Just a few hours, then I can be gone.

I'm sorry I lied to Polly about staying, but there's no way I can now.

I retreat to my room. On the way back I see her, clearing

away bedding from one of the rooms in my corridor. She gives me an encouraging smile.

I feel awful. Perhaps she's right. I'm going back tomorrow to London, into the vipers' nest, at my most vulnerable.

The hours tick by.

I go for a walk around the grounds, choosing to go while Reverend Newstead's Sunday Service is in full swing. The hymns drone across the lawn, accompanied by the agonised cries of the peacock.

I attract the attention of Sheppey, who has also ducked out of the service and taken a stroll. He accosts me as our paths converge.

"I say, old fellow, how are you?" he says. He is not in the least bit wary of me, although I can tell from his manner that he either witnessed or heard gossip about my night-time exploits.

"Tolerably well, Mr Sheppey," I say quietly. "Lovely morning."

"Listen," he says, leaning in, although there is no one who could overhear, "I heard about the incident last night. Everything alright, old boy?" He looks eager, like a dog following a scent.

I consider my response. "I'm afraid I'm not as familiar with what happened as everyone else. I was sleepwalking. I wonder if it's a side effect of the treatments here. It's all rather embarrassing."

"Well," he laughs, "it certainly caused a bit of a commotion. Sleepwalking, eh? Just make sure that you don't 'sleepwalk' into one of the other guests' rooms, if you know what I mean. I'm not sure that will wash if you're found getting into bed with the shapely widow Curtis, eh?"

I give a thin smile and we walk side by side for a while.

"I was sorry to hear about your father."

I stop, my feet scraping on the gravel. "What do you mean?"

"Edgeland, in't it? John Edgeland?"

"I'm sorry," I say, "you may be confusing me with someone else, with another..." I look away from him and make to move off, but he grabs my arm with his hand. I turned, shrugging it off, and glower.

He looks puzzled, then laughs. "Not likely, I did business with your father for years. I believe we've met before, several years ago at his offices in London and again at your home. I never forget a face. I wonder if we'll work together in the future, now you come into your inheritance?"

I give a razor smile, annoyed to have been caught in a lie.

First Waltz and now this vulgar little man. Is nowhere safe?

Tomorrow can't come quick enough.

"Don't worry," he says, sensing my shame, "I understand why you might be keeping yourself to yourself. As I say, I'm sorry for your loss. If you fancy a little drink sometime, I smuggled in a rather nice bottle of brandy."

I retreat. "No, no. It's fine, thank you. Anyway, I may head into town."

He looks hurt, then amused, then gives a little mocking bow.

ONCE I AM SURE THAT SHEPPEY IS OUT OF THE WAY, I double back, and I will go back to my room and read. Stay there out of the way, and then leave tomorrow as quickly and secretly as possible.

As I re-enter the hotel, though, I find Dr Waltz waiting for me.

I eye him warily.

"Good morning, Sir. I wonder if we might have a chat?"

I suppose I should have expected as much. I resign myself to it and followed him down a "Staff Only" corridor into his private office like a naughty school boy.

The room is in one of the corner towers of the hotel. It is circular and high ceilinged. Every wall is covered with shelves stacked full of leather tomes. It is as if the bottom of a well has been turned into a library. It's more like a medieval alchemist's laboratory than a doctor and businessman's office. Curiously there are no windows, but a gas lamp sputters and casts its sickly light across the broad, cluttered desk. Waltz reclines in the battered leather chair and beckons me to take a seat opposite him. He sits silently for a moment, studying me with steady, sympathetic eyes.

My anger from the previous day evaporates. I feel empty.

"I am very concerned about the incident last night," he says. "I do not know how much of it you are either aware of or can remember?"

I look down. "I remember nothing. I am only aware of what other guests have told me" (I do not want to get Polly into trouble) "and from their general reaction to me this morning, I can guess some of the rest. Were you witness to it yourself?"

"I was, Sir, and I want you to know that we have an ardent desire to help you and to ensure that it does not happen again. We take the well-being of our guests very seriously, and it is exactly this kind of malaise that we are here to treat. I can only say that this kind of somnambulism is relatively uncommon even in cases such as yours. Is it something you have experienced before?"

"Once or twice, perhaps. But I live alone, so I may not be aware of it."

He nods. "I think we can assume that it is not an isolated incident. I understand any embarrassment this is causing you, but rest assured that I've been considering how to treat you. Your full recovery is my main concern."

"Doctor," I say, "could you please give me your version of what happened? I need to know."

He runs his big hand over his jowls and leans forward. "One of the chambermaids saw you leave the building in your dressing gown. She followed you and found you by the fountain, led you back down to the hotel and then you began resisting our efforts to return you to bed. It was a delicate situation, we had no desire to wake you but you were becoming rather agitated, I am afraid to say. Some of your language was... unfortunate and I fear some of the female guests may have had their delicacies offended. There was one name, in particular, a woman's name, that you kept calling out, as if asking for help, or perhaps you were wanting to help her, it was uncertain."

My heart sinks. Here is the ultimate humiliation. I have exposed my inmost workings to an audience of bemused onlookers and can remember nothing of it. I hang my head.

"My wife."

"May I ask what happened to her?"

"She died. We were in India."

"I am sorry for your loss. This is still very painful for you and the grief you still hold is causing you pain. I want you to know that our facilities and the best efforts of my staff are at your disposal to help ease some of your sufferings. But only time will mend your grief."

"Of course."

"Continue with us, Sir. No matter what the temptation is to leave, especially after this incident. Have faith and patience in their efficacy and we can work together to ameliorate your anxieties."

I think about confessing, about telling him that I intend

to go, that this isn't for me. But I don't want an argument, or a sales talk, or a lecture.

He holds out his hand and, reluctantly, I shake it. I wonder what he will think of me in the morning when I am packed and heading for the train. He'll likely add cowardice and dishonesty to my list of ailments.

He guides me back to reception.

"Anything you require, Sir. Anything at all," he says.

I grit out a smile.

The rest of the day passes slow and sad. I spend some time in my room, lying on my bed.

The dinner hour comes and goes. I am fully prepared to go hungry as the price of solitude. I lie on the bed, my stomach growling. There is a knock. I shuffle over to the door and open it to see Polly with a tray of food.

"We saw you hadn't come down for dinner and Dr Waltz thought you might appreciate some food in your room tonight, Sir," she says.

"That's very kind."

"It's only this once, mind," she says. "You need to get out and eat. Don't think that I'm going to do this every night."

I take the tray. "I promise you, Polly, that you won't have to do this again. Thank you for all your kindness."

"You're very welcome," she says. "Sleep well, Sir. And no nocturnal wanderings. I won't be around to drag you back."

I eat my dinner and leave the tray outside the door.

The smoke on the moor has turned the moon blood red. I lay out fresh clothes to travel in. Then I dress for bed and crawl in.

I am afraid to fall asleep, but eventually, I give in.

When I wake up, I am in hell.

CHAPTER 18

I am standing outdoors.

The disoriented terror of waking in an unfamiliar place takes hold. I look around in desperation for something familiar to locate myself.

My head feels thick and tarry; my thoughts are viscous and slow.

I begin to make sense of what my senses are telling me. I'm like a baby separating and identifying colours, noises and sensations to create the world around it.

It is night, but I am surrounded by light.

The wind is cold, but I am hot.

There is fire all around me.

Above me the gibbous, furred moon is crimson.

Great whipping clouds of smoke billow and wash over me, making me cough. The itching, clogging fumes stick in my throat. The very earth seems to be smouldering and biting with flame.

I let out a cry of horrified realisation.

I am on the moor and it's on fire.

I look down and see that I am still in my nightshirt and

dressing gown. On my head is my nightcap; on my feet are my slippers.

I've somehow walked up onto the moor in my sleep.

What strange compulsion led me here? I felt anger, shame and confusion as I realise that I almost walked to my death in the flames.

Around me, the heather, bracken and grass fizz and hiss as the fire eats at them. I'm on a path, between fields of fire. I cough in great racking hacks and begin to run, panicking, not knowing what direction I am headed. Smoke obscures everything.

There is roaring heat on either side.

I look down and see that my dressing gown has caught. I stop for a second and stamp out the sparks that have taken root there.

The world is smoke and fire. I crouch low, retching and wishing that the wind would change direction.

As I run, I find a clearer patch, where the fire has either not taken hold or has already done its work. In the brief gaps between clouds of smoke, I notice the sun is coming up – the first faint washes of cold grey light spread across the sky as the night begins to dilute. I can see the outline of the horizon.

I pull up the collar of my dressing gown to mask my lower face. I head off again pell-mell down the path.

As the dawn slowly creeps in, I look behind and catch a brief glimpse of a familiar landmark through the morass of smoke – the sinister jagged splay of the Devil's Pinnacles. I am headed in the wrong direction.

Smoky tears streak my face, I have no choice but to retrace my steps along the path, back into the thickest part of the fire. Desperately I search for another way and see that the fire has not yet claimed an area to the east. The fire is still localised then, split from the main body of the moor by streams and tracks. To the east, seemingly undisturbed bog and heather stretch away and provide a potential detour if I'm willing to go back towards the depths of the moor and then take a circuitous route overland. This will take me around the fire, and the greatest risk will be submersion in any hidden bog.

The choice between that and a direct route back into the furnace is no choice at all. I give one more glance at the flames.

There is a figure in the smoke.

Someone is coming down the path from the centre of the moor, from the Blackmoor side, half-hidden by rippling veils of heat.

I squint through the fire and smoke.

It is a young woman, staggering as she edges forward down the path, but seemingly calm. She is wretched and ragged.

Her long blonde hair is plastered down over her face and she seems to wear a shift, torn and ragged around her knees. Her arms dangle limply by her sides and there is something queasy and strange about their length.

I wave and shout, but my smoke-ravaged throat offers only a dull croak.

The girl sways from side to side, and I worry that she might fall into the flames. I run as fast as my attire and creaking lungs will allow, covering my face with my dressing gown, itching, blinding smoke filling my eyes with tears.

On reaching her, I don't hesitate. I grab one of her thin arms above the elbow and pull her after me back down the path where she has just come from. She is stunned and unwilling to move, so I duck down and, pushing my shoulder into her midriff, lift her.

She is mercifully light.

I stagger down the path.

We go just far enough to be out of the worst of the smoke before I slump and lower her as carefully as I can, catching hold of her waist to stop her from falling.

Her face is covered by strands of hair, and she is streaked with soot.

"Where have you come from?" I say.

She stares at me, unseeing and mute. She appears to be paralysed by shock. I look down and see that her nightdress is caked in dirt and blood, and is burned at the edges. Her arms similarly are scratched and stained, and then I realise in horror why they appear so strange.

They terminate in grubby bandages at her wrists.

She has no hands.

They have seemingly been amputated.

I do not have time to consider why. I see that she is barefoot and that her feet are bleeding and raw from whatever strange journey she has been on.

The fire creeps in at every side. Our only option is to head overland into the boggy, clear area and risk any hidden smouldering that may lurk underfoot. I pick her up again and head out onto rough moorland. Soon I realise that progress is going to be tough. My feet catch on the uneven ground, turning my ankles, sinking into ruts, or bog. Carrying the girl makes things far worse.

I lower her and attempt to half support, half carry her through the thinning smoke, both of us stumbling over the uneven ground, irregular tussocks of sedge grass and heather. Now and again, we disturb a grouse lurking in the brush out of the way of the fire and it shoots up, burbling and desperately flapping to get away.

I'm effectively dragging the girl under my arm, her little feet trailing listlessly, her head lolling against my shoulder. She is light enough but I'm exhausted.

We come to a place of relative safety and rest.

From where we have come, I see the extent of the fire. It has spread over a good portion of the top of the moor. Vast clouds of smoke rise into the grey August dawn, blotting out the morning sun.

The wind changes and I inhale uncorrupted fresh air. I lie back, catching my breath, and then look at my companion.

She too is gasping, her eyes dull. Little wheezes come from her throat.

Her face, for all the soot and scratches, is beautiful. She is perhaps twenty years old and has a frail translucent quality as if she has lived out of the sunlight for all her life.

I look more closely at her arms and see that above the bandages, across her forearms, are the puckering and wrinkles of scar tissue, spreading in regular patterns up over the elbows to her shoulders. I cannot imagine what might have caused scars of such horrific regularity, scars which seem to have been inflicted more by mechanistic design than accident.

I ask her her name and what she is doing on the moor. Again, she looks blankly past me and doesn't acknowledge my presence. She opens her mouth to cough and I realise, to my horror, that she has no tongue.

I recover enough to proceed. I know that the way down to Cragside will take us over the Devil's Pinnacles. Our progress will be slow, so I resolve to take it in stages.

I lift her and we continue, staggering forwards. I notice that her mutilated arms cling around my waist, which gives me some comfort that her mind has not completely gone.

My back aches and I lose a slipper in a bog, hampering our progress even further. Still, I push on, never pausing to wonder what has led me onto the moor, or why I have happened upon this strange girl. All I know is that we have to get to safety and medical attention.

We clamber through the stones and gullies of the Devil's

Pinnacles until we finally crest the rocky outcrop overlooking Cragside.

The sun is up and everything in the valley below from the fields to the patches of woodland to the low roofs of Whitmoor seems perfectly bucolic, a world away from the hellish scene behind us.

A great wave of relief and joy lifts me.

The girl stares mutely down at the valley in confusion, casting her head this way and that as if attempting to make sense of her surroundings.

I feel a deep joy I've never known.

I've saved her life.

CHAPTER 19

The girl faints dead away and I only just catch her before she plummets over the edge of the crag. Still shaken by her mutilated mouth, I hoist her onto my shoulders and scramble down the stony gully that leads to the base of the Devil's Pinnacles.

My head swims, although whether it's from the inhaled smoke, the shock, or the effort of carrying the girl, I cannot say.

Despite my dream state, I'm able to carry her delicate form to the path that winds down to the clipped boundaries of the hotel and then through the grounds to the broad sweeping driveway.

The hotel is silent, the summer dawn still a distant herald to the day. I craft a plan in my exhausted mind. I can't let the staff know that I've been sleepwalking again, especially not up onto the moor.

I lay the girl gently on the gravel driveway and then run up to the front door and try it.

It's unlocked. It must have been when I set off on my

nocturnal wanderings. I enter the dark reception and shout for help at the top of my voice.

The echoes of my cry die away into the silent corridors and hollow parlours. The hotel feels uncanny, as if night has emptied it of all life.

I cry out again, "Help! I need medical assistance!"

I hear shuffling footsteps and turn to see a stocky, unshaven man who I take to be the night manager, returning from either his rounds or a nap. His fleshy mouth flops open as he stares at my dishevelled state. I grab him by the arm, pulling him to the doorway. "There is someone in trouble outside, come and see."

The man, who was likely witness to my performance the previous night, tries to resist. "Now, Sir. No need to be agitated, why don't we see if we can get one of the doctors to come and have a chat with you, maybe a nice cup of tea."

"I'm not mad, you fool, she's out here. There! She's injured and unconscious. She needs help."

The now alarmed night manager stands gawping like a fool, taking in the figure lying on the gravel.

"Mr Jeffries, I will take care of this," comes a familiar voice.

Dr Waltz steps into the pool of light thrown by the open door. "Show me," he says.

I lead him to the doorway.

He steps out and then turns, business-like.

"Mr Jeffries, escort Mr Weighton to my office. Get him some water. Then fetch Dr Locke at once."

I feel a flood of relief. "May I stay with her to ensure she is well? It would give me peace of mind."

Waltz shakes his head. "You go and rest in my office. I'll join you presently."

I nod and he heads outside, closing the door behind him.

My nostrils catch a kipper whiff of smoke. I smell like a bonfire.

More people have heard the commotion and are gradually emerging.

I'm painfully aware that this is the second night in a row that I've roused the hotel. Well, they will see this time that I have just cause.

Waltz opens the door again. "Jeffries, do as I say, man!"

She is still there on the driveway, lying very still.

Jeffries leads me to Waltz's office and then hurries off in search of Locke.

I sit looking at the glowering portraits, listening to the ticking of the grandfather clock in the corner.

Eventually, Waltz enters, mopping his forehead. "How are you feeling?"

"I am fine, but how is the girl?"

Waltz carefully folds the handkerchief, and then slips it into his pocket. He seems to consider his answer carefully. "Dr Locke is in attendance," he finally says. "They've taken her to a treatment room."

He sits down with a grunt in his leather chair. "Tell me what happened," he asks, looking very serious.

"I couldn't sleep. When I looked out of the window, I saw her staggering down off the moor. When I saw her collapse on the driveway, I came down at once and raised the alarm."

I hope that in the confusion Waltz will not remark on the soot on my face and the terrible smell of smoke, or else he will assume it is the residue of the girl and her scorched shift.

"You saw this girl conscious?" Waltz says, measuring his words. "Before she collapsed? What was your opinion of her condition?"

"Well, obviously I saw her injuries. Whether she's been in an industrial accident of some sort... I don't know. I think she

G.H. LUSBY

must have fainted through smoke inhalation. It looks like there is still a terrible fire on the moor."

Waltz nods. "We have... dressed her injuries. I fear you are correct about the smoke, she seems quite overcome. Time will tell if there is any permanent damage to her lungs. As to her wounds, do you have a view as to what could have hurt her so severely?"

I wince at the thought of the giant clashing machines in my father's mills. "I know that sometimes a machine can crush or sever unwitting hands, but to remove both of them... It seems highly unlikely. And did you notice the peculiar regular scarring up her arm? And her tongue? Oh, God, her poor severed tongue. Who could do such an awful thing!"

"Appalling," agrees Waltz. "I fear that there is a strange story attached to this girl, but unless she recovers, we will be none the wiser."

"We need to contact the police," I say.

Waltz nods slowly. "My primary concern is her well-being and recovery. Hers and your own. You've had quite a shock."

I cough.

He looks me over. I reek. It is blatantly obvious that I have been up on the moor, but still, I can't bring myself to admit to my sleepwalking.

"I think perhaps you will benefit from this medicine. It clears the throat and will act as a mild sedative." He goes to a cabinet in the corner of his office and retrieves a vial of vivid red liquid.

"Here, a teaspoon or two works wonders."

He pulls out the stopper and pours out some of the viscous stuff onto a spoon. Then he advances it towards me. I feel like a child being fed. I let the sweet sticky liquid slip down my throat. I taste the ethanol base and something inside me perks up. There then follows a second, and a third.

I instantly begin to feel better, lightheaded even.

Waltz summons Jeffries and he escorts me through a haze of corridors back to my room. The sun has risen and is very bright, making the plain walls shine.

Once safely alone, I strip and scrub myself with soap and cold water, trying to get as much of the bitter smoke out of my pores as possible. I keep coughing. My lungs whistle and wheeze with every breath. Some of my hair has singed and I snip at it with a pair of nail scissors until I am quite happy that any direct evidence of my exploits on the moor is erased.

It is only as I am dressing that I begin to wonder why I've not been allowed to see her. A suspicion takes root in my breast, and I feel a sudden need to be by her side.

My trunk still sits, open and packed by my bed.

I can't go now. Not when she's in distress.

I kick my smoky night clothes under the bed and grab my jacket.

I cough again and feel lightheaded. The sedative is becoming too much for me. I set off towards the door, fully intending to visit the girl, to make sure that she is getting the right care. The room lurches and I stagger to grip the bedstead.

That vast expanse of mattress looks very inviting.

I clamber onto it and fall fast asleep.

When I wake, Waltz is standing over me.

"Pardon my intrusion," he says. "I was concerned for you."

"How is the girl?" I croak, trying to raise myself and failing.

"My dear fellow, you may just have saved this poor unfortunate's life. The poor thing has smoke inhalation and some burns. We will be able to offer her some treatment, but I have telegrammed for a specialist to join us to assess the case."

"Doctor, I'm so glad to hear that. Is she conscious?"

He pauses, taking in my packed trunk. "She is awake, certainly, but unable to communicate. I fear that she is in a state of deep shock, doubtless caused by her trauma. I think it will be best if she is left to rest, although I don't doubt at some point she will be grateful to meet her saviour. She needs a friend, and as she recovers over the next few days, perhaps you can be that friend?"

"I only saw her from my window," I reiterate weakly. "She staggered down from the moor herself."

He nods and smiles.

"What of her other... injuries?" I say.

The Doctor's eyes flicker to his shoes. "I fear that this girl has been subjected to some terrible abuse or torture. Suffice it to say that once the specialist has been able to examine her, I will be contacting the police. Some families are living on the edges of the moor, and I'm afraid to say they are a little wild in their ways. Perhaps a drunken husband or father or rejected suitor meted out brutal punishment, eh? Who knows? Poor thing."

"Will she recover?"

"I am sure with the best care we can hope for the best. But now, my young friend, my concerns turn to you. You are yourself in a delicate state, this much is obvious, and I am keen that this latest shock does not knock back your recovery or trigger another episode like that of the other night. I think that you will benefit from regular doses of this. To take at your discretion."

From his pocket, he draws out a bottle of the red medicine I took earlier. He rolls it between his mighty palms and then holds it out to me.

"It will help you enormously."

Greedy for oblivion, I take it.

CHAPTER 20

I sleep and am beset by powerful, tugging dreams. My mind spins cobwebs that bind me. When I wake, I am wrapped tight in my own arms. The world feels changed.

I lie in a stupor for hours, slipping in and out of sleep, wondering what will become of the girl. I have become her champion, her saviour. Her protection is now my overriding duty.

There is a softening in the gnarled callouses that encase my heart. I think about her, holding her image in my mind as I lie there, wondering why the walls seem so unfamiliar.

Without moving from my bed, I find that I can keep an eye out for the arrival of the doctor, the specialist that Waltz has spoken of, by sending my mind out through the public spaces of the hotel where I can gain a secret vantage on the lobby and the corridor leading to the treatment room.

Eventually, a carriage pulls up outside and I see, or my disembodied spirit sees, a familiar tall, thin man emerge and stalk across the driveway. He is carrying a Gladstone bag and wears a frown. He is on dispassionate business. I see him speak in a low voice to the day manager before he is shown through. He doesn't see me.

He descends to the lower floor, my spirit floating behind him unseen. He enters a treatment room and the door is closed.

I hear a noise behind me. It is Waltz.

He can see me!

"My dear Mr Weighton, would you mind coming to have a word with Dr Strangler? He'd like to hear about how you found the girl."

I am confused for a moment, wondering how Waltz can see my spirit, but then realise that I am corporeal and standing, fully dressed, in the hotel reception.

"Of course," I say with a slight slur, and allow myself to be led back down the corridor. My heart races at the thought of seeing her again.

The girl has been moved to another room, past Waltz's private office and down a narrow flight of stairs to the lower, less frequently used parts of the hotel.

Her room is light and airy, with floor-to-ceiling windows looking out onto the lawns at the rear of the hotel. It has been made up into a hospital room, with screens, a table with a selection of towels, and in the corner a bed on which the girl lies, awake but still.

As I enter, the spider-limbed Dr Strangler unfurls himself from his position in a chair and stands to greet me. I feel his hand almost wrap around mine, such is the length of his fingers. His grip is bony, dry and loose.

"My dear Mr Edgeland. I am so pleased you took my recommendation to come to Cragside. I hope this incident hasn't disrupted your rest too much?"

His head extends and bobs as if keeping time as he talks. I am enveloped in a miasma of cologne, masking some deeper odour of corruption.

"You must have been brave and quick thinking to help this unfortunate girl. She owes you quite a debt, Sir." His voice is deep and sibilant.

I shrug off the compliment. "I happened to be at my window when I saw her come down from the moor," I slur. "If I hadn't gone to her aid, I am sure that one of the guests or staff would have eventually seen her."

He shakes his head from side to side. "No, no. This girl needed attention, your initiative in raising the alarm helped to prevent her from lapsing into a deeper state of catatonia. Now, tell me in your own words what happened when you observed her coming down from the moor. Please take a seat."

He gestures me into a chair and I retell my story. I have almost begun to believe the lie myself. When I finish, the Doctor crosses his long legs and sits back, observing me in silence. I wonder what is behind all this questioning.

"May I ask, have you been able to treat the girl? Will she recover?" I say, looking over at her.

He sniffs and looks across at the bed himself as if noticing it for the first time. "She is in a state of some shock, unable to speak. It would appear that she has been most horribly mutilated, her tongue severed, as you may have observed?"

I nod, then, with quick thinking, say, "I checked her mouth when I found her to ensure that she had not swallowed her tongue in her faint."

The Doctor smiles. "And she has had her hands amputated, whether by accident or design, who knows. In addition, she has suffered some burns and doubtless smoke inhalation. The doctors here are able to treat these things but she needs rest to recover. The larger issue is her current catatonic state, which is why I have been called in. It is unlikely that we will be moving her any time soon. The facilities at Cragside are more than adequate for her recuperation. I shall have to visit periodically to assess her condition and administer treatment."

I have been fighting off an urge to cough for some moments and finally give in. A low rattle erupts from my chest and I cover my face with both hands.

"Excuse me," I say, eyes watering.

"That's very nasty," says Dr Strangler, his head craning forwards.

"As you know, I have various ailments," I say with an embarrassed smile.

"I hope you don't mind me referring to this," he says, "but Dr Waltz has informed me, strictly between medical professionals, you understand, that you were intercepted whilst sleepwalking the other night. He said that you had made it out of the hotel and as far as the gardens, is that right?"

I glance at my shoes and nod.

"So your symptoms continue despite the treatments. That is not unusual. These things take time and you can't hope to recover in a few days. You are in the right place, Mr Edgeland. I urge you to stay, not just for your own sake, but also now, perhaps, for hers?"

"I wonder," I say, "will the police be investigating her situation? Presumably, she has family, or friends who may know who she is?"

The girl's eyes have opened. She is staring at the ceiling, quiet and calm.

I look properly at her. She has been thoroughly washed and dressed in a clean nightdress. Her hair has been combed. She is remarkably beautiful, although thin to the point of translucence. Her beauty, though, is offset by the skinny, scar-puckered arms terminating in freshly bandaged stumps.

The Doctor sniffs. "I fear that the local constabulary is not used to such unusual cases, and in truth, no crime has been committed. There is merely a mystery. I think there is a general desire for us not to raise too much awareness of this girl and her situation and we certainly don't want to alert her persecutors to her discovery. The police have been informed and will be conducting some discreet enquiries, but I don't hold out much hope."

There is movement behind me and I turn to see Waltz blocking the doorway. "As I have already said, we would like to keep this situation as quiet as possible. I trust that you will honour this request. Even amongst the other guests, there is no need to mention her residence here. We do not need a queue at her door. She is not a public curiosity or freak to be stared at."

"Also," says Dr Strangler, "given the nature of her injuries, we cannot be certain that whoever inflicted them won't come seeking to complete their work. For her protection, we must have silence. Is that understood?"

Waltz and Strangler have me cornered, and they make a compelling case.

"I only wish I could do something to help solve the mystery," I say.

Dr Strangler leans close, the sweet fog of his cologne enveloping me, making my head spin. He places a long thin hand on my knee and squeezes. "You have been a splendid help already. Of course, if you remember anything else, anything at all, you should let either Dr Waltz or myself know at once. And please do let Dr Waltz here treat that nasty cough of yours. I understand that he has given you some medicine. You must take it. We don't want your irritation of the lungs to develop into something more unpleasant."

I rise, unsteady, and thank the doctors, casting one last lingering look at the girl in the corner. She is so delicate and vulnerable.

"May I visit from time to time? I would like to know how

she is getting on, and I wonder if the presence of someone might help with her recovery?"

Strangler looks unsure. "Propriety demands the presence of an attendant at all times. The poor girl has been through enough. We cannot allow suspicion to fall on a guest at the hotel in such a strange situation, particularly a guest who has, if you will pardon my frankness, shown some signs of emotional distress and unusual behaviour himself?"

I smart at the obvious truth.

CHAPTER 21

I feel very confused after I meet with Strangler. So odd to see his familiar face here.

But I knew he was local to the hydro. And he had recommended it in the first place, so is it so unusual that he be brought in?

My head is fuddled.

Waltz escorts me back to my room, where a fresh bottle of red medicine is waiting on the dressing table next to a teaspoon on a clean napkin. It is odd, but I have never noticed the dressing table before. In fact, as I look around, I realise that there is something different about my room. There is light patterned wallpaper: twisting vines and roses. I reason that I have been wrapped up in myself since arriving and in all likelihood have never noticed.

I pick up the heavy-bottomed bottle and swirl around the thick vermillion liquid. It clings to the sides and settles slowly with a heavy viscosity. I squint at the tightly written script on the label but can't discern either the ingredients or the name of the drug. All that I can make out are the dosage instructions – one teaspoon four times per day. Or when needed.

I pick up the steel teaspoon and break the wax seal around the bottle stopper, then brush the sticky shards of wax on my fingers off onto my nightshirt.

Funny, I don't remember changing into it.

This medicine makes me feel strange. I wonder whether taking it is wise.

I pour out a measure into the bowl of the spoon and hold it up to the light. The medicine has a pronounced meniscus holding it together as if it were some kind of gelatinous deep-sea creature. It quivers in its metal seat as my hand trembles. I sniff it. There is a whiff of aniseed and a strong base of alcohol. The spirit makes my nose hairs tingle and curl as if they are recoiling inside my nostrils.

At the same time, I feel a sudden, panicky hunger for the stuff, an ache inside that needs removal.

Tentatively, I sip. There is a pleasant sweet numbing sensation on my gums and tongue. I swallow the lot.

Then, because it has been a difficult morning, I take two more urgent doses.

There is an immediate effect, stronger and quite unlike the previous times I have taken it. I feel the gloop warm my throat and stomach, giving me a feeling of deep reassurance.

Numbness floods my limbs.

I feel compelled to go lie on the bed and rest for a while. I place the bottle and teaspoon back on the dresser.

I pull both my legs up onto the bed and lie back, my head sinking into the fresh wonderful pillow, and a cool draught blows across my exposed feet. I look down at them, retreating into the distance, and marvel at how such strange alien appendages could grow on a human. How like animals we are. How strange that we keep all that animal nature tucked away inside leather casings. I resolve to never wear shoes again.

I begin to smile and as I do, the sun outside seems to become brighter and the sound of the birds louder.

I look out through the floor-to-ceiling windows at the lawn and vaguely wonder when I moved to a downstairs room.

My mind runs away with thoughts of the silver tinkling streams in the moor side, the waving of the grass and the soft burbling of the grouse tucked away in their nests sheltered by heather. They are out there now, tending their young, wrapping them in soft feathers.

How much love there is between a mother and her children. I remember my dear mother. I remember her embrace, safe away from my father.

My eyes become heavy.

All is well.

I fall asleep.

When I wake, I run a cotton tongue around my dry mouth and see that night has begun to fall. I swing my legs down and feel heavy-headed as my frame tips up, cantilevered into a sitting position.

Someone has left me dinner on the dressing table. I lift the cloche and see game pie. It is cold.

I pick at it and consider going for a walk.

I am still tired.

I consult my watch. I should check in on the girl. I am her protector now.

But I need to be fully well first. I'm no good to her sick and exhausted.

I take another two doses of the medicine then fall back on the bed, pulling the covers up and retreating again into sleep.

I WAKE IN A GREAT AND TERRIBLE PANIC. COLD MERCURY chills my arms and legs. My guts have tied themselves into impossible knots.

My eyes open wide in the darkness.

Something has woken me up.

There was a noise.

It was the sound of my door closing.

I spring from the bed and tiptoe across my room. A slight chink across the bottom of the door spills a fan of faint light across the floor. I listen, ear against the wood, and think I hear footsteps walking away. I slowly, carefully turn the brass handle and open the door a crack.

Peering out, I see the corridor is empty, but a shadow is flitting out of view as if someone is walking up the stairs past the gas lamp that sputters and roars there.

The corridor looks unfamiliar to me.

I step out of the room, my feet cold on the floor, and walk as quickly and as quietly as I can. I am certain that whoever was climbing the stairs has been in my room.

Suddenly I feel a terrible concern for the girl.

Whoever has mutilated her so horribly could have found out her location through idle village gossip.

Perhaps they have come in search of her.

I run along dark unfamiliar corridors. Get turned around, lost and confused. I reach a door. It is the girl's room.

There is the sound of whispering and scuffling inside. Then a gruff voice says something that sounds more like the grunt of an animal than English. There is a scrape of furniture and a metallic hissing sound not unlike the workings of a piston.

I try the door. It is locked from the inside.

On my attempt at the handle, the voice inside stops and then the scuffling begins again, quicker, more urgent, as if some terrible task has to be completed before I can gain access.

I pound on the door, crying, "Open up!"

Then I stand back and kick at the door, again and again, the wood splintering at the lock with a satisfying crack, and then with one last shoulder barge, it flies open.

I burst in and survey the scene.

The room is very similar to my own.

The floor-to-ceiling windows are wide open and the thin curtains blow in on the night breeze. A chair has been turned over.

On the bed, the girl is sitting bolt upright, her thin legs dangling over the side but not touching the ground. She is looking straight ahead in terror at something or someone outside. She is still in her filthy rags from the moor, her hair matted with smoke.

I run in and look into her eyes but see no hint of recognition at all.

I go to the window and look out onto the lawn. Out there in the gloom of the approaching dawn is a figure, human but somehow animal in his movements, running across the lawn. As he runs, he crouches, like an ape, weirdly long arms swinging by his side. The strange figure stops and looks back. Then he is gone behind a hedge. I pull the doors of the window shut and drop the latch.

When I turn, the girl is standing in the middle of the room, her jaw wide open and her awful stump of a tongue exposed in a silent scream. Her eyes are wide and mad. She slowly extends the stumps of her arms as if craving whoever, or whatever, had been in the room with her. Blood seeps through her bandages on her stumps and spreads, dripping onto the floor.

There is a knock at the door and it opens.

It is Polly.

She takes in the scene, looking nervous and somewhat surprised. "Good morning, Sir," she says.

It is indeed morning now. The sun has risen quickly. How long have I stood there staring out of the windows?

Then, in the morning light, I see something that I hadn't noticed in the darkness. On the far side of the girl's bed is a strange pallet on wheels, made from wrought iron and wood, and fitted with leather straps and a head brace.

Polly stares, strangely fascinated by me, her eyes wary.

"Thank God you're here, Polly," I say. "There's something terrible happening. They're after her, look!"

I gesture at the pallet.

"They tried to take her. I disturbed them in the very act and they took flight. I was so close to losing her."

I look at the girl. She has calmed and settled back onto the bed into a serene, exhausted repose. She is clean, in a shift of purest white.

Polly steps into the room and closes the door behind her.

"What do you suppose this is?" I say. "Some kind of stretcher?"

Polly nods, looking it over. "They meant to restrain her? To remove her from the hotel? The monsters! Who was it that you saw?"

"I don't know. But I do know that someone in the hotel has informed this girl's assailants of her whereabouts. I should warn Waltz he has a traitor amongst his staff. Did *you* know she was here?"

She blushes. "No. Well, not until Dr Waltz just told me. He asked me to look in on you both and see how you were doing. How are you feeling?"

For some reason, I can't lie to this girl. She helped me when I was at my most vulnerable. She showed me kindness and discretion. I decide to reveal the truth.

"I've been sleepwalking again, Polly, like the night you

guided me home. I woke on the moor, in the fire. I found her there and brought her down. It's just as well that I did, who knows what would have happened if they had recaptured her in that wild place?"

Something moves out on the lawn. I run to the patio doors and peer out into the morning mist. I think I see the figure moving again behind one of the hedges.

"They are out there," I say. "I'm certain they are plotting to come for her."

I look again but the figure has gone.

CHAPTER 22

E very day then, chaperoned by Polly, I sit in vigil.
     She lies silent as I watch over her, betraying no
     recognition of either my, or Polly's, presence. She
takes food, and is able to chew and swallow, but her
consciousness is elsewhere.

I am certain that my presence is helpful to her, that it's
her only hope of recovery. When I speak kind words, I
imagine that it's like someone calling to a distant shore where
a stranger stands lost and lonely, looking for a friend.

My fists clench in outrage when I see her scarred arms
and cauterised tongue.

I order flowers from the village: beautiful roses in the late
bloom of summer, just on the verge of corruption. They are
white to match her complexion. As the days go on, I order
more, great bunches of roses, pink and then red. The room
becomes like a hot house, the sun pouring in through the
windows and stirring up great waves of heady perfume. The
room is filled with colour and scent, and at the centre of it,
there she lies, beautiful and infuriatingly oblivious to my
worship.

I read to the girl. I hope my words might make it through the veil of silence. I plough through Wilkie Collins as the sunlight traces its arc around the room.

Her breathing, perhaps, becomes easier and more regular. As if she is soothed by my murmuring voice.

One morning, I exceed the boundaries of my duty by brushing her hair whilst Polly naps, marvelling at the soft feel of it in my hands. It is quite different to the tangled smoky briars that I felt against my cheek on our flight across the moor.

On turning over the brush, I see that I have inadvertently pulled out some strands and, checking that Polly is dozing in her chair, I place them between the pages of my book.

"You never know," Polly says one afternoon, "it may be kindness brings her back to us."

"Have you noticed anything strange about Dr Waltz?" I ask.

She flickers uncertainly, then answers my question with a question. "Haven't you wondered why this girl is being kept here when clearly her injuries would normally mean she should be moved to a proper hospital? She should be cared for by professional doctors, rather than the kind who make fat businessmen jump in cold plunge pools or sit broiling in steam."

She is right, of course.

I wonder in one dark moment whether she has been tasked by Waltz to watch the girl, or me.

I also begin to wonder if I dare cross the moor and visit Blackmoor, to try and find the villains who have done this. I begin to plot and study maps, making plans in my notebook.

I finally tell Polly that I intend to visit Blackmoor. She scribbles something in her notebook and I challenge her.

"What are you writing?"

She tears out the page and hands over the note. It reads:
QUIET, TRUST NO ONE HERE.

CHAPTER 23

Finally, I decide to cross the moor, in the hope of finding the truth.

I know I will need some kind of explanation for my inquiries, a pretext for exploring the town. I need an excuse to access private areas, and to interview the residents without arousing suspicion. I can't risk alerting the girl's persecutors that I am on to them. Not that I care overly for my safety, I'm more worried about them making another move against her.

I settle on the idea of posing as a visiting campaigner interested in the social care being given to the workers at the mill. I invent a Christian periodical and concoct a story that I am writing a piece on industrial practice and the betterment of the workforce.

With some reservations, I advise Polly of my intent, along with a clear instruction that she should not leave the girl unguarded. I reckon I can cross the moor and be in Blackmoor in a matter of hours should the way be clear. I study a map which hangs in reception. The route seems straightforward and so, taking a stick, I set off.

It is a disagreeable day; a foretaste of autumn. There is a glowering freight of iron cloud massing on the horizon, heralded by a nip in the air. Fat globules of rain fall on my coat.

I am still weak and feel a residual ache in my lungs. Added to that is the disorienting effect of the medicine and the heavy pressure in the air of the brewing weather.

I find it hard going on the slog up the side of the moor from Cragside to the Devil's Pinnacles. They rise above, their black shards framed against the lowering sky.

I push on up, through and past them, onto the crest of the moor and into the vast shallow bowl that leads finally up to the true summit. As the rest of the world falls away below the horizon, I feel suddenly very isolated and alone. I am a flea making its way across the back of a giant beast, a single point between earth and sky.

The fires have been out now for some days, but there still seems to be a seething heat running somewhere within the fabric of the moor, deep within the peat. I can see the extent of the flames, the blackened twisted fingers of heather and grass, burned to grey and brittle as a biscuit. The smoky stink of the burning remains, blown around in the wind.

I follow the path to the point where I found the girl. It's not far from the rough track that leads up to the Guardian Angels, the isolated stone circle that marks the apex of the moor.

I marvel at how far she walked in the flames. The blackened land stretches far into the distance. She must have staggered through that hell for some time before I found her. I wonder what terrible motivation pushed her on.

I begin the final ascent to the summit, heaving myself up the stone steps. The rain starts in earnest. The hot peat is so dry that it seems to suck up the moisture the moment it lands.

I reach the stone circle. I am not superstitious by nature but I take care not to step inside its bounds. I am struck by the irony that these ancient watchers have inadvertently marked not just the start of the wilderness behind me, to the north, but the industrial sprawl that lies to the south, on the other side of the moor.

I see now the towers, chimneys and drifting smoke of Blackmoor.

The path makes a long descent, down to a point where it passes through an open gateway in a drystone wall, and then on through fields to a narrow track. The track winds between two gritstone walls until it reaches a wider road, then that road snakes down a narrow gully bordered on each side by gnarled cliffs, till it emerges at a crenellated stone bridge.

On arriving at the bridge, which marks the boundary of Blackmoor, I can see for the first time the vastness of the famous central mill the town has been created around, a palace of industry, crowned with multiple sloping roofs and topped with an array of chimneys. The largest of these is designed to mimic a Florentine tower, exquisite and huge, but still tiny compared to the cyclopean mass below it.

I crane my neck back to look at the detailing on the facade of the mill. Some inflated ego, fed on images from Dante, Milton and Bosch, has been let loose on the design with no thought for any consistent cosmology. Gargoyles and dragons cling to the buttresses, heralding angels surrounding a bas-relief of Atlas holding the world on his shoulders, glowering down at the pathetic mortals below him. The whole carries a gothic intensity, as if a cathedral has been transplanted to this northern valley. Yet the only veneration is to capitalism and the sheer will of its master.

The mill sprawls even across the river itself, like Chenonceaux. Brown choppy waters race through dark arches into hidden channels and tunnels, driving who knows what massive engines deep in the cellars.

I hear them hum and roar. The noise makes the cobbles vibrate. The whole town resonates with a nauseating low buzz that permeates my flesh and rattles my bones. My head aches and I feel suddenly as if I am rotting from the inside.

I cross the bridge and follow the cobbled ribbon of road up to a perfectly ordered town. It seems designed in a grim pastiche of the Italianate, pleasant enough. But the regimented houses give away the mechanistic intent behind them. The dwellings are extensions of the mill itself, and it is obvious that all housed within them exist only to serve it.

The air is dense with smog. Noxious chimney fumes cascade over the town and creep through the streets, staining the golden sandstone with a dire blackening fungus.

There is something peculiar about the whole place, an almost biblical, fantastic thread of design seems to run through all the buildings, as if the whole town is a place of heretical or occult worship. The streets are named after angels, Gabriel, Cassiel, Azreal, and Belial. There are other larger buildings positioned around the town, each impressive and perfectly proportioned. There is a church set back in a clipped neat park; a neat hospital in a cobbled square.

There is none of the organic messiness of other towns where the patterns of streets and buildings have a reassuring fluidity, as if they have developed and adapted to shifting needs. Blackmoor seems perfect and precise.

I cross a road and enter the empty park in the hope that I might move away from the terrible insidious din of the mill, but the noise follows me, vibrating the very blades of grass on the tightly cut and rollered lawns, trembling in the blackening petals of the dusty white, pink and red roses, and resonating off the stained-glass windows of the church.

The church is not the usual gothic-spired affair, rather it

looks Byzantine, with four cupolas at each corner and an inlaid mosaic image above its door that I cannot decipher. The front door is heavy oak, studded with iron, more like the door to a Florentine bank than a place of worship. I chance a look through a window. There are no pews, merely a plain altar at one end of the room and a clean marble floor zig-zagged with black and white stripes. I wonder if there is a standing room only there on a Sunday.

I haven't seen a soul.

I go to the hospital and climb the few stairs to the open doorway. Inside, I hear voices. There is a clean corridor leading to a single ward. Half a dozen patients are lined up neatly in beds. They all seem happy enough, sleeping or reading.

"Excuse me, can I help you with anything?"

I jump and turn around to see a nurse with a prizefighter's face.

"Ah, yes," I remember my cover story, "I am a writer for a Christian periodical and am new in town and was interested in finding somewhere to find some refreshment?"

"This is a hospital, not a restaurant. I suggest you try the next town, Bridgestone. There's nothing here. There are no public houses in Blackmoor." She folds her arms across her chest, her piggy eyes are suspicious.

I look around. "I must say, this is a splendid little hospital. How many patients can you care for at any one time?"

She looks unimpressed. "Up to fifteen, but we've never had reason to. Conditions at the mill are very safe. We rarely get an accident or poisoning. Most of the folks in here have family health problems."

I decide to chance a direct approach. "I don't suppose you had a patient here, a dear friend of mine. She had blonde hair, a pale face with blue eyes."

"I'm sure I don't know."

"She was quite distinctive, also she had unfortunately lost her hands, perhaps in some sort of accident."

The nurse sniffs. "Are you sure you've got the right town, Sir? What was the girl's name?"

I realise, too late, the flaw in my plan. "I wonder have you seen anyone of that description?"

"I'm afraid not, Sir," she says, emphasising the "Sir" as if it is a substitute for a cruder epithet, "and to be honest, I'm not sure I'd be straight with you if I had. Do you mind me asking who you are, Sir? It's normal for all visitors to report to the mill, seeing as the whole town is private property. Haven't you seen the signs?"

I feel the nurse's hard eyes on my back as I head down the steps and back across the deserted square.

I thread my way down the hill along narrow cobbled streets to the base of the mill and, looking up, become quite dizzy at its immensity. I wander around its base and eventually find what looks like its main door. There is a heavy iron knocker, which I lift and drop.

The door opens at once. The noise of machines bursts out of the doorway and makes me flinch.

A tough-looking man in work clothes steps out. It's as if he has been waiting for me. He has a barrel chest, cauliflower ears and a neck so thick that it seems to taper up to the top of the head.

"Can I help you, Sir?" he shouts above the din.

I abandon my cover story and get straight to the point. "Yes," I shout back in the most officious tone I can muster. "I am here to see the proprietor. I am looking for information on a person I believe to be from Blackmoor and would like to interview him."

"Do you have an appointment?"

"I'm afraid not."

"Then I'm afraid that it's out of the question – the owner

is a very busy man and doesn't accept visitors without appointments."

"You could tell him it's about a missing girl. She was found on the moor."

"Are you the police?"

"Just a concerned citizen."

The man considers my request for a moment.

"Wait here," he says and swings the door closed with a heavy clunk.

I pace in the cold shadow of the mill.

After a while, I turn and began to walk away.

As I do so, the door behind me opens again and the man steps out. "I've been asked to escort you out of the town. So you can be sure of the way."

CHAPTER 24

I have no need and no desire for an escort.

I am not done with Blackmoor. Something is going on here. I am sure of it.

But I don't dare challenge him. He's huge.

The man walks alongside me as we descend the stone steps back to the cobbled street, then he escorts me over the bridge, past the dark arched under-vaults of the mill, to the gulley beyond. Only there, at the boundary of the town, in the shadow of the overhanging gritstone cliffs that guard the way up to the moor, does he finally take his leave of me.

"You'll find the path back to Whitmoor at the top of this road. I suggest you follow it carefully, and quickly too, mind. The moor is no place for a man after dark. It's easy to lose your way or drown in a bog. There are deep secrets in the pools up there."

Then he looks me in the eyes and begins to chant:

"Away on the moor, far, far from the town,
Where the weak and unwary may stumble and drown,
The sisters lie sleeping in pools dark and deep,
Till the summer fires come, and the waters retreat."

He turns away and heads back down the road towards the bridge.

"I'll be careful," I mutter.

I WALK UP THE ROAD, CERTAIN THAT THE MAN WILL BE looking back and checking my progress. Eventually, I stop, panting from the climb and glance back. He is standing there at the end of the bridge, staring at me. I give him a friendly wave (which he ignores) and continue.

After another few minutes, I chance another look back and see that he has finally turned and is crossing the bridge back into town.

I dart behind a rise and flatten myself against the turf, peeking up to watch his progress.

I know that I have to go back into Blackmoor. There is foul play somewhere down there. I wait until I am confident that my escort has made his way back to the mill and then consider my route of descent.

Crossing the bridge is not an option, it's far too exposed. I peer down the river to see if any other crossings are available. In the distance, I can see just one, a footbridge some way downstream.

I begin to tack across the fields and fringes of the moor, trying to keep myself low, using gorse bushes and rocks for cover, till I reach a low drystone wall which provides excellent protection from spying eyes. I slide down through some rough coppices of hazel and finally re-emerge near the footbridge.

I scurry across it, lunging for the shelter of the stone houses on the other side.

What will they do if my repeat incursion is spotted?

If the owners of the mill are culpable for the terrible

injuries suffered by the girl, they will not be overly worried about a lone man looking to fix the blame on them. I have to tread carefully.

I zig-zag back through the neat narrow streets of workers' cottages until the mass of the mill rises above the slate roofs and I find myself again near the centre of town.

I decide that the best course of action is merely to observe. With this in mind, I duck into the neat park and find a vantage point behind the empty bandstand where I can watch the town unseen. I have an excellent view of the hospital, the church and the front of the mill.

I wait.

At around eight o'clock, a hooter sounds somewhere in the mill and the main doors are thrown open. Out marches a silent army of workers, all dressed in a distinctive brown uniform. I am surprised at the general lack of chatter amongst the workers. Instead, they seem perfectly calm and at ease walking in silence and then filtering off down the side streets to their respective homes.

I decide to follow one small group of women down Abaddon Street. Leaving my hiding place, I run across the park and catch up with them.

"Excuse me, I wonder if you could help me?" I say, puffing.

The group of three turn around in surprise and look at me with silent amazement.

"I'm looking for anyone who might know a girl who comes from this town. She has fallen into my care in Whitmoor, and I'm trying to locate her family or friends. She is blonde, and somewhat frail, about twenty years of age. Do you recall anyone of that description?"

The women look at each other and I catch warning flashes between them.

One of them, a scrawny girl with a pinched, hardened face, says, "No, we don't know no one of that description, and you'd be best getting out of here. It's not wise for strangers to be wandering around chatting with people. We're good God-fearing people here and outsiders are not welcome. Good day!"

"She may have had an accident of some sort," I persist, "injuries to her hands. They've been amputated."

Another woman crosses ropey arms and snarls at me, "She said to be on your way. We don't know anything about no girl, and if you talk to us, you'll get us into bother. Get home to Whitmoor, Sir, that's my advice."

I bow and retreat, apologising for any inconvenience I have caused them.

I try the same approach on two other groups of stragglers and get a similar response. My presence is being noted. Groups of men are staring, muttering to each other. I dare not approach them.

Then, one of the women I approach shows shocked recognition when I describe the girl. She denies anything and scurries away. I follow her.

I hang back and let her group disperse into their respective streets, watching my quarry head up Jeremiah Street. Once the others are out of sight, I pounce.

"I'm sorry to bother you again, Madam," I say, "but I couldn't but help notice that you seemed to recognise the description I gave?"

She looks terrified. "You'll get me into trouble talking to me like this alone on the street," she says. "What if someone sees?"

Her gaze flits up and down the street. Then she glances up in holy terror at the mill tower.

"Come in, quick," she says, and opens her front door, bustling me in before slamming it shut behind me.

Her cottage is bereft of ornamentation, having only the bare minimum of plain furniture. The only decoration is a needlepoint framed above the small table bearing the words: *Beware of sin, for it bites like the serpent and has the claws of the lion.*

The woman checks at the window and then turns to me, angry.

"I'll tell you what I know, but you have to leave. It's not safe for you here. The girl you're looking for went missing some weeks ago. No one knows where she went. Her name was Lavinia."

Lavinia! My love has a name.

"She was a good girl," continues the woman, "worked at the mill, she got the attention of the bosses. The last anyone saw of her was one night a couple of weeks ago after church. Not been seen since. She's not the first either. Maybe she was in the hospital, maybe she had an accident. No one knows for sure, but we know it ain't safe to ask too many questions either. I don't want my pay docked, that's for sure, not with the prices in the company store."

"Does she have a family? Friends?"

"Her old man died last year of flu, her mother ran off when she was little. She didn't have anyone, apart from me and a couple of others as made pals with her."

"Do you have any idea what might have happened to her? She's been injured."

The woman looks frightened. "I won't say, Sir, and you don't want to know. You need to get out and leave me be now, I don't want any attention. I've only been in town myself a year. I moved here from Bradford looking for work. I don't like it. It's not right here. Please, go."

She seems desperate and so I can only oblige, glad at least that the girl is known to someone, and that she has a name.

"Have they come looking for her?" I say as I turn to leave.

"No one has mentioned her since she disappeared," the

woman says, "not the bosses, not the other girls I work with. That's the strangest thing of all."

I thank her and leave as discreetly as I can, moving with stealth in the lengthening shadows.

A disappearance and a conspiracy of silence!

I make my way back to the hospital and decide on one last look before heading back over the moor. I have no desire to be lost in the dark on the way back to Cragside.

I peer in through a window. Perhaps I'll see others with similar injuries to those of Lavinia.

However, the only patients are asleep and whole. There is no evidence of industrial accident, just routine illness. A doctor is tending to one particularly pale patient, administering a red medicine that looks very familiar.

As if sensing my eyes on his back, the doctor turns and looked directly at me, his eyes widening in shock.

It is Dr Strangler.

CHAPTER 25

I duck below the window.

My mind and heart race each other.

All of a sudden, the conspiracy is made real.

Strange, but my overwhelming feeling is a relief. For days, I've doubted my perceptions and perhaps even sanity, but here is the final proof. I hurry back down the road, clinging to the wall, glancing back at the hospital, wondering if Strangler will emerge.

I don't doubt my presence has been registered, and that my look of recognition will have spoken volumes.

My only priority now is to get out of Blackmoor in one piece. I have to return to Cragside before my exploits are reported back to Waltz.

I JUDGE THE DISTANCE BETWEEN THE HOSPITAL AND THE bridge and calculate that it will be a five-minute walk. It takes me past the entrance to the mill and the hulking doorkeeper.

I have to chance it.

There is no time to work my way back via the footbridge. I begin to walk, eyes straight ahead, feigning confidence. My breath and pulse echo in the chambers of my skull. In my peripheral vision, I see the shadow of the mill loom on my right.

With my tweeds, I cannot be mistaken for a worker.

Blank windows stare down from the walls of the mill. Any one of them could be hiding an observer. I see no movement. The bridge grows ever nearer.

Then I hear a new noise rise above the ever-present throb of the mill. I hesitate to call it music, but distinct notes drift across the park. The atonality and the repetitive pulsing nearly stop me in my tracks. It seems to be coming from the strange Byzantine church. Is the clamorous dirge generated by some infernal organ? Or is it the singing of a hellish choir? There is something unholy about it, the melody warped by deliberate dissonances. My heart threatens to break from its moorings.

Then I see the profile of the thuggish doorkeeper framed in the open side entrance to the mill. He is lit from behind by grisly flares, and in the half-light, his size seems magnified, like a monstrous golem. He gives that strange flourishing gesture again, beckoning me in.

I walk on and amazingly he doesn't move from his post. I pick up the pace, almost breaking into a run, striding with dissolving composure for the bridge, hitting its sudden gradient at such speed that I power over it, legs pumping beneath me. With sudden hope, I see the cobbles winding up through the rocky gully.

My reserve breaks. I run, fuelled by all the adrenaline that has been building in my system. It surges like compressed steam through me. My limbs have been released from iron fetters.

I have to be away from that terrifying music. That

hideous drone is an affront to decency. I sense in its strange pitches an intoxicating siren call.

Oh, God. What do they worship?

I pound the cobbles, up through the gorge. I dare to look up at the crags on either side, half expecting to see shadowed figures waiting above me in ambush. But there is nothing save the tangles of roots, the branches of trees and the darkening blue of the summer night.

The music echoes off the walls of the gully, maddening me and blurring my vision. I have half a mind to stop, rest and give myself over to it.

Finally, I emerge at the top of the gorge, feeling the fresh air of the moor on my face. It carries the dreadful music away.

My lungs heave and there is a queer bubbling sensation beneath my clothes. I pull open my waistcoat, unbutton my shirt and examine myself in the dying light.

There are gills between my ribs, tiny slits in the skin, and thin filamented filters, like the underside of a mushroom. The gills are blackened with smoke. I watch the rise and fall of my chest, the opening and closing of the striated slit-mouths as they suck in the fresh moorland air with a wet hiss. I feel sick and sit down. I close my mouth, clamp my hand over my nose, and let my lungs breathe of their own accord.

Then I shake my head and come to, look again at my chest and see nothing but pale skin.

I can't waste more time.

I press on, desperate to be free of the malign influence of the town, feeling my spirits return with every step.

Then the ground beside me fizzes and pops with a tiny explosion.

It's nearly a second before I hear the gunshot echo across the valley.

I fling myself to the ground and hear another bang. I

glance back at the mill and see a tiny wisp of smoke from one of the windows of the Florentine tower. I am being targeted by a marksman.

I crawl forward, keeping myself under cover. Another pop and the earth beside me explodes. Again I hear the delayed gunshot echo. My frayed nerves can take no more and I decide to run for it.

I gather what's left of my strength and sprint up the path. Up and onwards, knees and elbows pumping. I run for my life, thinking that at any point I will feel a thud like a punch in my back, or my arm, or my leg, and then it will be all over.

CHAPTER 26

I run till I can bear it no more, then fling myself down into a dried-up streambed. There are no further shots. Darkness is falling quickly now. I appear, for the moment, to be safe.

I crawl along the little gully as it snakes up the side of the moor and glance back, noting with relief that the town has finally sunk out of view.

I stand, dust myself down and hurry along the path.

Am I being followed? Will they send dogs?

Better death, I think, than to be taken alive back to Blackmoor.

But I see no one, hear no more shots or any evidence that I am being tracked. Still, I look over my shoulder every few minutes, duck behind the gorse and fling myself into the heather whenever I hear a noise. It's not a comfortable journey.

The darkness doesn't help. Every third or fourth step, I stub my toe or stumble over a stray rock embedded in the path. My ankles throb from having turned so often.

I give into wild speculation as to what will be waiting for

me back at Cragside. I know now, beyond any doubt, that Waltz, at least, is in cahoots with Strangler and therefore the masters of Blackmoor. As my mind spins frenzied scenarios and picks apart evidence, I hit upon a single realisation.

What did Waltz say? "Our dear patrons and investors."

It all falls into place. The conspiracy to extract Lavinia from the hydro back to the town; the lies to cover up the true identity of Dr Strangler. It explains Waltz's insistence on keeping me drugged with this medicine which still numbs my skin and fogs my mind. Perhaps they think that I rescued Lavinia from the town, or at least aided her in her flight. They are covering their tracks. Both the girl and I are clearly in mortal danger.

And what of those machines, with the tortured faces and entwining limbs?

My mind turns to Polly and I worry for her safety. She has been left to watch over Lavinia on her own for the day. She has family and more to lose than I.

I pick up the pace, sure that my absence will have been noted. A search of my room will already have taken place. Perhaps Polly is being interrogated.

The night, in conjunction with the medicine, blurs the edges of the world, softening the horizon. Rising before me, casting a pall over the sky, is a bloated harvest moon the colour of pus.

Its appalling light guides me. I pass the Guardian Angels, silent and watchful. Their long shadows stretch like fingers over the shimmering heather. I follow the now familiar path down towards Whitmoor using gravity's momentum to push through the fatigue. I am desperate to get back, yet at the same time dread what I will find.

I come to the Devil's Pinnacles and gaze down upon the hydro. I don't remember thinking of the building as malevolent before, but with these new associations fresh in my mind, it seems to emanate evil. The sharp tourelles and crenellations look like bitter defences rather than ornamentation. The narrow windows catch the cool flame of the moon.

I bound down the narrow paths that lead to the grounds and then run through the gardens.

I feel eyes on me as I walk up the driveway, panting, cringing from the pressure of their gaze.

Forcing myself, I saunter with a bold air through the entrance and across the lobby, intending to go straight to my room.

I immediately catch sight of Polly. She has been waiting for me. She throws me a look and gives a slight shake of her head, so I continue up the stairs and along the corridor to my room, leaving the door ajar.

Sure enough, within a minute, she joins me, glancing back down the passage before closing the door behind her.

"I can't be caught in here," she says. "They've been up to something. Waltz has been in with the girl and I could hear him talking to her. I think that the other doctor was here in the morning. Where on earth have you been all day?"

I tell her my story and she listens with growing horror.

"I know her name, Polly, it's Lavinia!"

She sits back as if I've struck her.

"Does the name mean something to you?"

Polly says nothing, merely stares at me with something approaching pity.

"What do you think we should do?" I ask.

"It would be best if you packed and left right now. There is a night train back to Bradford that leaves in an hour, you can make it easily. Go and find a doctor. Get help for yourself. You are not a well man."

"I can't leave her, not now," I say.

"I don't know what we can do," says Polly, her voice cracking. "This isn't some little play mystery, it involves powerful people, people I depend on for a living. You're in great peril."

I flush. "You've done enough, Polly, please go back to work, keep to your duties as inconspicuously as possible and leave this to me."

"And what are *you* going to do, exactly?"

I stare into her frightened eyes and then turn to look out at the darkness outside.

"I will keep watch tonight," I say. "They are going to make their move."

CHAPTER 27

The Pleiades launch, and the Milky Way blossoms across the night sky. In the dark, the trees and hedges melt into vague presences. Then, without warning, a bank of clouds shifts and the moon is revealed again, now blood red. Its rusty glow spreads over the gardens, warping the landscape into a hellish half-light.

I settle into position behind a hedge opposite the girl's window and try to make myself comfortable. The last train moves off from Whitmoor station and chugs along the valley. The noise of the engine echoing off the crags.

The leaves and branches around me stir in the breeze and I pull my coat tight. I listen to my breath and feel my legs stiffen. I shift, trying to soothe the pins and needles buzzing in my feet.

So it goes for three hours. I settle into a meditative state somewhere between waking and sleep, my awareness held on her window. Occasionally my eyes unlatch, and trace the most obvious side route down to the road, then back again before resuming their vigil.

When they finally come, it's not by the route I am expecting.

They stride up the main drive and brazenly work their way around by the main path. I watch them wheel a strange iron stretcher to her room.

One of the men simply knocks on the patio doors and a light goes on inside.

I heave myself up from my vantage point and hobble towards them, gripping my stick tight, not knowing how I'm going to tackle multiple adversaries. I feel the lawn turf churn under my boots as I begin to run, losing sight of her room as I level with the borders of rhododendron. I thread my way through the beds, then I round the corner and see the patio doors open, the light spilling out in a golden fan across the green lawn.

Clutching my stick, I creep towards the light, listening to the sounds inside the room. The men are whispering. I don't doubt that after having been disturbed on their previous attempt, they will be armed.

I peer around the window and see them.

There are two of them, both hunched over Lavinia. They are strapping her onto the stretcher. She is placid. The men are both dressed in dark coats. One is tall, with abnormally long arms giving him almost a simian appearance. He has a thick jaw and pugged nose, his eyes set far back under a protruding hairy brow. His companion is whip-thin with lank blond hair that seeps from under a grimy cap.

Watching over them from the lit doorway stands Waltz.

His hulking form casts an even vaster shadow over the high corniced walls of the room.

He sees me before they do and howls at the men, "Look to the window. He's here!"

They turn, see me, and charge.

I raise my stick and swing it, catching the thin man on the

side of the head and knocking him down. Then his larger companion catches hold of me and I know I am in trouble.

With terrible strength, he lifts me and throws me down onto the patio. The back of my head smacks the flags and the scene whirls.

Then they are on me, pinning my arms and legs. I smell their oily breath on my face, and feel their grubby hands grip my wrists and ankles.

They hoist me up and carry me, kicking and writhing, into the room.

I let out an almighty scream for help but am immediately silenced by a fist to the stomach. I double up in pain and feel my gorge rise. I try to catch my breath but the wind has been knocked clean out of me. They drop me to my knees and I clutch my stomach, dry heaving. I look up as Waltz stands over me.

He is impassive. He looks like a man who has finally made a long-delayed decision. The two ruffians look to him for guidance.

I notice another figure in the room. Standing behind them all, watching from the shadows, is Dr Strangler.

"I'm afraid, my dear Sir," says Waltz, "that you have worn out your welcome at this establishment."

"I know your intentions, Waltz," I say. "You can't have her."

Waltz nods sadly. "I was hoping that we could spare you this humiliation but you have left me no choice."

Dr Strangler steps forward into the light and walks towards me, carrying a syringe. On seeing it, I begin to stand but am seized from behind again by the two thugs. I buck and thrash as the Doctor carefully pushes the needle into the side of my neck.

CHAPTER 28

W hen I wake up, I am no longer at the hydro and am no longer dressed. I am stripped to my underwear, lying on a wooden platform, my ankles and wrists bound by tightly buckled leather straps.

Craning my head, I can see that I am in an arched stone chamber, like a cellar or the inside of a tomb. The walls are lined with bracketed instruments and a trolley has been wheeled next to me. On it stands a bowl of what, from the smell, I guess is an alcohol-based sterilising fluid. Next to the bowl is a heavy surgical saw.

From above me, in the curves and shadows of the ceiling, comes a noise.

It is the sound of dripping.

That same dripping that has haunted and followed me around the hydro, the same noise that haunted me in London the night I woke in the bathtub.

It is the same noise that came from the bathroom, the night she died.

I struggle and strain against my bonds, arching my sweaty back up off the wooden platform. The leather straps bite into my wrists and ankles. There is no give in them, no room to wriggle and prise myself free. My eyes bulge and I stare at the saw. Its vicious teeth glint in the flickering light.

I look around me at the patterns of the light on the walls and think, for an insane moment, that I see the familiar patterns of wallpaper. A twining of briars and blooming roses, maddening in their regular repetition. I blink the sweat and tears from my eyes, the salt stinging.

My vision swims and as it clears, I find myself in the girl's room.

In my room.

The curtains are drawn. The door is shut.

The single roaring gas lamp in the corner spins shadows and sputters filleted spasms of light across the walls, casting shadows that almost make it seem as if I am in an underground chamber.

My vision clears and I see the stone walls again. The dripping water is torture in its arrhythmic stutter. It cuts through the silence, bedevilling any attempt to find a pattern.

The wind rattles the casement in the bedroom and the curtain stirs.

But there is no curtain or window. Only stone walls.

I blink again and bellow for someone to come, to have done with me.

I glance down at my bound ankles, strapped to the brass bedstead. My sheets sopped with sweat, the mattress damp and sticking to my back as I arch and writhe.

But there is no mattress. The wooden platform grates against my shoulder blades as I let myself down again.

The door opens.

A figure stands in the gloom. I see her face, staring at me from across the room. She is soaking wet and pale. That waxy skin, the eyes wide with horror, at the dreadful realisation of what she has done. Wild panic has contorted her face as she tries to stanch the consequences of her ridiculous act, her stupid, weak, fatal act. She looks at me, naked and dripping, bedraggled and dying.

She takes a faltering step forwards into the light and, as she does, becomes something more tangible, different, but no less horrifying.

Dr Strangler.

I let out an animal cry. I am certain there are words in it, erupting in a stream that I neither control nor understand. My mouth shapes sound, biting out chunks of meaning. He does not understand or care. He simply observes me with cold eyes. He takes hold of my wrist with his hand, reading my pulse.

I yank my hand away, but the bindings and his wiry strength hold me tight. He clasps cold, dry fingers around my wrist and I close my eyes.

Warm rivulets of blood run down my arm.

I open my eyes and see my wife by the side of me, staring in blank horror, mouthing words I cannot hear. I look down and see her hand gripping me, the blood from her own shredded wrist pulsing in hot red gouts, threading rivers down my arm, my elbow and pooling on the wooden boards. Running and soaking my back.

Pooling on the sheets of the bed.

I contort my body again, and Dr Strangler steps away, making a note with a pencil.

My wife is nowhere to be seen.

I feel my mind begin to give.

I see the walls of our bungalow, the hot wet reed curtains, the scuttling of a lizard across the wall and hear the cries of other people's children outside in the dusty early evening. The walls still carry the heat of the day. I hear the irregular dripping of the bath, the slithering of someone inside it.

I breathe heavily to try and regain my sense of place in the world.

"My dear chap. All you have to do is sign. You will feel better. That's all there is to it."

I open my eyes and see Waltz.

I remember.

They mean to make me confess.

Yes, it had been my choice, not hers, to go to India. It was my act of rebellion against my father, my rejection of his legacy. But they can't lay what happened to Isabella at my door. It wasn't my fault. Who could have suspected the effect of the heat, of the disease on her, and our little one, lost inside her?

My poor wife. She wasn't weak, she was heartbroken and sick.

I will not sign.

We had to stay. We had to see it through and recover together. There was no way she could have travelled home in that fragile condition. It would have been murder to go. It wasn't my fault.

Was I kind enough? Attentive enough? I struggle to remember. I thought I was, but perhaps I bottled it up.

It was not my fault.

"Just sign. Here's a pen, old boy. Make it all better."

Strangler stands behind Waltz.

I remember the funeral, a scattering of mourners in the baking afternoon, the breeze hissing in the banyan, the dust rising like a spirit from her dry grave.

The fires by the river.

I couldn't stay in India after that. I had to return and leave her out there, alone under the dust.

It's true.

I abandoned her. I abandoned her before and after her death.

Where have they taken me?

The chamber is stone and there is a sputtering gas lamp in the corner sending shadows scuttling like spiders across the walls and vaulted ceiling, shadows like twisting briars and blooming roses repeated over and over again.

The curtains billow. They have opened the window and are letting in air. I am grateful for the sheet.

I sit in bed eating something like gruel, the pillows behind me.

I pull at the bonds that tie me to the platform. Waltz releases one of my hands and holds out a pen.

"SIGN!"

I refuse. They beat me.

They strip the sheet from me and flog my emaciated form as I squirm, weeping, away from them.

They bring the girl to see me helpless there. Her wounds have opened again and she is bleeding from the stumps where her hands once were. She opens her mouth and laughs in a silent tongueless laugh, mouthing something, wanting to be understood.

I run down the corridor towards my wife's bathroom, feeling a terrible presentiment. There is something very wrong in that slithering, in that wet scrambling panic coming from behind the door. Is she drowning?

I run towards the door of the room where the girl is being kept.

Is she being taken away by the men from Blackmoor? I have to save her, to stop them.

I run down the corridor towards my room in the hydro, towards the sanctuary, away from the prying of the other guests.

I run, lost, through the mill, tears streaming down my little face, my nerves shattered, machines on every side. I turn and see my father slowly shaking his head in shame. Feel his boot in my stomach.

Such a disappointment.

"Simply sign. Here's the pen, John. I can call you John, can't I?" says Waltz.

Behind him, Strangler is uncorking yet another bottle of the red medicine.

I shake my head. I will not confess.

"Then I'm afraid we don't have any choice," says Waltz, his eyes narrowing. "Strangler, I think we need to be more persuasive."

Strangler steps forward with the bottle, forcing it between my lips. I choke down the familiar aniseed liquid.

"We don't want to hurt you, John. We are trying to help you," says Waltz, then he looks away, bracing himself, biting his lip.

From all around me, instruments of industry spring out of the walls like a sudden growth of briars. Great metal hooks bite into my soft skin, piercing the white flesh which seems to rise to suckle on the iron that penetrates it. Blossoms of rose-red flesh erupt like pouting lips. I am bound with heavy chains and held firmly.

Faceless workers come from the shadows and split open my shoulders with surgical instruments, combing out the muscle fibres there and burning them with hot irons, crisping their meat to form a hardened scab-like, crab-like armour across the top of my torso. Great spinning gears descend from the ceiling and I feel the hooks take hold, the chains tighten and begin to heave me up, drawing me into the grinding guts of whatever dark mechanism lurks above me.

I feel a trembling in my spine, an ecstasy of pain and utter submission to whatever this alien mechanism is. I feel my willpower begin to dissolve and be replaced by a milky, alien certainty. There will be no more railing, no more resistance, only submission and a flat, featureless peace.

On the moor, in a pool, lies a girl with blank eyes. Flowers float around her. Her hair swirls like petals.

Strangler comes to my bedside with hard eyes. He pulls back his fist and punches me in the face.

A very real pain lurks somewhere in the red fog, under layers of narcotic featherdown. It spits through the mist at me. I hear my groans but am merely an observer within my own body. It is all abstract, unreal somehow.

Then the second punch comes and the fog clears. I cry out and the world snaps into sharp, crunching focus.

The room. The room in the hydro where the girl is held.

I am still in the hydro.

But where is the girl?

Has there ever been a girl?

Strangler punches me again. Waltz turns his face away, extending the paper and pen towards me, waiting for me to sign.

Strangler goes to the bureau and advances towards me, clutching a steel surgical hammer. He grabs my left wrist and holds it flat against the bedstead, the cold of the brass on the backs of my knuckles.

"We judge that you are guilty of the most heinous of crimes, that of the murder not of some enemy, or stranger, but one closest to you. Your wife, Isabella. Do you confess? Will you not sign the paper before you end all this? Will you not meet your God with a clear conscience and a glad heart?"

Strangler smashes the hammer down on my fingers. I scream in pain.

"Confess!" booms Waltz, still turned away. "Confess! Murderer!"

It's true.

I did kill her.

With my good hand, I take the pen, and scrawl.

I glance at the paper. It does not look like any kind of confession to me.

It looks like a legal document.

I cry out a name, the only name I can think of. The only person I wish could be there with me in that moment of awful clarity.

I cry for Polly.

CHAPTER 29

I kick open the door of the Rose and Crown and barge past a couple of hefty farmers.

"I didn't think women were allowed in here!" quips one of them, and his mate brays with laughter.

Faces, all male, most of them leathery with weather and bloated with booze, turn to stare at me. I storm through the tobacco fog of the taproom to where my father is propped in the corner.

"Ey up, Hardacre, here's trouble!" laughs one man by the bar and a joyless laugh, more like a pack animal howl, goes up around the pub. Fat red faces, mouths wide open. Stubby yellow teeth on all sides. I wish I could slap their gobs shut, every one of them.

My dad is sprawled across the bar, shirt tails out, casting his head around with lost, bleary eyes, straining to make sense of what's going on. He's still singing the last of his song, the one I could hear as I was striding down Brook Street. Something German, maybe Schubert. There are cries to get him to stop.

"Philistines!" he slurs at them. "Maybe you want another poem then?"

Cheers.

"Very well. Here's some Milton...

A virtuous girl named Sapphire,
Succumbed to her lover's desire
She said, 'It's a sin, but seeing as it's in,
Could you push it a few inches higher?'"

A great cheer goes up, then dies as they see the look on my face.

My dad notices me and squints to check he's not deceived. "Polly! My dear sweet daughter, saviour of my diminished family. This girl," he addresses the crowd, most of whom have turned back to their conversations, "this beautiful girl is the man of the house. She's a daughter, a mother and a father all in one. We're very lucky to have her." He wags a finger at them and then points it at me, the end of it ranging, waving around my face. I can tell the mental effort involved in keeping it on target.

"Come on, Dad. You need to go home," I say, trying to get under his arm to hoist him off the stool.

"Nox nova est. Nox tenera est."

"No, it bloody isn't. Stand up, you drunken idiot," I hiss at him. God, he's heavy. There's more laughter.

"Can't any of you help me?" I shout at the onlookers. There are shrugs and smirks all around, then they turn away, as if helping me would give their daughters and wives licence to come and extract them in the same way.

"Bloody men," I say and heave him up.

I'm not a strong girl, but when I've got my temper up, I can surprise myself. Up he comes and I haul him, jelly legged, across the taproom. One pock-faced farmer, with mock chivalry, opens the door and bows as we tumble out onto the street.

The fresh air hits him and he regains his footing, straightening up and smoothing down his shirt front, slick with spilt beer. He takes a deep breath.

"Oh, I don't feel..." Then he braces himself against the wall of the pub and throws up rancid, vinegary swill all over the pavement. He regathers his strength, panting, drool ribboning off his lips, then blows again.

Eventually, he wipes off his mouth on the back of his sleeve and staggers back to me. "Take me home," he says.

I take his arm (the other one) and lead him up the street, pulling him back into position when he drifts off towards the gutter. I don't tell him off, what's the point? He'll be back here again in a few nights' time, popping out for just one then drinking the place dry.

"You're a good daughter, Polly, better than I deserve," he says. "They turned me down again today, the governors."

"Do you wonder why?" I say, harsher than I intend.

He shakes his head, sniffing. "I'm not the man I was," he says. "I'm not the man your mother married."

"Come on, Dad, let's go home."

At the end of Brook Street is the poor end of Whitmoor, mean cottages from another century, some of them, like ours, still thatched with mangy heather. It's where the unfortunate families live. Where we live.

Samuel is with Nelly. She was the one that let me know that Dad was making a spectacle of himself at the pub. He's probably asleep now, oblivious to the racket across the street as Dad bundles through the front door and into the kitchen, knocking over a pile of books. I follow, closing the door behind me.

He falls into the chair by the stove, which is still crackling, and sinks with his head in his hands. I'm not in the mood for his self-pity tonight, so make myself busy making a pot of cocoa.

"There's some stew if you can keep it down," I say.

I say stew. It's a slurry of oats and turnips. The usual for the end of the week before my pay comes in. I can't remember the last time we ate any meat. Samuel is small for his age and is there any wonder? Funny how there's always money left over for Dad's drinking, though.

I push him back and unbutton his filthy shirt, wrenching it off his narrow hairy shoulders. I'll have to wash that tonight. The rest of it will have to wait till morning.

"What did the governors say, Dad?"

But he's nodded off, stubbled chin on his chest, snoring in soft purrs.

I think about picking him up again and dragging him to his bed, but it's been a long day, I've been at it since five and I can't be bothered.

I prop an embroidered velvet cushion, one of the few things still left from happier times, under his head. I drape a woollen blanket over him. Then I use the hot water to wash the shirt, hang it dripping over the stove and take myself to bed.

Without Samuel in there with me, I can stretch out, and for once, I don't mind the lumps in the straw mattress. I need to sleep. I'll be up again in a few hours and I'll have to clean out the stove before I head back to Cragside.

I pray to God for some kind of change, for something, anything to happen.

But my heart's not in it, and I'm fairly sure he's not listening anyway.

CHAPTER 30

The next morning, I let my aching muscles lead me through the routine of preparing the house, cleaning the grate, lighting the fire, and making the tea. Then I dress and head up in the early light to the hydro.

All the girls at Cragside (there are ten of us) have seventeen rooms each to make up every day. In the old days, I've heard there'd been more, fifteen at most, doing twenty-four rooms each. That was in the heyday. Now some areas are virtually closed, including the whole garden floor downstairs. The hydro just isn't as busy now. I suppose people are losing the taste for all that cold water, suffering and preaching.

It isn't terrible work and certainly better, from what I've heard, than life in domestic service. The girls are silly, but generally good-spirited and there's only ever occasional nastiness between them. The worst bit is that some of the guests, the male guests generally but not always, think that for some reason all the chambermaids are flighty and some look to take advantage of that. There's one girl I know who made twenty-five pounds in tips one year and who Mrs Hubbard sent on her way.

There were strict talks after that from Dr Waltz and Hubbard about the importance of moral behaviour, neat appearance and comportment. They said that our guests were here for their ill health and that any degeneracy or wantonness would endanger their recovery and would be cause for instant dismissal.

There's no need for all the girls to live on-site, which is just as well. Some, such as myself, are from Whitmoor, or Woodley further down the valley. Those that do stay at Cragside have poky little quarters in the east wing of the hotel, where you can hear mice scurrying around in the winter. I'm glad I have to walk up from the village every day. It's the only time I get to think.

So I tend my rooms, change sheets, clean and make up fresh fires. During the day, most of the guests are in the treatment rooms, or out taking the air. Some go off for day trips up the valley, up to the rocks and the waterfall at Grimston, or out to the priory at Carlside. I'm pretty much left to my own devices and am glad of it.

I think about Samuel, and my dad, and wonder what I can do beyond this.

Deborah Jenkins finds me as she's passing and pokes her nose into the room I'm working on.

"Hi, Pol, do you want in on the Fell race sweep?"

I turn with my fists on my hips. "Do you think I've nothing better to do with my money than put it on some scrawny sheep farmers running up a hill in their underwear?"

"It's a good field this year. Joseph Ashdown is running again. He did the Burnthwaite Feast Day race in under twenty minutes. And barefoot too. There could be a good pot. Maybe even five pounds."

"Not interested," I say. "Well... maybe. Let me think about it."

She laughs. "You come and see me later and put in. All the

other girls are in, well, apart from Esther Brown, she's far too goody-good to be interested in a flutter."

"What about the waiters and porters? Are they running their book this year?"

"No, we're pooling the lot. It's all Mr Morris's idea." Morris is the head waiter. He's a character – rumour has it he made over four hundred pounds in tips in one year and has refused a duty manager post because it'd leave him much worse off despite the salary increase. He has a way with the guests that's a marvel to see, although once you get wise to his patter, you can tell how he does it. He gradually worms his way into their favour, never seeming ingratiating, but working the charm till they come to feel they're somehow special. Then, on their departure, he rakes in it. A clever fellow but always with an eye for the main chance. In his management of the dining room, where we have to help out sometimes, he's strict in public, but behind the servants' door, he's kind enough, and always organising schemes like this.

"I'll think about it," I say.

Deborah shrugs, then looks me up and down. "What's this I hear about you charging into the Rose last night?"

"Never you mind that," I say. "It's nothing for you to worry about."

"So it's true then? Go on, tell us! No? Well, you keep your secrets then. I suppose that's what you get for being educated above your station, Polly Hardacre…"

"Be off with you. It's a private matter. And don't you be spreading rumours about it with the other girls, Deborah Jenkins, there's a saying about people in glass houses, you know." I give her a meaningful look. Her dad's a right one.

She sticks her tongue out and struts off.

I'm busy enough as is, what with the beds to make up and always hanging about waiting for the one chance I have to change over rooms when the clients go to get their treatments. And Mrs Hubbard has her eye on me. I don't know what I ever did to annoy her, but she's put a mark against me for some reason. It's always "Polly Hardacre" this and "You, girl" that. She doesn't care for me, hasn't ever, not since I started. I reckon word has got to her about Samuel and she's put one and one together and come up with "hussy".

Later, I'm making up one of the rooms on the top floor.

I don't care for the top floor, particularly on these hot days when the heat in the whole place seems to float up and gather there. That's why we seldom have guests up there, not that we have a lot of guests anyhow. Certainly not like the old days, Mrs Hubbard and some of the other older girls are always saying. Back then, it was full to the gunnels with fat tourists coming to take the waters, to freeze, half boil and pray themselves better, taking long walks across the moor and breathing in the air that I've been breathing all my life. It's never done me much good.

I'm running a hand across the flat sheets, the mattress that's so much smoother than my own, when I hear a voice at the door.

"Dr Waltz wants to see you."

CHAPTER 31

I t's Maureen, with a glint in her eye and a tone that I don't like. "Looks like you're either in trouble or..." She winks.

I feel a sense of dread. Waltz is an odd man and he smells of pomander. His big hands frighten me.

"Or what, Maureen Donnelly?" I say, defiant-like, as I shake out a sheet.

"Or he's going to try and get you in trouble."

I shudder at the thought of his big flabby body. "That's wicked to suggest," I say.

Maureen smirks, helps me tuck in the sheet around the edges of the bed and smooths her hand over the flawless cotton.

"Well, you've heard what happened to Margaret Yeadon. She went to see the Doctor on her own a few times and before you know it, she's out the door being driven to Leeds by her grandad. Not been back since. Still, I hear she didn't go to term."

"I don't believe a word of it. That was Jack Micklethwaite, the lad from the bakery. Everyone knows that."

"Well, you'll find out anyhow. He wants to see you at your earliest convenience if you can spare the time, milady."

Maureen stands aside and presents the door to me with her hand. I sigh and push past her and she gives a little curtsey as I go.

"Don't forget to tell him to pull out before he spends," she whispers.

"You're disgusting, Maureen," I say, stifling a snigger. I go out with as much dignity as I can muster.

On the way down to the Doctor's office, I run into Mrs Hubbard. I see her before she sees me. I try to duck out of her way down a corridor, but she catches me. I swear that woman sees everything she isn't supposed to.

"Polly Hardacre, what are you doing slouching around the corridors on your own? Are you idle, girl? Do you want for productive work?"

"No, Mrs Hubbard, I've been..."

"Well, there are more rooms that need airing on the top floor. If they've not been started yet, then I'll be very annoyed. I thought you were up there with that silly creature Maureen Donnelly."

She has a face like roast beef – all wrinkles and red with years of being indignant and sour. Her forearms are thicker than my poor legs.

"Dr Waltz sent for me, Ma'am."

She doesn't like that one bit. She straightens up and looks me in the eye.

"And what would the Doctor want with a flighty girl like yourself?"

I bristle. "I'm not flighty, Mrs Hubbard. Not at all, and I work hard, not like some of the others. You know that, don't you? And I don't know what the Doctor wants."

She catches me a right clip round the ear, making it proper smart. "Don't you give me any of your sass, young lady.

I know you and your father and what you've got at home. I won't have you lowering standards in this place. If you're going to see Dr Waltz, I want you to come to me straight afterwards and tell me what the matter of your conversation was. I'm not a believer in tittle-tattle and I don't want you telling the poor Doctor your life's woes. Do you hear?"

My dad says he remembers when Mrs Hubbard was a girl, how she used to be quite the prettiest little thing in the town, and knew it. That was before she'd dropped a few babies, put on some poundage and let her worse nature get the better of her. She's bad to all the girls, but she holds me in special contempt.

I give a curtsey (she likes that sort of thing) and go down-stairs. Out in the main reception, there's a group of guests hanging around, getting ready for some walking expedition up the moor. That handsome Reverend is leading them. Some of the other girls have tried to give him the eye but I always think he isn't interested. He only cares about God. Well, God and the boy who works in the stables. I've seen him following him with his eyes.

It's amazing what you see when no one pays attention to you when you're just another silly girl in a uniform.

But I'm not a silly girl.

I've learned well at school and from my father before the drink got the better of him. I've read books, lots of them. More than any of this lot.

I KNOCK AT THE HEAVY DOOR TO DR WALTZ'S OFFICE AND he booms out in his thick accent to come in.

I've heard the rumours, of course, everyone has, and I believe them more than most. Dr Waltz has always seemed a little too good to be true. Too pure to piss in a pot, as the saying goes. Still, I'm not as pretty as Deborah Jenkins, or as "well developed", shall we say, as Esther Wilkinson. The truth is, though, I need my job more than either of them.

I wonder what I'll do if the Doctor does get fresh with me; what choice will I have? I decide to worry about that if it happens and not otherwise. A person can drive themselves to distraction with all that imagining.

I push open the door and go in, a bit sheepish.

He's sitting there behind his enormous desk, big hands clasped together, sausage fingers interlaced in front of him resting calm and heavy on his blotter. He has a placid, benevolent look on his face that tells me he has been waiting for me and planning for how this little meeting is going to go. I feel some tension rising in my chest and I swallow hard.

"Ah, Polly, thank you for coming by. Come and take a seat." One of his hands gestures like a seal flipper at a chair that's arranged and waiting in front of the desk.

I curtsey and scurry across the room, my head bowed, shoulders raised as if bracing for a thrashing. I sit in the chair as demurely as I can, afraid to make eye contact with him, although I can feel his stare tracing my body. It feels like hot ants marching all over me.

"I've been hearing good things about you, Polly. I understand from Mrs Hubbard that you are a girl who does good work, who can be trusted to do what she's told and not make a fuss. That's important in a place like this when the clients are here to relax and not be bothered with a lot of needless fuss."

That's news. When did Hubbard ever put in a kind word for anyone?

"I try my best, Sir."

"I also understand that your family situation makes this job very important to you. How is your father, girl? I am a governor at the school in Whitmoor, so I am well aware of his condition and the unfortunate events leading to his current situation."

I flush. I can't blame the governors. It's my dad's own doing that he lost his teaching post.

"He's well, Sir, thank you for asking. He is not working, alas, but in good health. Well... better than he has been."

"I see. And is he exercising moderation in his daily habits? Losing your mother must have been a terrible blow."

I look at my chewed fingernails. What business of Waltz's is it what my dad does? I think of him, drunk from lunchtime most days, asleep when I get home, stinking of the filthy stuff that's rotting him from the inside out. I shudder to imagine him trying to look after Samuel, drunk.

"I'm sure he does his best, Sir, but I'm afraid it's a terrible struggle for him."

Waltz nods his big bear head slowly, his soft eyelids lowering in contemplation. "Indeed, there are many of our clients who have faced the same struggle with the evils of drink. Do not give up hope, my girl. Perhaps I should ask the Reverend to call on him someday?"

I imagine the reception he'll receive.

"That would be kind, Sir. But I fear my father has little care for the church."

Waltz sniffs and gestures dismissively as if to say the subject is closed. He takes a deep breath. Here it comes, I think.

"I need assistance with a private, personal matter that is of some delicacy. I've thought long and hard about which of the girls could help me and I've settled on you as the likeliest candidate. Someone who can be trusted with discretion and, to put it frankly, secrecy. Does that please you?"

I feel my heart sink. The old rake does have his eye on me, after all. All that talk of my father was just to remind me how dependent I am on him and his sweaty patronage. I know if he chooses to terminate my employment we'll all be in real trouble, and so does Waltz.

"Yes, Sir," I say, and then without being able to stop the flow of words, blurt, "I've always tried to be a good girl, Sir. I wouldn't want to do anything that would jeopardise that."

Waltz sits up. "Good Lord, no, girl. I would never ask you to do anything immoral. What must you think? No, this is quite the opposite. I require your help with a particularly delicate matter involving a guest. The poor man is at his wits' end, and I need someone to help me keep an eye on him and his movements and report if anything odd happens. The poor man has lost his wife and his father in the space of a year, and as I'm sure you can appreciate, it has taken a grievous toll on his emotional state. He has come here to recover and rest but having met the man, I'm convinced that it will be a long road for him. My doctors and I can only monitor his progress intermittently, we have so many other responsibilities, you understand. I need someone, I need you, to keep a friendly eye on him, without him knowing."

I remember something I saw the previous evening. I'd been coming back up the drive late from checking on Samuel before it was time to change and light up in the rooms. I'd been at the main gates after half running all the way from Whitmoor when I'd seen a man approaching, dragging a trunk behind him down the drive. I'd thought that looked odd, the case was going to get scuffed and scratched. He'd been a young man, not bad looking, but in a bit of a state, as if he'd been running away from something. When he saw me, he'd stopped, and raised his hand to his eyes to shield them from the sun, which was directly behind me. I'd regretted coming in the main entrance, which wasn't something we were supposed to do, but I'd been late and I'd thought all the guests would have been at dinner.

Then I'd seen Waltz barrelling down the drive after him.

That was a very odd sight. Dr Waltz doesn't run. Dr Waltz doesn't even walk if he can help it. He'd shouted after the man.

I'd known I was late and that I was going to get it in the neck from Mrs Hubbard anyway and I hadn't wanted trouble from Dr Waltz, so I'd ducked back behind the gates and went round to sneak in the servants' entrance around the side.

I guess that the man must be the guest that Dr Waltz is speaking of.

The job doesn't sound too bad and I'm so relieved that it's nothing more sinister that I smile and nod my acceptance.

"Will you come and report to me each day on what the gentleman has been doing, his movements, habits and behaviours? You will need to be circumspect. We can't have him thinking he's being spied on, can we? That's not the sort of atmosphere we want to create when he's trying to get better, eh?"

"But Mrs Hubbard, Sir. Won't she think that I'm neglecting my duties?"

Waltz smiles leans across the desk and pats my hand. "Don't you worry about Mrs Hubbard, girl. I'll let her know that you're doing some special work for me. After all, it was she who recommended you."

I doubt that. I wonder what their discussion was really about. Waltz seems to know a lot about my family, all of a sudden.

"Of course, Sir," I say. "I'd be happy to help. Who is the gentleman, Sir?"

Waltz looks down at a ledger in front of him, but I know he knows the name off by heart. He was shouting it as he floundered down the drive after him.

"It's a... John Weighton. He's freshly returned from India."

No, it must be someone else. The man he was chasing had a different name. I can't remember what, though.

"I'll do my best, Sir," I say.

"Good girl. I knew I could count on you and if you do this thing for me, I'm sure we can see our way to giving some sort of special remuneration that might help your domestic situation. It can't be easy being the sole breadwinner in a family. I understand there is a little one as well?"

I say nothing. I know what they all think, but I'm not going to give them the satisfaction of telling the truth and having them think it's a lie. Let them speculate and gossip about Samuel.

He's all I care about.

CHAPTER 32

So, I ask a couple of discreet questions and soon find our Mr Weighton.

Turns out it *is* the man I saw.

I first see the poor man at breakfast the next day, sitting at the table that matches his room number. He sits there fiddling with his eggs and toast and taking tiny bird sips at a cup of that foul spring water they force on the guests.

He looks like he's been in the wars. He's thin, painfully so, and brown, from his time in India, I imagine, although that's wearing off. He has a sort of wasted appearance, as if he's been eating himself from the inside and all his skin is being sucked in towards his heart. It's his eyes, though, that give me a start. They're big pools of nothing, beautiful really, but empty and blank as if he's looking at something beyond the clatter and chatter of this world. He seems to be carrying a slow, seeping sadness around with him.

Also, he's younger than I expect. Maybe twenty. Barely a man. He has a tainted innocence, like a fragile doll that's been battered and now fears he might fall apart at the slightest touch.

I understand how he must feel. I've lost those close to me (who hasn't?) but I've found solace in worry about the living, and hard work always drives any self-pity from me. This man doesn't look like he needs work, he's well dressed and staying in one of the best rooms in the hotel. I wonder if having space and time to spend with his loss is going to help him. A soul can spin round on itself with no distractions.

I watch him for a bit before Mrs Hubbard tells me to go about my business. I know from Waltz that she doesn't know what my special work is, and I sense her curiosity and bitter frustration. That said, I have ten more rooms to make up before lunchtime and she'll be on me if I slack off more than she thinks Waltz's commission warrants.

I pull the trolley with sheets past the doorway and as I pass, clattering along, I give him a surreptitious glance. The noise of the trolley seems to jar him out of his reverie and he looks up at me. I give him a polite smile and nod good morning and he just turns those big empty eyes back to his egg. "We've got a real jolly soul here, Polly Hardacre," I think to myself.

After breakfast, he goes for some of the treatments and, as the girls aren't allowed near the steam rooms when the men are in there, I lose track of him.

Instead, I pay a little visit to his room and have a quick look around to see if there is anything in there that might help with my observation. I feel bad for the snooping, to be sure, but going into rooms is all part of a chambermaid's role, after all.

It feels quite exciting, like I'm carrying around an important secret that no one else knows, not Mrs Hubbard, not the girls, not anyone apart from me and Dr Waltz. I feel immune to any accusations they can throw at me, secure in the knowledge that I'm protected.

The view from his room is lovely. You can see the slopes

of heather, the crags of the Devil's Pinnacles and, nestled below them, Whitmoor. It's a windy day and stipples of grass and heather are cascading down the hill in giant uneven waves. Smoke is trickling up from the chimneys in the town. I try to see my little house but can't.

I look around the room. His heavy battered trunk is of good quality, stowed under the bed and emptied. The wardrobe is stocked with fine clothes, more than is needed for a normal stay at the hotel. There's little odd or interesting at all. Then my eye is attracted to a picture frame at the side of his bed.

It's a heavy, beautiful cameo frame in silver, more suitable for a centrepiece in a parlour than as a travel item to bring on a rest cure. It shines in the morning light, and I think it's likely worth far more than I earn a year.

But the oddest thing about it, and the thing that makes me nervous for what it implies, is that it's empty.

Whatever photograph or sketch has been in there, it's been removed, and all that remains is the blank black felt of the reverse, a pitch black that seems as dark and impenetrable as the silver frame is lustrous.

Beneath that strange gap, the silver is engraved in fine scrolling lettering with the name "Lavinia".

There's something not right about the thing. It has pride of place where he can see it before sleep and on waking, but where is the photograph? Has there ever been one?

My skin crawls as I hold it and I turn to place it back in the exact spot on the nightstand.

As I do, I hear a key fumble at the lock.

I put the frame down and look around for a hiding place. I'm not thinking straight so don't realise that it's the most obvious thing in the world for a chambermaid to be alone in a room mid-morning, but that frame has rattled me.

The key turns in the lock and, given the door is unlocked

(by me), it can't turn. Mr Weighton, for it's surely him, strug-gles with the key, assuming it to be stuck. But the door could be opened any second. I run to the only place I can think of, the wardrobe.

As I hurry passed the nightstand, I clip it, tipping over a porcelain jug of water. I juggle the thing in mid-air for a moment and manage to grip its smooth heavy belly before it hits the floor, but not before it spills most of its contents all over the floor.

The water splashes and runs everywhere.

Unable to think what to do, I carry the jug with me and fling open the wardrobe door, clamber inside and close it behind me, just as I hear the room door open.

I sit in the dark, my heart racing, cursing myself for being so foolish, clutching at the half-empty jug as if it's a baby, water dripping from my skirts.

The door of the wardrobe is not completely closed. I had pulled it behind me as far as I could but it's still ajar. There's a finger's width gap that I can see out of, or, more to the point, that he might see me through. I look down and realise that part of my skirt is sticking out.

I hear footsteps cross the floor.

They stop just outside the wardrobe, and I hear the water on the floor disturbed. There is the sound of him pacing back and forth, testing the window. Then there's a groan and a creaking of springs as Mr Weighton gets onto the bed. I hear heavy breathing and I try to make my own breath match his rhythm, as if that's more likely to hide the sound of my own.

The cupboard and clothes are musty and I feel my nose running. Unable to help myself, I sniff.

I try to breathe through one nostril to see if that's any quieter and when it isn't, I breathe through my mouth. In the dark, the heavy clothes hang all around me and a harsh tweed overcoat brushes my face. I have to fight myself not to push it away.

There's the sound of gentle snoring.

I risk a peek out of the gap in the doors, shifting my weight carefully. Weighton is asleep, curled over and cradling the empty photo frame to his chest.

If I wasn't in such a precarious situation, I'd feel a wave of sympathy. As it is, all I want to do is to get out of there.

I carefully edge the cupboard door open and step out, still carrying the jug.

The floor of the wardrobe gives a horrible creak and I stand as quickly as I can, wincing at the rattling of the coat hangers behind me as I disturb the suits and coats.

Mr Weighton sleeps on.

I close the wardrobe door gently behind me, rehearsing excuses and stories should his eyes open, but mercifully they don't.

I tiptoe to the door and turn the handle, open the door and step out.

Then, with great care, I close the door to the room behind me, but with the wetness of my hands, the handle slips and snaps back with the tiniest of clacks.

I walk swift and quiet down the corridor. Then I hear the door open behind me.

"Miss!"

I turn. It's him, standing in the doorway, bleary-eyed.

I flush. It's all up. Less than a few hours since I've been charged with this job, I've already made a mess of it.

I walk towards him, clutching the jug, putting as brave a face on it as I can.

"Yes, Sir?" I say in as normal a voice as I can muster.

"I seem to have a leak or something in my room. There is water all over my floor. Would you mind seeing if anyone could come and help with it?"

"Was this here when you just got in, Sir?" I say, looking in at the mess and feigning surprise.

"It was, although the stain was there when I arrived yesterday. Is there a leak somewhere? I heard dripping last night."

I look at the ceiling, wondering if he had seen me through half-closed eyes as I tiptoed across his room a moment before. Perhaps this is all a test to trap me.

"I don't see one. Perhaps there's a pipe running under the room that has burst. I'll see if I can get someone to have a look at it."

I'm trembling. I am not the sort of girl that lies easily. There's something wicked in lies that rocks me to my bones and grates against the world.

I hurry to the door again and down the corridor. I get rid of the water jug as soon as I can.

I find Scrimshaw, the caretaker, sitting smoking his pipe behind the kitchens. I tell him fairly snippily what's happened (sort of) and that the guest is one of Waltz's special concerns and that gets him moving right away. We go back up, him carrying his mop over his soldier like he was still in the army, the old fool, me carrying a bucket, my brain spinning stories.

I stand at the door as Scrimshaw sucks his gums and looks at the ceiling. Mr Weighton is pacing, and agitated. I wonder why he doesn't just go downstairs to the library or something. The poor man doesn't look well at all. I stare at the water, then when Scrimshaw's investigations are fruitless, I mop up the mess once and for all.

Mr Weighton suddenly grabs his coat and pulls it on, as if seized with a new idea. He strides towards the door and I step aside to let him pass, half wondering if he's on his way to report the whole incident at reception.

He stops and looks at me with his big eyes. I look back at him and realise that he's scared of something.

"Excuse me, girl. Do you think there's something odd about that water?" he asks in a low voice. "You've been staring at it in quite a peculiar fashion."

My heart leaps. Is he on to me? I speak without taking a breath, feeling the words run out in a stream, my throat drying as I lie. "No, Sir. It's just this room hasn't been used for some months. It's odd that it should choose to leak the moment that someone takes occupancy."

"Why was it left vacant? I thought Cragside was more or less fully booked over the summer?"

I flush and can't think of anything to say. How can I compound the lie? I'm wading into untruth and a simple query to reception or Waltz will reveal my dishonesty. I decide to play the shy chambermaid and look away, muttering that I don't know about such things while giving the damp floor another cursory mop.

Weighton stands in the doorway for a moment. Then he turns and strides down the corridor.

Scrimshaw looks at me. "That was a spill, not a leak, girl. What are you up to? I hope Mrs Hubbard doesn't find out about this."

"Well, there's no need to go blabbing to her about it is there, Albert Scrimshaw? There are lots of things it's probably better she doesn't find out about," I say, giving him a hard stare. I know all about his afternoon naps and his bottles of gin in the tool shed. I'm certainly not going to be threatened by him.

He harrumphs and goes on his way. I take the opposite direction and go down the servants' stairs two at a time, seeing if I can catch up with Mr Weighton before he reaches reception.

I see him, stick in hand, striding towards the gardens.

I wonder what I should do. I know my commission from Dr Waltz allows me to duck out of my afternoon duties and follow after him. I'm not dressed for it, certainly, but it's a mild enough day.

I decide to chance it. I scurry out through the servants' entrance, across the gravel driveway and into the ornamental gardens, keeping him in sight but hanging back. I wonder what excuse I can use this time if my pursuit is discovered.

It's a warm afternoon but most of the other guests are either at treatment or milling around the lower gardens.

For a convalescent, he has enough strength in him, I can say. He keeps a brisk pace, stabbing at the path with his stick, pausing occasionally to take deep lungfuls of air. He strides over the little bridge that crosses the beck.

A couple is taking the waters from the fountain. That horrendous Mr and Mrs Garstang who come here every year. Mr Weighton stops for a word with them. I freeze under a yew tree and wait till he moves on. Then I duck behind a hedge and work my way around till I can rejoin my pursuit unseen by them.

I realise that he seems intent on hiking up onto the moor.

There's a cool breeze up here, despite the warmth of the afternoon, and I clutch my arms as I walk, feeling more and more ridiculous being out in the open in my black and white uniform.

I follow, peering from behind hedges and trees, trying not to look like I'm stalking him, racking my brain as to what possible reason I can give should my presence be discovered.

It does make me laugh how when you're born with it looming above you, the prospect of a walk on the moor seems like some penance rather than a healthful pleasure. Most of the villagers, myself included, would rather do pretty much anything than walk across the moor for exercise.

Still, on he goes and so on I go, feeling more and more exposed as we rise from the gardens up to the stone wall that marks the boundary of the hotel grounds with its iron gate. He passes through and heads up into the heather.

I decide to stop.

It isn't just the risk of being discovered, although out on the open moorland that would be considerable. Explaining why a chambermaid might be in the gardens is one thing, but explaining why she is on a remote moorland path when she should be at work is quite another. It also isn't the sudden, slightly odd thought that to a certain mucky-minded kind of person, it might look as if we were on a pre-arranged assignation away from prying eyes.

No. The real reason I stop is that something in Mr Weighton's gait and the way he looks around makes me want to give the poor man some privacy. He's alone with his thoughts, and for all the job I've been given by Waltz, he is here with us to recover.

I feel like an intruder.

CHAPTER 33

I 'm fair shattered from all the intrigue, not to mention all my actual work, which doesn't let up one bit. Some girls, like Esther Wilkinson to name names, would probably take Dr Waltz's "little job" as an excuse to slack off completely and to lord it over the others, but I hope I'm not like that. As soon as I get back, I set to my rooms with a good dose of elbow grease.

Also, I'm not sure what Dr Waltz will think of me being off for the afternoon, but I've had it booked for ages, and I suppose that with Mr Weighton probably being busy with treatments, there isn't an awful lot else he can be getting up to. I collect my wages from the day manager on the way out and tuck the envelope into my apron pocket. At first, I think he's made a mistake as he hands it over, in fact, he double checks the ledger himself, but sure enough, there's a note alongside my name, instructing an additional payment. It wouldn't be anything to the more senior staff in the hotel, but it's more money than I've ever held before. The day manager raises an eyebrow at me but says nothing.

I go home, grinning from ear to ear, and almost don't

notice the burning up on the moor.

My dad looks a little pale and puffy but no worse than usual. He's reading to Samuel and has not taken a drink yet, as far as I can tell. They're both hungry, so I go grocery shopping. I have a fairly set route I take with my basket, going to the greengrocers, bakery and finally, as a treat, the butchers on Moor Lane. I even buy Samuel a little treat, a bar of Fry's chocolate. It's just when my basket is about as full as I can manage that I see Mr Weighton.

He's outside the bakery and I'm so used to looking out for him now that I recognise him immediately.

I hurry over to the other side of the road, but it's too late. He's seen me.

"Good afternoon!" he calls, trotting over the road to join me.

I've no wish to engage him in conversation. It's not encouraged to talk to the guests outside the confines of the hotel, and for an unmarried chambermaid to do so with a young male guest is highly inappropriate. To say nothing of my special reasons.

"Good afternoon, Sir. Is there anything I can help you with?"

He laughs (that's new). "No need for formality, I was just wondering if I could help you with your basket. It seems rather heavy."

Now, this really is crossing the line. I look up and down the street to see if there's anyone from the hotel who can see. There may not be, but there are plenty of folk from the town who I recognise, and who won't be slow to gossip if they saw Polly Hardacre being squired by some rich young man up the main street. He begins to look troubled.

"I don't mean to put you in an uncomfortable situation. If it is improper for me to converse with you outside the hotel, then I apologise."

"Well, it's not particularly encouraged by Dr Waltz, and to be honest, Sir, this is the only afternoon I have off in a week."

He apologises and backs away, then offers to carry my basket. It's mortifying really, but my basket is so heavy. I've gone a little wild with my shopping, what with the extra money. And so we walk along together, him making faltering attempts at conversation and me staring straight ahead and blushing to my roots.

I find it very odd that someone who's rich and from a "good" family would condescend to making conversation with someone like me, and out in the open as well. He doesn't seem to have any ulterior motive, he just seems completely oblivious to the difference between us. I don't know whether it's sweet, or if he's just a bit "dateless", as my Granny used to say. People like him should know better, and I guess it won't do him many favours with his sort, mingling with the lower orders.

It's funny but I feel like he's casting around, looking for someone to talk to, maybe not even a woman, but just someone with ears who'll be willing to use them. I steal little glances at him. He seems shy but full of things that he wants to get off his chest. I'm not a Catholic but I imagine he needs a good dose of confession to clear his head.

Halfway along Brook Street, Mr Weighton, out of the blue, says, "I think I may be packing my bags tomorrow."

I stop short. This is bad news. The extra pay has been lovely, and if this man leaves the hotel, then that will be the last I see of it. Of course, he's going to be going home at some point, but I need that money. My family needs the money. Not to mention the fact that this poor distressed man needs to get better.

"I hope I haven't offended?"

I turn to stare at him. I really could do with at least one more extra pay packet, and he's booked in for several weeks.

"I think you should give the treatments a chance, Sir. What harm could there be in them?" I say, a little harshly.

He stands, shamefaced on the road as, embarrassed by my outburst, I snatch the basket from him and hurry home to my family, who are waiting to be fed.

This isn't going to plan.

I UNLOAD MY SHOPPING AND FEED MY FAMILY. CHEESE, fresh bread and tomatoes. It's lovely to see them pounce on it and to have to wipe the juice from Samuel's mouth.

All the while, though, I'm stewing about my conversation with Mr Weighton. He mustn't go, for his own sake, but to tell Waltz would be to confess that I've talked to him. I'm torn.

Samuel gives a little burp. My father pats him on the back and they have a cuddle.

"Did you call in the bottle shop, Pol?" he says, a hungry edge to his voice.

"I didn't, Dad. I got interrupted by someone from work. Sorry."

"Not to worry." He looks agitated, but then he remembers something. Sure enough, two minutes later he finds an excuse to head up to his room where I know he's got one stashed. He's managed to hold off this long. That's quite good for him.

I sigh and plonk Samuel on my knee, look at the remnants of their tea on the table and decide that after a day of lies, honesty is the best policy with Waltz.

AS SOON AS I ARRIVE BACK AT CRAGSIDE, I GO TO SEE DR Waltz.

"Is he with a patient?" I ask the day manager.

He isn't, having just finished his meetings for the day, so I head along the hallway and down to his office door and knock.

"Come."

I lean my weight onto the handle and push it down, letting the door glide open.

Waltz might as well not have moved since my last visit. He's still sitting there, the same blank expectant look on his face across the enormous slab of polished oak that's his desk.

"Ah, Polly, this is a surprise. Close the door, please."

I do so, letting the latch snap back up with a clatter that fills the room. The only other noise is the heavy ticking of the grandfather clock in the corner.

"Come and take a seat." Waltz's voice is soft, low as if he's about to break bad news.

I wonder if he's had a word about the spillage in Mr Weighton's room. Or if word has got to him about our meeting in town. If I'm to lose my position, it won't go well with Dad, or with Samuel.

I scurry to the chair in front of Waltz's desk and he gestures at it.

I sit, folding my hands demurely on my lap, and brace myself for the worst.

"How have you been doing with the little favour I asked of you this morning?" says Waltz. "How has Mr Weighton been?"

"He went up onto the moor for a walk, Sir," I say, "and I believe he's been taking his treatments. He also... went for a walk into Whitmoor this afternoon."

"I understand there was a bit of a disturbance in his room this morning. What was it?"

"A leak, Sir, or a spillage. Either way, it was sorted out as right as rain. Nothing to worry about."

He pauses, then lets it pass.

"And what do *you* make of our guest, Polly? Have you had any dealings with him?"

I wonder if Waltz has set one of the other girls, or male members of staff, to watch over me. Perhaps he doesn't trust me to do my work properly. I rack my brain to think who might have been spying on me in Whitmoor.

"I've... I confess I've met him briefly a couple of times, Sir. It wasn't my intention, but he approached me. He seems very sad, if I may say so, Sir. Sad and tired."

Waltz takes off his glasses and nods. "I think you might be right."

"He's not been doing anything untoward, or unusual, but he does seem exhausted and a bit... frayed, if I'm honest, Sir. As if he's not quite all there. More than is usual for the clients here. And, begging your pardon, Sir, I got talking to him briefly in Whitmoor, it was my afternoon off and I've had it booked for ages. I needed to go shopping for my family, you see. Anyway, he saw me on the street, and he told me in passing that he was thinking of leaving tomorrow."

Waltz looks up sharply. He thinks for a moment, then gets up and starts pacing around the room like a tiger in a cage.

Finally, he stops and rounds on me. "Do you know what happened in the pressure chamber today?"

I shake my head.

"Speak up, girl."

"No, Sir. I've not heard. I'm sorry, I'm not permitted to go into..."

He waves away my obvious statement as if swatting at a butterfly. "Well, it seems our Mr Weighton had a bit of a turn. An attack of some sort that nearly laid the poor fellow out."

"It does get very hot in the treatments, Sir. It has happened before."

"Of course, but this wasn't a simple reaction to the heat

205

or the pressure. I think the poor fellow had a fit of some sort. The guests who were with him said that he was having convulsions."

I feel a twinge of sympathy.

"I have met with the gentleman," he says. "I examined him myself this afternoon, and want very much to help him. But I fear he is stubborn." He seems to consider, then speaks slowly and calmly. "There is a tonic that is of great efficacy in circumstances such as this. It is administered orally, but I'm afraid that Mr Weighton is unlikely to be willing to take it. Now what I have to ask of you, you may find hard to credit, but given the severity of his symptoms, I need to take this step. I believe this is the only course of action. I'm afraid my oath as a physician doesn't allow me to stand by and watch this poor man wither away. I suspect that without the correct medicine, Mr Weighton will deteriorate, and the convulsions that afflicted him in the pressure chamber today will manifest themselves in other ways, to the injury of his body and perhaps to the risk of his life."

He looks at me and breathes through his nose. There is a vague whistling in his nostrils and his bulk gently rises and falls in the chair.

"I need you to administer the medicine to Mr Weighton. Put it in his food. It is a simple liquid that can be put into any solution. I need you to do this without his knowledge. One of the aspects of his condition is a tendency to paranoia, which may be aroused if he suspects he is being treated without his knowledge."

I wonder if it counts as paranoia if your suspicions turn out to be true.

"You want me to put medicine in his food without him knowing? Oh, Sir. I don't think I could."

Waltz nods. "I understand your reticence, my dear girl. Indeed, it is not something that I would ever normally countenance, but I am so afraid for the poor man that I'm not sure I can see any alternative. Well, short of seeking some kind of legal instruction to detain him at Highroads, at the asylum, for further examination. You wouldn't wish that on the poor man, would you? Think of his reputation."

I think of my own dad. He was there for a few months after Mum died. It wasn't long, but the memory of walking down those long, whitewashed corridors listening to the wailing and shouting behind each of the cell doors has stayed with me.

"I wouldn't wish Highroads on anyone, Sir," I say.

"Well, then, will you be the good Samaritan and help this bereaved man in his hour of need?"

I swallow, it's one thing to keep an eye on someone and quite something else to drug them without their consent. The question hangs in the air between us, my response caught in a spiral of conflicting thoughts.

"I'm counting on you, Polly," Waltz says, his meaty hand reaching out across the plain of oak. He places it flat and outstretched, fingers pointing at me, as if he half expects me to reach out myself and place my little hand on his, as if that will offer some form of comfort, as if Waltz himself is the one in need.

"But Sir..."

"Your family are counting on you as well," says Waltz with a threatening tone to his voice. The sausage-like fingers of his outstretched hand curl, retracting into a fist. What was soft and fat becomes hard, gristly and dangerous.

I have no choice. I nod.

Waltz brightens immediately. "Good girl," he says. He pushes himself up to standing and walks over to the cabinet in the corner. "The dosage is very important," he says, unlocking and opening the door. He takes out a small unmarked bottle. It's made of opaque red glass and has a cork stopper. "One teaspoon only. That will be enough to calm his nerves and relieve him of this brain fever. You are doing the right thing, Polly. This relief will allow Mr Weighton the time and space to recover and heal himself. After all, isn't that what we are about here at Cragside?"

He paces over to me and hands me the jar, cradling it like a mouse. "I'm so glad I can trust you with this," he places his big hand on my shoulder and tightens the grip, his eyes meet mine, "and that I can trust to your discretion."

❧

I LEAVE WALTZ'S OFFICE, MY HEAD SPINNING. THE JAR OF medicine is tucked into my apron pocket, swinging heavily against my legs as I walk back to my duties. I feel like I'm being dragged deeper into something which just feels bad. Why is Waltz taking such an interest in this man?

It's early evening now. There's a nice muffled silence in the hallway. All the guests must be either outside, enjoying the evening, or taking their rest before dinner. The only sound is the scratching as the manager scribbles at the ledger. The whole world seems calm and unsuspecting of the mission I've been tasked with.

A wicked little worm of a thought wriggles into my mind. What if this isn't medicine at all? What if it's a kind of poison and I'm being used as an instrument of murder?

I could hang.

I touch its smooth body through the material of my skirt.

But Waltz is a doctor and sworn to protect life.

He knows best. He's created this whole place. Why would he want to harm an innocent guest?

I dismiss the suspicion as nonsense and set to planning how to carry out my orders.

CHAPTER 34

Mr Weighton arrives very late to dinner when half of the other guests have left. He sits in his customary place, looking more fragile than ever. Most of the other guests at the hotel make at least some basic attempts at conversation with others, even if they're on their own, but Weighton seems completely and utterly alone in the world, as if he isn't in the room at all. He's like an illusion or a reflection of someone miles away.

In the end, administering the medicine, whatever it is, is relatively easy. I've managed to build it up in my mind to be some kind of elaborate sleight of hand that'll require planning, lying and treachery. At dinner time at Cragside, though, the entire staff is rushed off their feet and no one has time to notice anything other than what is in front of their faces. All except Mr Morris, the head waiter.

He sees everything.

Morris is bidding goodnight to guests as they drift off from dinner, oiling them up for his eventual end-of-stay tip, his payday. He smiles, asks polite questions and offers advice on the bill of fare and things to see nearby.

I sidle up to him. "Good evening, Mr Morris, I don't know if you've heard but..."

"Well, it's all anyone's talking about, Hardacre. It seems you've been singled out, girl."

I flush. So much for discretion.

"Well, I need to know what food he's having, how much he eats and the like. Could I possibly ask to see it before it's delivered?"

His benign smile never leaves his face. "What's in it for me, Hardacre?" he says out of the corner of his mouth.

"My week's tips?"

"How about two weeks'?"

"Mr Morris, I need that money for my family."

He sniffs. "One week then, but you come in on the sweep." He winks.

I sigh. "I'm in."

"Now go see Jenkins and put your stake in. And mind you bring me your tips tomorrow morning."

"Yes, Mr Morris. Thank you, Mr Morris."

"Go talk to Charles, he's waiting on Mr Weighton this evening."

And so I intercept Mr Weighton's soup course, a thin consommé. Checking I can't be seen, I fish out a teaspoon I pocketed earlier, measure out a dosage and drop the red medicine into it. I'm relieved to see it melt away as I stir the liquid. Like a witch mixing a cauldron.

Charles takes up Mr Weighton's soup and places it before him. He looks up with tired eyes. Then, like an automaton, begins to eat. He doesn't notice a thing.

On his way out, he surprises me by approaching.

"I'm sorry if I embarrassed you this afternoon. I trust you managed to finish your errands?"

I nod but my eyes can't hide the shame I feel. It was as if

he knows my guilt and is twisting it deliberately. My stomach aches with anxiety.

"Yes, Sir. Thank you. Have a pleasant evening," I mutter, unable to make eye contact.

I force myself to walk with a measured pace back through the entrance to the kitchen, letting the door swing shut behind me.

NORMALLY AFTER DINNER, SEEING AS ALL IS LIT UP AND THE beds turned down, all we girls need to do is mind our bells until ten. I, however, am on a late shift that night, having had time off in the afternoon, which is as well given what happens next.

Mr Weighton retires early and I put the unpleasantness of dinner behind me and throw myself into some menial work in the laundry. I'm bone-tired, the stress of the day has put such a weight into my limbs I fair feel like I could sink through the floor.

It's Maureen who comes to grab me as I stand there vacant, running a hot iron over a sheet.

"There's one of the guests wandering around in a daze in the dining room, Pol. I don't know what to do. He looks like he's stark raving mad."

"What concern is that of mine, Maureen? Go and get one of the porters." Then I think for a second. "Who is it?"

When she tells me, I nearly drop the iron on my foot.

I hurry upstairs.

All is quiet and dark in the dining room. There's little evening entertainment at the hydro, the guests being encouraged to have long restful nights of sleep. Echoing down the hallway, I can hear a few stragglers in one of the parlours. The summer sun has long set. The furniture and paintings are indistinct, like ghosts, their edges vague.

I hurry in between the tables towards a single line of light splintering the dark: the slightly ajar doorway to the main hallway.

I stop as the light is blotted out. Someone has stepped between me and the door.

I try to breathe quietly, watching the shifting mass of shadow I now see as my eyes adjust to the gloom, a darker shape against the dark of the far wall.

Then the door opens. It's like someone has spilt a bucket of light across the floor, stretching from the far wall to myself. I'm pinned in its beam and stand helpless as the shadow of Mr Weighton, for I catch his face in the light as he turns to leave, moves through the doorway into the hall.

He's wearing a nightshirt and cap.

He doesn't see me, or if he does, bears me no mind.

I follow fast, running up the stream of light to its source.

In the hall, I see him padding in his slippers towards reception. I give chase, calling, "Sir, can I help you?"

He ignores me and walks on, at a strange deliberate pace.

I catch up with him, flushing to see him in such an unseemly state. I try to block his way but he ignores me. His gaze is fixed ahead of him and, I swear, he doesn't even see me.

I dodge him as he brushes past me, moving forward with a steady, relentless will.

On reaching reception, he doesn't, as I'm expecting, talk to the night manager who sits reading a book behind his desk. Instead, he walks straight past and out through the doors, which are still unlocked.

I turn and snap at the oblivious man behind the desk, "Get one of the doctors! One of the patients is sleepwalking!"

The fool looks up, half asleep himself, and then gets to his feet and trots off.

I push open the front door and go after Weighton.

He's crunching in his slippers across the gravel driveway.

The night is cool, but not cold, there being no breeze and there being heat still in the earth from the day. The moon has been swelled by a thin layer of smoke, giving it a bloaty gauziness. Across the horizon is the odd orange flicker of flame, as if the whole hillside is a pile of dying coals.

Across the deepening blue lawns, the black cypress trees stand against the sky watching us.

He carries on, across the lawn now, a ghostly figure in a white nightgown, his cap bobbing as he walks, to what destination I can't guess.

I wonder if it's something to do with the medicine I gave him. Maybe it's a side effect, or maybe it's his melancholia that has infected his sleeping as well as his waking life.

Either way, I realise that he's heading in the same direction as the walk I followed him on earlier, and at this rate, he's going to wind up on the moor. I don't fancy his chances if he goes up there in the dark. There are cliff edges, and bogs, to say nothing of the fire. At the very least, he'll break an ankle in a rabbit hole.

I glance back at reception, hoping that help is coming, but all's quiet.

Weighton has found his way to the paths running through the trees and he slips into deeper darkness.

I give chase, wondering if what I've heard about the dangers of waking a sleepwalker are true. I'm not sure that I'll have any choice in the matter.

I run across the lawn, my skirts hissing across the grass.

At the trees, I struggle to see the path and have to grope with my hands, feeling my way, using the tree trunks as fence posts as I stumble and edge along, wishing that the moon was fuller or brighter. Every so often, I catch a glimpse of a pale shape ahead of me. He doesn't seem to have any such difficulty and I wonder what strange inner map he's following.

I call after him with no hope that he'll either hear or respond. I struggle on and finally emerge into the clearing with the fountain, still burbling and splashing in the dark.

Mr Weighton has stopped and is gazing around as if looking for the right path to follow. I seize my opportunity and run up to him, being so bold as to grab his hand.

"Sir! Are you quite well?" I say in a loud voice.

He looks past me into the darkness and I know that he's oblivious to me.

"Sir, you need to come back to the hotel. Sir?"

Then he lets out a low moan, a long indistinct cry that his mouth takes and gradually works into a long extended howl of "Isabella!"

He raises his hands and pulls off his hat, then starts pulling at his hair, writhing and contorting like he's having a fit.

A wave of tingling goes through my body in sympathy, like a basket of spiders has been tipped over me. My throat is all thick with choked emotion.

He sounds like my dad did when Mum died.

"Sir, come back to the hotel with me."

Instead, he turns again to the path, to the narrow winding stair reaching up through the trees up to the moor above us, where massive black clouds, edged with silver, move in a slow march across the sky.

I hold on tight to his sleeve and tug him back, a single idea suddenly forming in my mind. I rack my brain for his first name.

"John, darling, come back. It's cold out." I make my voice all soft and what I imagine is seductive.

I have no idea what I'm doing.

If Mrs Hubbard could hear me, she'd have had my guts for garters, or just laugh out loud.

He hesitates, though.

I try to speak with a posh accent, rounding my flattened Yorkshire vowels. "It's time to come back in, darling. I've missed you."

I blush to hear myself.

In the dark, I can see his eyes glistening as if dew is gathering on them.

"Isabella?" he says.

"Darling, come back to bed." I wince at my boldness. I hope to God he really is asleep because I feel awful cruel twisting his grief like that. Still, it seems to work.

I take his dry hand in mine again and pull him gently. He is led as easily as a horse.

We walk through the trees back to the lawn. We must cut a strange and scandalous pair, me in my chambermaid clothes and him in his nightshirt, holding hands together as if we were on some late-night tryst.

I realise as we go over the wooden bridge over the beck that Mr Weighton's night cap is still up by the fountain. Well, there's no going back for it now.

I take care to lead him into the pools of light cast by the now buzzing lobby. The night manager has managed to rouse not only Waltz and another of his doctors, but also some of the staff and a few guests who seem to have stopped by on their way to bed.

Oh, there's a regular crowd there to watch the fun.

Mrs Hubbard is there as well, big arms folded across her bosom. Her jaw drops when she sees me, I can tell you. I slip his hand in shame but take hold of his arm again, steering him towards the front entrance where there's quite a hubbub.

The doctors come down the steps to greet us, Waltz looking concerned. I hold up my hand in warning.

"Mr Weighton is just returning to his room. He's quite asleep, I think," I say in a low voice.

Waltz peers at my companion and says, "Perhaps I can escort you back to your room now, Mr Weighton."

Weighton looks at Waltz's fat face and then around him at the gathered crowd, as if seeing them for the first time.

"No! No!" He stares frantically around him, his eyes wide, but dead. They seem visionless and wholly mad. The poor man is deep in a trance. He looks like sheep do when they're killed.

He yanks his sleeve out of my grip and sets off back across the lawn away from us. The doctors give chase, followed by the night manager.

"Don't hurt him!" I cry, then feel Hubbard's glare on me and realise how silly that must sound, shouting after my betters. And doctors, at that.

They catch him and take both his arms.

He struggles, his face twisting into a grimace as if he's being led to his death rather than a comfortable bed.

"Can you get my medical bag from my study, please," Waltz asks the night manager as he grapples with the struggling man.

I hear a couple of the other guests sniggering to themselves at the sight of the man in the nightshirt being led, still dreaming, feet kicking, by two doctors back to the hotel. It isn't my place, but I can't help but shoot them a glare. That poor man, if it isn't bad enough to have endured such a loss, he's now to suffer a public humiliation.

I imagine that most of the other guests will be aware of his shame by the time breakfast is over tomorrow morning.

The doctors lead him back up the stairs, and he seems more compliant. It isn't clear whether he's awake yet, but Waltz keeps murmuring to him in a soothing tone and it seems to have calmed him somewhat.

I wipe a tear out of the corner of my eye and feel a presence move next to me, giving off heat in the cool night air.

"You've got some explaining to do, Polly Hardacre."

Hubbard is staring at me down her nose. I quail in fear.

Then Waltz returns. "Well done, Polly, good work. That poor man has your quick thinking to thank. The Lord only knows where he might have ended up wandering off into the night like that. Mrs Hubbard, will you excuse us? I need to know the detail of what happened."

"Is he going to be alright, Doctor?" I say.

"Oh, yes. I've given him a mild sedative and he's being escorted back to his room. I didn't know that he was a somnambulist, otherwise we might have offered to lock his door on an evening. Still, no harm done, I think, other than a bit of embarrassment in the morning, I imagine. Mrs Hubbard, may I?"

Hubbard sniffs and bustles off, shooting me an evil kind of look on her way past.

Waltz leads me to his office. "Brandy?" he says. "You must have had quite a shock."

"No, Sir. I don't partake."

"Medicinal purposes only."

I pause and nod. He seems relieved and goes to his fancy cabinet and pulls out two little glasses. "I think I'll join you," he says, quite eager.

Then, once poured, he flops down in his chair, the leather straining with the sudden weight. He runs his big hand across his face and I realise how tired and careworn he looks.

"You did a good deed tonight, Polly. Did you administer the medicine as we discussed?"

"I did, Sir. In his soup."

"Just the dosage I instructed?"

"Yes, Sir. One teaspoon, just as you said."

He nods, looking around his office, shifty, as if reluctant to make eye contact with me.

"I think that we may need the help of another colleague of mine. I would like you to continue to keep an eye on Mr Weighton, Polly, now more than ever. I think we have seen tonight that he is not in the most stable of conditions and potentially poses a threat to himself and very possibly others."

"I'm sure Mr Weighton would never harm anyone, Sir," I say, "begging your pardon."

Waltz looks at me, suddenly reassuming his authoritative air. "Thank you, my girl, for your opinion on this. I don't believe that you have received medical instruction, particularly not in nervous conditions. Don't forget your place."

"I'm sorry, Sir. He just seems very helpless," I say, lowering my eyes.

"Yes, and we must therefore help him. Continue to observe our patient, Polly, but after tonight, it is best not to initiate any further direct contact with him if possible. I imagine rumours will fly around the guests after this little performance. I will need you to be supportive of our needs should you receive any direct questions from Mr Weighton on the matter. What will your story be?"

"The truth, Sir."

He looks at me with a hard stare over his glasses. "And what is that?"

"That I saw him wandering out into the gardens in his nightshirt, raised the alarm and gave chase, persuading him in his sleep to come back to the hotel. That he was a bit confused."

"Nothing else? No mention of the medicine?"

"No, Sir."

He gives a grim smile and murmurs, "That's a good girl."

❧

I GIVE A CURTSEY AND LEAVE. THERE IS NO ONE IN THE cloakroom of the servants' quarters but I can hear low gossiping coming from the kitchens as I tiptoe past. Mrs Hubbard is in there, muttering something spiteful, I'm sure. I unhook my cloak as quietly as I can and creep out of the servants' entrance into the cool of the night.

The hotel is dark. There are only a few lights still on in the guest rooms. I glance up to try to identify Mr Weighton's room but can't. The cypress trees hiss as I crunch down the gravel driveway and out through the gates. The road to Whitmoor is indistinct but the moon reveals itself in brief waves of half-light and keeps me on track.

My mind is in turmoil. I turn over the events of the day, trying to understand my part in what's happened. I wonder how much of Mr Weighton's distress and wandering is my fault. I'm sure the medicine, whatever it is, if not the cause of his late-night wanderings, then at least hasn't helped in the slightest.

I also consider Dr Waltz's behaviour. I've been working at the hydro for a year now, and I've never seen this kind of personal medical interest taken in a patient before.

Certainly not by the head doctor.

I think about how I'm bound into this whole mess. Perhaps my engagement as a spy for Waltz is rooted in his concern for the patient, as he claims.

Still, my own guilt bubbles to the surface and I don't like it one bit.

I'm an honest person, by and large, and don't care for lies. I feel ashamed. I've let myself down. But what choice do I have when Waltz is all-powerful at the hydro?

When I need the job so badly.

Still, something writhes in my brain, something that says,

"Polly, you know this is wrong, don't you?"

I bristle that I'm going to be forced to lie to Mr Weighton tomorrow. I bet he'll ask me about what's happened when he gets wind of it. Assuming he can't remember anything.

As the lights of Whitmoor come into view through the trees, I pull my cloak tight. It would have been a cold strange awakening on the moor for Mr Weighton if I hadn't stopped his little expedition. The breeze comes in great random gusts over the moor, scudding the clouds across the moon.

I wonder who the other doctor is that Waltz mentioned.

As I get near our cottage, I know that my father's still awake.

He's singing again.

I cringe as I push open the front door. He's in the parlour, sprawled in his chair, one leg over the arm and a bottle of his filthy rot-gut by his side. His head is lolled back and he's belting out "Come into the Garden, Maud" at the ceiling. His waistcoat is unbuttoned and his shirt is undone to his belly. His spectacles are dangling precariously from one ear. He's so wrapped up in his song that he didn't notice me enter.

The fire in the kitchener's almost out, and badly in need of a rake. There are books strewn on the floor, some open and face down, spines all bending, which annoys me more than anything. I pick up *On the Origin of Species* and my copy of *David Copperfield* which has splayed on the hearth rug and put them neatly back on the little bookshelf.

Samuel must be up in bed already. I hope for his sake that he's asleep.

"Dad!" I hiss, picking the specs off his head and folding them.

"I said to the rose, 'The brief night goes, in babble and revel and wine.'"

He drones on in his cracked baritone, oblivious.

I shake him. Immediately a rubbery hand lunges and

grabs my wrist. His bleary eyes open.

"Pol, my girl, where have you been? You've left your father alone to look after himself and see what a mess he's made of it, girl."

"Oh, Dad. Where's Samuel?"

"Abed, abed, where all good children should be. He ate dinner tonight, my love, with the wonderful food you bought. He had it when he got back from Nelly's. I've not had anything."

I look at the half-empty bottle of spirits. "Well, that's not true, is it, Dad? Where did you get the money for that?"

I know he's been in the biscuit tin where I put the rest of my wages. I'm about to tell him off but I stop myself. "I'm sorry about the school, Dad. We are going to talk about this. But not tonight."

He flushes and for a moment I think he's going to get angry, but he doesn't, instead, he folds up with his hands clawed, clutching the sides of his head, fingers digging into his bald scalp. "Oh, Pol. I always wanted better for you. You're a bright girl, and now you've got to suffer because of my weakness. What's wrong with me? What's to be done? I'm a bad man, Polly, I'm a bad man."

"You're not, Dad, you're not a bad man."

I sink to my knees and embrace him. He's hot and sweaty and reeks of the booze. He clumsily embraces me back, breathing on my hair.

I wish I hadn't promised to give up my tips to Mr Morris. I obviously can't trust my father with money anymore. He's worse than ever. I'd thought after Samuel's birthday things would have gone easier for him, but he's taken a step down and stayed there. Poor Samuel. He'll never be able to have a birthday without everyone thinking of the mother he's never known.

My father is compliant as I help him up, and lead him to

his room where he sprawls, fully dressed, on the bed. I yank off his boots and leave him snoring gently.

Then I go to our room and find Samuel, fast asleep, tucked under the covers. He's in his nightshirt and has been washed. Although he's four years old, he looks younger asleep. A book sits on the bedside table, *Perrault's Fairy Tales*, and I guess that my dad read it to him before he went to sleep.

At least he managed that before he started drinking in earnest.

I change and crawl into bed beside my little brother, drawing him to me and wrapping both arms around him. He stirs and half opens his eyes. I stroke his hair and whisper, "Shush, Samuel, go back to sleep."

Tears spring into my eyes. Why has all this been landed at my door? I can barely keep the household running straight. I think about my own discarded book. How vain and presumptuous to think that a woman, especially a girl of my station, could write something. Yet it's still in me, a whole churning world, dormant now, but still there in my heart.

Why did my father set me up for so much disappointment?

Why couldn't he have left me alone? Kept me ignorant.

Normal.

Happy with my lot.

Then my practical Yorkshire inner voice returns. "Now, Pol," it says, "this kind of thinking won't do any good. You've got people that depend on you, so all you can do is crack on, for their sake." I rub my tears dry on the pillow, then run my hand over Samuel's little tummy, full thanks to my extra work for Waltz. I hold him close, for the first time in weeks not feeling like I have to squeeze the hunger out of him.

I will do what is needed. For them.

Like I always do.

CHAPTER 35

I'm like two penn'orth o' drop-dead, eyes itchy and limbs aching. Still, I've no choice but to get up and about it, so I stagger to the washstand and do my ablutions. Then it's downstairs to make some tea on the ashes, before cleaning the grate, blacking the kitchener, and lighting the fire. All the while listening to Dad, still snoring in his room, fully dressed.

Then, when the house is all set up, it's another wash to get the grime off and back into my clothes from the night before.

Then back to Cragside.

It's a warm summer morning carrying the promise of a hot day. A thin mist hangs in the valley, already starting to burn away. Sparrows scuttle in the undergrowth and dart, fluttering across the path, perching on the drystone walls, as I climb out of Whitmoor towards the looming hydro. Behind me come the sounds of the village waking, men drawing back stanchions from the windows of shops, the clopping of a lone dray horse, coughing and laughter from some early rising tradesman, the crying of a child.

I renew my resolve to follow Waltz's orders.

The kitchen and laundry are fair buzzing with discussion about the previous night. I avoid all questions and stares as I go about my work, brushing away the sarcastic comments of the other girls.

Whenever I'm near a window, I keep half an eye on the gardens. I half expect to see Mr Weighton out there again.

Then, as I'm cleaning one of the empty rooms on the first floor ready for a new arrival, I see him.

He's walking back from the gardens, and I see that in his hand he's clutching something white.

It's his nightcap.

Without thinking, I flee the room and hurry down the stairs into the lobby.

I wait there, not knowing what to do as he enters through the double doors and strides towards the stairs. I nod and say, "Good morning," looking for some acknowledgement, a memory, or understanding of what had passed the night before. He seems oblivious but rested and sane compared to his condition only hours before. He smiles back, a slightly puzzled look on his face, and greets me before heading up the stairs without any break in his progress.

I'm stuck there, my thoughts in knotty torrents, all the arguments I wrestled with last night coming back to me in a jumbled flood.

I look out at the gardens, at a couple of nattering guests who are watching Mr Weighton climb the stairs. My self-control breaks. I turn and head up after him.

I know he's aware of my presence before I catch him. I have one moment of doubt, and then take the final plunge and reach out to grab his attention.

"How are you this morning?" I say.

He looks startled. "Very well, thank you. It's beautiful out there." He pauses. "Is anything the matter? I have noticed that people are acting rather strangely this morning, has something happened that I've not heard about?"

"I'm probably not the one to tell you, Sir, but seeing as I found you... Better from me than one of the other guests."

"What do you mean? Has there been an incident overnight? Has someone died?"

"I shouldn't tell you out here. Perhaps in your room."

This is really bad behaviour for a chambermaid and I know that it's not only my job and my family's livelihood, but also my reputation that's at risk.

He hesitates, then opens the door and gestures to me to take a seat.

"Now, what is it?" he says, business-like but concerned.

"Do you remember what happened to you last night?"

"To me? I dined alone, went to bed early and woke to feel refreshed, whereupon I went for a morning walk up to the fountain. What is the matter?"

"This may be a bit of a shock, Sir, but it's not the only walk you've been on since you went to bed."

"I don't understand."

I tell him. As I reach the part about the fountain and my attempts to bring him back to the hotel, he takes the nightcap out of his pocket and places it beside him.

All the hope and colour drain from him as I tell my tale and when I mention the name he cried, he's aghast. He seems to curl up in himself and put his face in his hands.

I can't help it, I shuffle next to him and put my hand on his shoulder. I tell him about the scene in the lobby.

"Oh, God, what am I going to do? I need to leave at once," he says.

I'm so far outside the bounds of myself that I don't know who I am anymore. I'm terrified but somehow exhilarated as if there's a bigger me that I didn't know existed rising up behind me and taking control.

For once in my life, I'm doing something!

Bold, I lift his face with my hand and stare directly into his eyes, speaking as I would to Samuel. "You're going to go down for breakfast, Sir. You're going to look them all in the eye, smile and eat. Then you're going to go about your scheduled treatments and you're bloody well going to get better."

"What is your name?"

"Polly, Sir."

"Thank you, Polly. You have done your best to save me and my dignity. I'm only sorry that I have brought you into this mess."

"Now, Sir. I don't want to hear any self-pity now. You have a duty to yourself. Go and eat breakfast. And I'd be grateful if you don't mention this little chat to anyone, Sir. It'd be my job if you did."

"I promise, Polly," he says, and I'm sure he means it.

I curtsey, out of habit more than anything else, and leave him to get ready. On my walk back down the corridor, my heart races.

I feel alive.

But oh, God, I'm in trouble.

How am I to spy on Mr Weighton for Waltz when he now thinks of me as his secret protector and friend?

CHAPTER 36

Of course, given I'm feeling confused and vulnerable, I inevitably walk straight into Mrs Hubbard. I swear that woman has a nose for weakness.

"Hardacre!" Her voice is like a rusty knife.

She flanks me down one of the side corridors as I reach the landing.

"Where have you been, girl?"

"Just doing my rounds, Mrs Hubbard."

"And does doing your rounds involve talking to young gentlemen in their rooms? I think not!"

I flush. I feel her eyes crawling over me, probing for lies.

"I don't know what your game is, girl. I heard about your little adventure last night with that same gentleman. I won't have my staff mingling with the guests, certainly not in the gardens after dark. It's scandalous, that's what it is. I know you think you're marked with special favours from Dr Waltz, but it won't wash with me."

I know it's useless to say anything. I just mutter, "Yes, Mrs Hubbard," knowing that submission is the quickest way to end the conversation.

She presses her hatchet face close to mine. Her breath comes in warm gusts that smell of cooked liver.

"I'm watching you, girl. I know you're up to something and if I see you bend the rules, take a step out of line or start to get ideas above your station, I'll have you out of here before you can say Jack Robinson."

"Yes, Mrs Hubbard."

"Don't try and appease me, you little hussy." She puts out her hand and pinches my arm, twisting the skin beneath my dress. I squirm and bite down on a cry, but she doesn't let go.

"What were you doing with that man in the gardens?"

I shoot her a glare and she twists her fingers harder. Her eyes bulge with pleasure and her face flushes scarlet. She's having a fine old time, the dirty old cow. I wriggle and pull myself free of her grasp, only to meet her other hand as it comes round fast with a meaty slap on the side of my head. My ear rings and I stagger.

"You get back to your work. I'll see you right, my girl. Once you're out of favour with Waltz, I'll be down on you like a tonne of bricks, and then you'll wish you'd kept below stairs where you belong."

She turns and walks off and I hear her heavy breathing recede as I turn in the opposite direction, hot tears in my eyes, my arm and face smarting.

All I want is to get back to work, to make up beds, to go about my business with no more intrigue, no more strangeness. I want to be an anonymous chambermaid again, ignored by everyone.

I reach the stairs and hurry down, my skirts swishing against the banister, sniffing back the torrents in my nose, wishing I had a handkerchief.

"Girl!" I turn away from the guest and dab my eyes with my sleeve before turning.

"Girl, do you know who made up my room?" It's a scrawny

old man with granite mutton chops on either side of a sallow face. His skin hangs in folds around his skull. He doesn't look happy.

"I believe I did, Sir. Is there anything amiss?"

"Well, yes. My bed was half made! There are sheets pulled off the mattress and just left like that!"

I realise with a sinking feeling that his must be the room I'd been making up when saw Mr Weighton returning from his morning walk.

"I'm so sorry, Sir. It's my fault. I was called away. I'll go and finish up now."

"Well, it's not good enough. I'll be mentioning it. I have been in treatments all morning and I get back to find complete disarray. I thought that thieves had been in the room. I don't know what sort of establishment this is, but I expect better for the money I'm paying."

"I'm so sorry, Sir. Let me go and make up the room now."

"No, no. It's too late. I've done it myself. What's your name?"

My arm and head are still throbbing and before I can stop myself, I blurt, "Hubbard, Sir."

"Well, Hubbard, I'll be mentioning it to the housekeeper. Now go about your duties."

I scurry away and down the stairs, feeling like my world is collapsing.

"Hardacre! Dr Waltz wants to see you. Again..." says the day manager as I hurry past.

I stop, dizzy, take a deep breath and change direction to head towards the office yet again, feeling as if the day can't get worse. As I approach, I wonder if it can.

Waltz isn't alone. He's deep in discussion with a thin, well-dressed man with a long, scrawny neck.

"This is Polly Hardacre, who has been an enormous help

to me in this matter, Doctor," says Waltz and gestures to me to take a seat.

Both of them have already been discussing me.

"Polly, this is Dr Strangler of Highroads. You are familiar with Highroads?"

"The asylum, Sir?"

Waltz winces. "That is not a term that is in favour. They tend to the sick of mind, it is a hospital."

I think about my own dad's experience there and shudder.

"Polly, I promise you, this is the last time that you will need to help us," says Waltz. "The Doctor here has been appraised of Mr Weighton's situation and I am confident that he will be willing to submit to his care. It is a great relief to me personally as the one thing that I cannot stand is a fellow human in a state of suffering."

I wonder what they expect me to do.

Waltz has a freshly determined look in his eye. All the softness has drained from him.

Dr Strangler stands on the other side of me. He's as thin as Waltz is fleshy. His face is gaunt and pale, his hair a mere collection of wisps scraped across a bald head. He says nothing.

"You have Mr Weighton's trust now?" Waltz's question is more of a statement.

"Yes, Sir, and I don't wish to abuse it."

"There is nothing wrong with caring for a patient, especially one who is not of sound mind, Polly. I merely ask you again to administer the sedative to the poor man so we do not have a repeat of last night's embarrassing episode."

I flush and have to fight my immediate urge to comply. I feel trapped.

"The good Doctor here has given me a stronger batch, one that will have greater efficacy in giving poor Mr

Weighton a decent night's sleep. And so I need to call upon you one more time. Will you help, Polly?"

I feel like I'm standing at the centre of a see-saw. On one side is my family and on the other my sense of what's right. I've been brought up a certain way and what Waltz is asking goes in the face of all that. My body aches with the test.

"I can't, Sir, I'm sorry. I don't think it's right." My voice is smaller than I intend. I sound like a frightened child.

"Then I'm afraid I will have to terminate your employment with us, girl," says Waltz.

His face flushes and he walks away. The other doctor watches with no expression at all. Only his bulging eyes move, following Waltz around his office as he paces.

"You know what this means for your family, don't you?" says Waltz. "You are a most ungrateful girl. I have singled you out for special work, with rewards that would make your life easier and now you throw it all away with this silly selfishness? What of this poor young man? What care do you offer him in his time of need? That is not the kind of attitude to guests that I expect here at Cragside. I expect better from my staff and therefore I no longer wish you in my employment. Do you understand?"

I understand, alright. I understand why I've been picked for this task. They think they've power over me because of my circumstances.

And they're right.

I feel the see-saw tilt and I think of Samuel. He won't understand why there's no dinner, why we're hungry again. He won't understand why we are moving to the city so that his big sister can get a job at some awful factory and not see him at all. He'll most likely join me there in a couple of years, those little fingers picking scraps from the tines of clattering machines.

Didn't I already do the same thing last night? What does it matter now anyway?

All of a sudden, my high-minded resistance feels selfish and hollow. My real duty is to that little boy, to keep him fed and dressed and housed and as loved as I can manage in between shifts.

To hell with morality. I can't afford it.

"I'll do it, Sir."

Waltz stops his pacing and smiles.

"It is the last time. Tomorrow we are going to discuss extending the care for Mr Weighton to allow him a private consultation with the good Doctor here. I am sure that we can help him."

I don't care for him at all now. I know when I'm being bullied. And I knew when I'm beaten.

"Please don't ask me again, Sir."

Surprisingly Waltz smiles. "I promise, and I know that you mean well. But you are not a doctor, you are only a woman, and cannot understand what is needed here. You have made the right decision."

The other doctor stalks away across the room and opens a black Gladstone bag in the corner. He brings out a tiny vial of a red syrupy liquid.

His deep voice is as dry as old straw. "Put all of this in his evening meal, girl. All of it, mind. Leave none spare."

"Do as the Doctor says, Polly," says Waltz, "and then we'll have an end to this."

I GO THROUGH THE REST OF THE DAY IN A DAZE, PREPARING myself.

That evening, the dosage is delivered just as they ask. Mr Weighton has requested to take dinner in his room. I take it up and before I knock on his door, sprinkle the medicine liberally into the stew, mixing it in with my finger. I resist the urge to lick it clean, wiping it instead on the inside of my dress pocket.

The deed is done. I say a few encouraging words to him. He looks more abandoned and tired than ever. But he manages a smile back at me.

On the way back to the kitchen, I feel as if the corridor is tipping and rolling beneath me like the hull of a galleon in a storm.

Later, as I walk out of the grounds, I'm still wrapped in this strange inner fog. It deadens and warps everything.

What upsets me most is the look of gratitude on Weighton's face, the sense of hope in his eyes that he had found an ally, someone who he can trust. In my mind, I try replaying Waltz's justification for the medicine but no matter how often I repeat his words in my mind, it can't counter the feelings that course through me.

I've betrayed a vulnerable man.

Another voice rises in me, telling me that I'm being foolish, sentimental, idealistic, that I should follow the advice of my betters and simply do as I'm told. But even that voice, normally so strong in my practical Yorkshire mind, is shouted down by my conscience.

I suppose in my everyday way I tell lies all the time. Certainly, raising a child, I've told my fair share, simply to get things done. What is it about this one? I feel as if I'm wriggling to be free of a web.

I look up at the moor and see smoke blotting out the stars. If the wind turns, all that muck will roll down off the heather and fill the valley with peaty fumes.

I turn down the Whitmoor road and, as I descend, its lights rise to meet me. The low houses and church spires of my childhood offer some comfort.

The bells of St Anne's chime ten as I pass. I take my normal shortcut through the graveyard. The stones are arrayed in neat rows, the path threading through them to the far gateway. As I pass my own mother's grave, I lay my hand on it as I always do.

It feels especially cold tonight.

I pass under the yew tree that arches across the gate and I'm submerged in shadow. I'm unseen and alone. It's as if I've suddenly vanished from the face of the earth.

No one can see me. No one can ask anything of me.

I want to stay there all night.

CHAPTER 37

The next morning, there's no sign of Mr Weighton. I allow myself to settle back into a routine, methodically making up room after room. I begin to think that life might even return to normal. Still, there's a nagging in my mind. Where is he?

Finally, my curiosity gets the better of me and I go up to his floor. I'm sure that Hubbard will string me up if she finds me away from my work, particularly in the vicinity of that man.

I put my ear to his door and listen but can hear nothing. I fumble through my set of keys and unlock it, giving a bright little knock and calling, "Make your room up?" as I always do.

There's no response. I open the door and scuttle in, closing it after me.

The room is empty.

It's not that he has stepped out for treatments or breakfast. The room has been cleared and cleaned ready for the next occupant.

I open the door again to check the number, but I'm not mistaken.

I look under the bed and in the cupboard, but there's no trace of his trunk, any clothes or personal effects at all. He has checked out, just as he said he would.

I feel a funny brew of puzzlement, relief and sadness. It's good that life will get back to normal, but I realise that I did quite like him. I hope he'll get better, wherever he's gone.

I look out of the window, half hoping to see him rattling in the carriage down the driveway to the station. But the grounds are empty apart from that bloody peacock. The moors are still smouldering, but the fire looks under control and the wind has turned.

I turn to leave and see something that stops me. Under the wardrobe is a glint. I crouch and fish around in the darkness. My fingers touch something cold and I pull it out.

It's the silver picture frame. For a moment, my heart breaks a little, thinking that he has left it by accident. Then I feel suspicions crawl all over me like mice. I'm certain that Mr Weighton would never, ever leave this behind.

I search the room again and check the sheets. They have been scruffily tucked in, certainly not to the exacting standards that Mrs Hubbard has drilled into all the girls. The pot on the washstand is still half full of brackish water, not freshened to the required level, and the towels are hung messily. The more I look, the more I see mistakes and slackness.

The room hasn't been made up properly, and not by Betty Poulton, who's working this floor today. She's a stickler.

I step out of the room, tucking the picture frame into my pocket as I go, feeling its heaviness against my leg through the petticoats. This thing is dangerous. If it's found on me then I'll be branded a thief.

Going down the stairs, I see Betty coming up with her basket and a pile of laundered towels. I smile and greet her as we pass. She smiles back and then looks puzzled. I quicken my pace.

In the laundry, some of the other girls are chatting and laughing as they work. I push my way in and try to act as normal as possible.

"Save any guests this morning, Polly?" says Maureen. She and Jane Jessop giggle at each other as they scrub at sheets in a bowl of hot scummy water. Their sleeves are rolled high and their wrists pink.

"No, I'm having the day off today," I reply. "Besides, the gentleman has left."

Maureen shrugs. "I don't know about that. But did you see the gentleman in 104? I swear he's the size of an elephant! I'm not sure how he's going to get on with the meagre rations they dole out here. I wouldn't be surprised if he's got a suitcase full of pasties in his room!" They giggle and I join them. Then I crouch to pick up a pillowcase and feel the corner of the frame against my leg.

After a while, it's time to help clean the dining hall, so I grab a bucket of cloths and polish and head off.

On the way I see Dr Waltz, striding with his bag towards the back stairs. He gives me a business-like nod, with a patronising half smile as he would to any of the girls. I half turn to watch him as he walks on. Then, once he's out of sight, I hurry after him, down the stairs to the lower ground floor.

The garden floor, as it used to be known, isn't open to guests anymore and is badly in need of renovation. It's still fitted out with smelly coal gas lamps, rather than the electric lights that are in the main areas upstairs. Parts of it are just used for storage and there are boxes and old laundry stacked up at the far end. It's a shame, I've always thought, because some of the empty rooms open out onto the rear gardens, although their patio doors are fair riddled with woodworm.

I peek around the foot of the stairs and spot Waltz at the end of the dark corridor. He's stopped at one of the rooms.

He looks around and I duck back.

I hear the door of the room open and then close behind him, and the key turn in the lock.

I tiptoe down the corridor. There are men's voices coming from inside the room, and something outside the door. As I get closer and my eyes adjust to the gloom, I recognise it. There can be no mistake.

It's Mr Weighton's battered leather trunk. I notice for the first time it's inscribed with a monogram.

J.E.

Is he under lock and key now? Is he a prisoner? I hear a scrape inside the room and hurry back, up the stairs and into the light, my mind spinning.

THAT EVENING, I GO HOME, VERY AFRAID.

I stash the picture frame under my mattress. I know I should have handed it in. Now I'm a thief as well as a liar. If I'm caught, it'll be prison or transportation, I'm sure.

I sit beside the little fire, watching Samuel play with his ragged teddy before bed. My father has set to on the bottle immediately after finishing whatever mean work is available to him up at Hag Farm.

I try to forget my curiosity about Mr Weighton and resolve to put him from my mind. But still, the nagging worries won't go away. They bob in my mind like corks that won't sink.

The next morning, I'm still musing, but I resolve to crack on, trusting that time and hard work will put the gentleman from my mind.

CHAPTER 38

Making up rooms offers some solace, but whenever my work takes me near the stairs to the lower ground floor, I feel my stomach hollow out. I can't leave it alone.

I scrape together excuses to go there, listening hard for any sound from below.

I head back to the laundry and help out there for a while before, to my shock, Waltz comes to find me.

"Miss Hardacre. If you please, would you spare me a few minutes?"

Well, you can't believe the looks on the girls' faces. Dr Waltz himself, come down to the laundry to ask me to go with him. He doesn't even act like I'm in trouble or anything.

No one has ever seen him down here.

Hubbard's expression is a treat.

I nod, with a twisting pleasure at the amazement on the faces of the other girls.

I follow and he leads me out onto the rear lawn. We walk, in full view of the girls, who I know have their faces pressed to the steamy laundry window. I can imagine their whispers.

He looks more mithered than usual. He's not slept.

We reach a bench and he sits with a grunt. I remain standing, looking down at him.

His big hand covers his face as if shielding it from my gaze. He looks up, through the bars of his fingers.

I brace myself.

"I'm afraid I have not been frank with you," he says in a low voice. "I did so to protect the integrity of Mr Weighton."

"I assume he has left Cragside, Sir? His room is cleared."

"I am afraid something quite unexpected has happened. It seems our Mr Weighton has been taking the night air again. He was found in the most pitiful state in the lobby this morning just gone five o'clock. I'm very afraid to say that he seems in quite a deep state of emotional disturbance, so much so that I had to move him to one of the lower ground rooms. We have considered our options and the best approach at the moment seems to be *not* to move him from the hydro, but instead, to minister to him as best we can here."

I wonder who "we" refers to.

"I'm sorry to hear that, Sir. What do you mean by distress? Is he a danger to himself?"

"I am no alienist, but I think not. Of course, we are more used here to treating the everyday strains and illnesses of our guests. This new development is quite beyond my capability and so I have had recourse to summon Dr Strangler again. He will be over again later in the week to assess the patient."

He goes quiet as two guests saunter past. I nod good morning to them.

Poor Mr Weighton. I wonder what had happened to the poor man to bring him to this condition. Why not simply move him to Highroads immediately where he could be treated properly?

Waltz watches the guests disappear, then he looks up at me. I swear there are tears in his eyes.

"What I have to say to you now, Polly, is in the strictest confidence. No one else here knows. I have already trusted to your discretion and I have been pleased that you have discharged this duty very satisfactorily."

"Thank you, Sir."

"I fear I am going to have to lean on you in new ways, however, and hope that your natural compassion and intelligence, of which you have shown great depths already, is enough to carry you through what I am sure will be your most testing challenge."

He is slowly getting to the point. I feel my stomach tighten.

"Mr Weighton is sadly afflicted by powerful delusions. Their origin is unknown to me."

"Perhaps the loss of his wife, Sir? Or his father?"

I should not have spoken. It's not my place.

"Then he has said something to you?"

He stares at me momentarily then continues. "These delusions seem to have developed somewhat aggressively throughout the last two nights. As I say, two nights ago he was out of his room again. We cannot tell where, although from the smell of smoke on his nightshirt and dressing gown, he may have gone as far as the moor. Parts of his attire were badly singed."

"Is he burned?"

"No, thankfully. He was found in a state of considerable distress. Now prepare yourself, my girl, for the nub of the matter."

He pauses, licking his lips, checking we are alone.

"He believes that he brought back someone with him from the moor. He has created an imaginary companion, one who he assumes everyone else can see. A woman, injured in some way. He believes he rescued her from the flames. You understand, Polly, that there is no one. He returned alone."

He hangs his head in sorrow.

"The poor man," I say, and mean it.

"Indeed. This development has persuaded me to take precautions with him for the sake of our other guests. He has now been moved to one of the rooms on the lower ground floor. The season is ending and the hotel is becoming quiet. He will be quite safe and protected down there and should create no further disturbance. It will allow us to address his situation."

"May I ask, Sir, what your thoughts on Mr Weighton are? Will he recover?"

"You show an unusual level of curiosity, Hardacre, for a girl of your station."

"I'm sorry, Sir. I'm just worried about him."

"That is good. Good girl. It is Dr Strangler's opinion that you may be able to support the gentleman in his recovery. He will require care while he rests and recovers. I am looking to you for that care, Polly, but listen well. I have two conditions for this work, and they are iron laws. I cannot countenance either of them being breached for a moment. To do so would risk Mr Weighton and pose some risk to the reputation and future of this hotel. I cannot allow this, and the repercussions for yourself would be equally serious."

"I understand, Sir. What are the conditions?"

He nods and takes off his spectacles. His red eyes look tired, he must have been awake much of the night. "Number one, no one must know that he is here. He is out of the way for a reason. As far as the other guests and even the other members of our staff are concerned, he has left the hotel and is at this moment returning to London to tend to a matter of business. I cannot emphasise this enough. If word gets out that he is here under these conditions, it will ruin his reputation, and possibly that of Crag-side. Is that clear?"

I nod.

"Second, and this will require all of your efforts. It is Dr Strangler's considered opinion that Mr Weighton's delusions need to be humoured, that allowing them to play out will be a natural part of the healing process."

I frown. "I don't understand, Sir."

He smiles. "Of course, I know it is asking a lot for you to grasp this."

"I mean I don't understand why encouraging these delusions will reduce them. Surely they will send him further into madness?"

Waltz frowns. "Polly, I am trusting you to execute this charge. Indeed, I am torn about the process myself, but I am assured by the Doctor that this is the best thing for our patient."

"You want me to lie to him?"

"If necessary, yes. Think of it as a means to an end, the end being his recovery and avoidance of a worse fate in the asylum. I will, of course, ensure that you are rewarded for your efforts. As you know, I am a governor on the board of All Saints school, where I believe your father formerly worked. I have some influence on the other governors. Certainly enough to ask that your father's reinstatement is considered again."

My heart leaps.

We set off again, reaching the back entrance to the lower ground floor.

"How do I humour his delusions, Sir?"

"Well, that is down to your discretion. He is in quite a deranged state and it is difficult to predict where the fantasies will take him. My advice to you is to just listen and validate where possible. I will do most of the work to support the treatment and Dr Strangler will supervise when he can leave his other duties at the asylum. If, of course, the patient appears to be descending further into this madness, Strangler will intervene or reconsider the approach. He may need to take him into more permanent care. We will continue to administer the medicine as before. It has been proven to be wonderfully sedating to him and will help keep him calm. Will you help us with this difficult task, Polly?"

What can I do? I say yes.

"He has not yet had lunch. I will let you work through the other arrangements that need to be made. Do not fail me, Polly, and more importantly, do not fail Mr Weighton."

He reaches into his pocket and hands me a little plain notebook and pen. Then he hands me a fresh bottle of medicine.

"For your observations. I know that you are an educated girl. Report back to me alone."

With that, he strides off.

I nod, reeling from what I've been told.

I've misjudged Waltz. He is willing to risk everything for this stranger's recovery.

I've been trusted with secrets that could bring down the hydro and Waltz's reputation.

Me! Polly Hardacre!

More than that, I've been allowed to do something, something beyond fetching, carrying, and serving others. And not just sneaky little tasks like spying either. A man's sanity depends on me alone.

It makes me stand tall for what feels like the first time in years.

The girls are still staring at me from the window, awe on their faces.

"Well, Polly, my lass," I say to myself, "it looks like this is your moment. Don't mess it up, for God's sake."

CHAPTER 39

I get some lunch for Mr Weighton and, composing myself, carry it down the stairs.

The rooms on the lower ground floor of the hotel face eastwards. They back onto the rear gardens, not nearly as well tended and impressive as those to the front, but they do give a certain peaceful atmosphere. It's been many years since the rooms down there were in regular use. They are smaller than the upstairs rooms and lack views of the valley. The lower ground floor is away from the currents and flows of the rest of the hotel and is therefore out of sight and out of mind.

Perfect for Mr Weighton's recovery.

On the windowless corridor, lit only by sputtering coal gas, only one of the rooms is now occupied and I don't know what to expect when I reach it.

I listen outside the door and hear nothing, then, taking a breath, I give a polite rap. There's a scuffling noise inside.

"Mr Weighton, are you decent? May I come in?"

There's no answer.

I open the door and peer in. The room is modest, but it's

clean and pleasant enough. There's a nightstand, empty of any mementoes; the walls are decorated with a rather busy wallpaper of twisting briars and roses. There's a bed, of course, with a brass bedstead, and above it hangs a painting of the Devil's Pinnacles, as if to make up for the lack of view. The curtains are thin and open, although the light that makes it through the window is weak, sapping the colour from everything in the room and making the whole scene gloomy.

In the bed itself, under the coverlet, lies Mr Weighton.

"Good morning, Sir," I say, trying my best to sound brisk and normal.

He looks pale and drawn, more so even than usual. He's dressed in a nightshirt and his cap sits awkwardly on his head. He hasn't shaved for a couple of days, by the look of it. The shadow on his lower face, combined with the dark bags under his eyes, make him look sick and, truth be told, disreputable. His eyes, though, are the most alarming thing. They're wide and panicked, and somehow seem to look at somewhere I can't see.

I recoil a little and have to check myself.

"Thank God you're here, Polly," he says, "there's something terrible happening. They are after her, look!" He gestures at the empty air next to the bed. "They tried to take her. I disturbed them in the very act and they took flight. I was so close to losing her."

An adoring look crosses his face. He is so sweet and so pathetic that I feel tears well up inside me.

How am I supposed to react to this lunacy?

"What do you suppose it is?" he asks, looking again to his right, his eyes tracing the outline of an unseen object. "Some kind of stretcher?"

I remember my instructions from Waltz to support his delusions, to follow them and see what they will reveal about the workings of his mind.

It's easier than I expect. With all the respectful kow-towing I have to do in my work, and all the patience I have to show at home, I have a great pent-up imagination. It's time for make-believe.

"They meant to restrain her?" I say. "To remove her from the hotel? The monsters! Who was it that you saw?"

The words come out in an angry torrent. I'm surprised by the sweet relief they bring.

"I only caught the backs of them as they ran out through the patio doors," he says. "I've turned the latch, although I doubt that will stop them. I don't know who to suspect, but I do know that someone in the hotel has informed this girl's assailants or previous captors of her whereabouts. I should warn Waltz that he has a traitor among his staff." He looks at me with a quick, suspicious glance. "Did you know she was here?"

I flush. "No. Well, not until Dr Waltz just told me. He asked me to look in on you both and see how you were doing. It must have been a long night, the night you found her, I mean."

"You can't imagine. I was sleepwalking again, Polly, like the night you guided me home. I woke on the moor, in the fire. I found her there and brought her down. The Doctor has been very kind and has let me keep vigil over her. It is as well that I did."

He stares again through the patio doors and then pulls back the covers and runs to them, peering intently at some-thing, although all I can make out is an empty lawn.

"They are out there even now. I am certain they're plot-ting to come for her again."

So it begins. I tell him I am to chaperone the girl and that he'd better get used to me being there with him.

And, at first, it seems to go well. He swears me to secrecy, to not mention the break-in to the other doctors. I agree, of course, and in doing so am brought into his confidence. Then, once I've gained his trust, the full extent of his madness becomes clear.

He truly believes that the girl is with us. He believes that she is being hunted still by her persecutors and that it is only his presence that's protecting her.

I have no choice but to drop myself into the mysterious rapids of his mind and trust that I can be of service there. And stay afloat myself.

So persuasive are his fantasies that I can close my eyes and imagine that they're real, that the girl is with us as a constant silent catatonic presence, and that we are under threat from some unknown enemy.

It is, I suppose, like the kind of games that Samuel plays, except that to my new playmate, it's a deadly reality. His misguided senses infect me to the point that I feel my pulse racing with the drama of it all, and I have to remind myself of what's real.

At first, I think I have the measure of his madness. There are long stretches of silence when I know he's lost in reverie, sedated by the red medicine (Waltz makes me mark on a checklist when he has taken his dose). I'm not shy about force-feeding it to him if need be. I'm sure my experience of doing the same with Samuel stands me in good stead. If need be, I grasp his nose and have the knack of slipping in the loaded spoon when the opportunity, and his gasping, open mouth presents itself.

My other duties are fairly light. I bring him food and drink which he either eats, glassy-eyed and distant, or ignores. I try to keep him clean and brushed, but the poor man is soaked in a permanent bitter sweat. When he does notice me or engage in conversation, it's with vague questions and statements, random to my ears. I'm ignorant of their place in the ongoing drama that's being enacted within his poor head.

"Is she safe? How is she doing?"

"Is there a way around the back of the hotel and up to the moor?"

"Does she seem paler to you today?"

I attempt to answer these questions, but to keep him calm, and consistent, I keep my answers as short, simple and vague as possible. I don't want to challenge his view of the world. I don't know what he'd do to himself if he were upset.

He asks me to order her flowers and I say that I will, telling him that I have arranged for great bunches of white roses, hoping that they'll appear in his imagination, which they duly seem to (much to my relief). I even go so far as to sneakily clip a bunch of roses from the garden myself and place them in a vase by the side of his bed.

"There," he says, "with fantastic garlands. Of cornflowers, nettles, daisies and long purples."

I make a note.

I'm growing in confidence. For the first time in my life, I'm doing something. Something worthwhile. I go home each day buoyed up.

One time, I pretend to sleep and I watch him crawl across the bed towards me and begin to brush my hair. I can smell his sickly breath on my face as he whispers tender words. I sit motionless, dreading whatever is to come next. But he sits back on the bed and pulls strands of my hair from the brush and places them between the pages of my notebook, which I've left inadvertently beside me on the chair.

I'm glad that he doesn't read the scribbled notes I've been making on him.

Then the next day, on his instructions, I bring stocks from the little glass-house by the side of the hotel. They fill the room with their heady sweet perfume, adding to the air of unreality. At least they mask the smell of illness.

"You never know," I say to him as he gently rearranges the flowers for the fourth time, "it may be kindness that brings her back to us."

He looks at me with grateful, blank eyes. A fleck of spit stands at the corner of his mouth.

Suddenly, I realise I'm leading him further into his madness, not out of it.

A horrible truth occurs to me.

I have no idea what I'm doing.

It undermines all my newfound confidence.

CHAPTER 40

As time goes on, my twice-daily reports are not well received.

Waltz starts to lose patience with me. That hurts.

He's frustrated at the calmness and lack of irritation in the patient, and the lack of meaningful interaction. He tells me to draw Weighton out, to learn more about his fantasies. When I weakly protest, he encourages me to lie. To play along and see what happens.

"The man needs to be moved beyond this state of torpor! I want detailed information on what he talks about. Dr Strangler is coming in a few days, and it is essential for Mr Weighton's treatment that we understand his delusions, and what they might indicate about his state of mind. They may provide the key to unlocking his malady and then curing him."

"But Sir. I'm scared he won't be able to come back if I lead him on. If I excite him, isn't there a chance he'll turn violent, and try to harm either himself or me?"

"Have faith in Dr Strangler's advice. He lives amongst the

G.H. LUSBY

insane. He knows their ways. I'm sure he would never put
anyone's safety at risk."

❧

AND SO, RELUCTANTLY, I STEEL MYSELF.

When he asks me how "she" is, I ask him questions, in
turn, trading information.

He tells me in detail about his adventure on the moor and
I make detailed notes on it. I blanch a little at his vivid
descriptions of her brutal injuries.

On another occasion, he begins muttering, speaking as if *I*
were the girl.

"What did they do to you, my darling? I don't even know
your name. Perhaps I will give you one. I wish you could
signal in some way to tell me, but no, I will give you a name
and you can nod if you think it will do for you. Or perhaps I
shall stumble upon your true name by fortune. Do you even
know it anymore?"

I shake my head, pretending to be her, and his eyes,
tender in his mania, fill with tears. "Then shall I name you?"

I nod, but he slips into a reverie.

Another time, he fantasises at length about taking the girl
into his care and as these fantasies develop, they begin to take
on other, more sensual aspects that make me blush to note
down in my little book. I've already noted, one morning on
entering his room, the sticky wet stains on his nightshirt and
their sweet ammonia smell.

I'm intrigued and appalled at the livid fantasies that seem
to infect his mind, and the terrible cause of them which, even
to my untutored opinion, is now becoming more apparent.

But my suspicions feel too raw, too personal and powerful
to simply make a callous note of them in my little book.
When he finally sinks back into a stricken dream and I clear

away his untouched dinner, I check over my notes and go again to see Waltz in his office.

"Has the patient taken his medicine?" is his first and usual question, and this time barked at me.

"Yes, Doctor."

"And how does he seem to you? Is he more coherent? Alert?"

"He is agitated, Sir, but has been very communicative. The girl is constantly in his thoughts. He talks to her, to reassure her. He wants to give her a name but hasn't yet, to my knowledge. He sometimes seems to think that I am the girl, but other times he talks as if she's elsewhere in the room. It is not easy work, Sir."

"Of course, of course," says Waltz, "and yet you seem to be gaining his trust. When I enter the room, he shows alarm and entreats me to leave. At times, he seems to suspect that I am one of those trying to do this imaginary girl harm."

He looks out of the window at the farmland down in the darkening valley below. "We must persevere."

"I think there is something valuable in this girl's name." He turns again to me, his face half in shadow. "Double your efforts. Draw him out."

So, I use my imagination. I try something different, something forbidden.

I hold back the medicine.

Oh, I fill out my journal like I'm supposed to, but I let the appointed dosing hour slip past and then watch Mr Weighton to see what happens. At first, I don't notice the difference in him, but after two missed doses, there is a change. Instead of dissolving into frantic anxiety, he becomes calmer and his obsession with the girl seems to fade.

What is this horrid stuff they're giving him?

I decide to press him with questions.

"Sir, tell me about your wife."

He squirms under the covers and hides his face in his pillow.

"Was she beautiful, too? Like the girl, I mean, not me."

He looks at me, a mask of grief descends over his face and he says the first coherent, truthful thing I've heard from him in days.

"She was a woman, therefore to be wooed, a woman, therefore to be won. She was my wife, therefore to be loved. But I lost her, Polly. She took herself away from me."

CHAPTER 41

I sit back, watching as he slips back into a half-doze, his terrible sadness fading into sleep.

So, I think I understand some of what lies behind this broken man, and what an awful burden he carries. I've found a root of his misery.

I wonder what to do about the medicine. Waltz will have my guts for garters if he finds out I've withheld it. So I do my usual trick of slipping in a spoonful to give him a restful night.

I think about taking my new knowledge to Waltz on my way out, but something stops me. It's as if Mr Weighton has shown me something so secret and tender that I don't want to betray him and turn it over to a man whose motives I'm again none too sure of.

Instead, I go home to my own family, thanking God for them.

When I return the next day, I see that matters have taken a turn for the worse. I see immediately that he is back to his delusions and very distressed.

He's out of bed and furtively checking the windows, the locks on the patio doors and even under the bed. When I enter, he looks up, anxious, then bids me close the door.

"Oh, thank God, Polly, it's you. Is there anyone else about?"

"What are you doing, Sir?" I ask, seeing that the night-stand has been tipped over.

"I think someone was in here last night," he says, "she indicated to me that the patio doors had been opened." He gestures at his bed and I guess that, in his imagination, the girl is lying there.

"Do you remember our talk yesterday, Sir? You started telling me about your wife. Do you want to talk again?"

He looks at me with blank eyes. I have never seen eyes like that before. They seem to see me, and yet not see me, staring at some point beyond the back of my head. They are wide with panic and madness.

"I need to give you your medicine," I say, a tremble in my voice. So used am I to seeing him lying there, deranged perhaps, but at least prone, I'm shaken to see him up and about, full of this new fevered energy. I don't want him to be a threat to me or anyone else. Oh, God, what if he gets out and amongst the other guests? Is this my fault?

"There's no time for that now," he says, waving me away. "Can't you see that they've tried to take her? To take her before she can tell us what happened over there? In Blackmoor?"

"Come and sit down," I say. There's only one way of dealing with him when he's agitated. It's to play along. "If someone comes, they may be suspicious to see you up and checking her room like this. Who knows, there may even be someone in the garden watching right now."

The moment the words leave my mouth, I regret it. He runs to the window and looks out, peering from behind the curtain at the lawn.

"Do you think so?" he says. He retreats from the window. "I've seen the doctors look at her strangely, and Waltz in particular seems to have some knowledge of her. As her appointed protector, I must know!"

I raise my eyebrows at this. "And who, Mr Weighton, appointed you as this poor woman's protector?" I make my voice deliberately provocative and disapproving.

"Well, God, of course. Or fate, or whatever force moves the universe forward and guides our passage through it. Why else would I have walked up onto the moor to find her? I was called there! And why else would she have walked through the flames to find me if not guided by some hand of providence? God has given me this charge and I must fulfil it."

From then on, he becomes more and more paranoid.

He begins to turn on me, saying that I'm too inquisitive, that it's inappropriate for me, a mere chambermaid, to be showing so much interest in his relations with the girl. He becomes withdrawn, then launches into spates of yammering mania.

He thinks he sees more intruders at the window and crouches in vigil, looking out over the empty grounds.

I end up shouting at him to sit, and to my surprise he does.

He looks so drawn. Days of not eating have drained the puppy fat from his cheeks and hollowed his eyes. There's a waxy sheen to his pale skin and his hair is matted. He looks every inch the lunatic that the doctor from Highroads will surely take him to be.

"Have you noticed anything strange about the doctors?" he asks, eyes rolling.

I have. God knows I have. I feel a devil move inside me. "Haven't you wondered why this girl is being kept here when clearly her injuries would normally mean she should be moved to a proper hospital? She should be cared for by professional doctors, rather than the kind who make fat businessmen jump in cold plunge pools or sit broiling in steam?"

It's wrong of me, I know.

He springs from the bed and paces the room.

"Look at her!" he says. "She could be a sleeping angel. If only I could have saved her before whoever did this to her did their foul work."

He sits again on the bed and his hand caresses an imaginary head on the pillow.

"Look how soft her hair is, Polly. Come and feel it!"

I hesitate, then sit on the opposite side of the bed to him and let my hand trace what I imagine he sees in his mind's eye, trailing my fingers through imaginary hair.

"You see?"

"Yes, it's beautiful," I say.

His fingers briefly touch mine and in that strange moment, I can feel hair beneath my touch, silky and smooth.

Then I notice something on the bedside table. It is an empty cup, and not one I've brought here. Inside are the dregs of some tea.

Someone else has been here in the night. Waltz?

He starts to get up again. I've got to keep him talking.

"Who was it, do you think?" I ask in a low voice. "Who did this to her?"

His face darkens and he eyes the door, nervous. "I suspect much. Have you heard of Blackmoor?"

I nod slowly. "Of course. I've never been."

"I have been reading up on it. What a place! It is as if hell had broken through the fissures of the earth and kept growing, sending up blackened claws into the sky in the form of chimneys, and towers. The smoke and soot, Polly. It's as foul as this place is fair. It is a wicked place and I... I intend to visit it."

"Do you think that the girl came from there?"

"I am sure of it!" he says. "I'd like to believe that her injuries were simple industrial accidents and that she wandered, confused by some infection, from a hospital." At this, he leans close, conspiratorial. "But her tongue! Polly, I intend to go there myself and investigate!"

I know of Blackmoor. There's an impressive mill there, to be sure, but it's a modest, well-run little town. It's certainly not the sinister hell that Mr Weighton has described. I shift in my chair, making notes carefully.

He notices.

"What is it you are writing?" he says, suspicious.

Flushing, I turn the page and scribble something, the first thing that comes into my head. Then I lay a finger against my lips and lean forward, showing him what I've written...

QUIET, TRUST NO ONE HERE.

He reads it, wide-eyed. "I suspected as much," he says, "so she must be protected from those inside this place as well as those without." He gives me a pointed look then turns away from me and curls up on the bed.

After that, he refuses to eat, and takes only his medicine, which he seems almost eager for. I've noticed that this latest bottle seems to have a more potent effect on him than previous ones. I hold it up to the light, staring into its ruby viscous depths, wondering if it's stronger.

Finally, he falls asleep but tosses and moans.

I reckon he's in a powerful, bitter dream.

I sit by his side half the night. In the end, I have to leave him just to clear my head and step out of the room, locking the door quietly behind me. I can see what this "leading on" has done to the man's mind. I'm helping this poor sick creature drive himself to his grave. I lean against the banister that leads up to the ground floor and feel sick.

What are Waltz and Strangler really up to?

His fantasies have wormed their way into my mind, twisting it.

What if there is a conspiracy, but the victim isn't this imaginary girl, it's Weighton himself? Why is he being kept here against all common sense?

I wonder whether Waltz visits Weighton at night when he is fully under the influence of the drug and whether he does or says things to feed these fantasies of persecution.

As I walk down the corridor, I start to shake. How have I allowed things to develop so far? There's something wrong with what I've done. I don't give a fig now for the opinion of the learned doctors. This isn't right.

I hear a cry from back in the room.

I run back down the corridor, wiping my tears away with the back of my hand and fumble the key into the lock, turn it and push the door open.

Mr Weighton is lying on the bed, on top of the covers, stretched out and rigid. His neck is straining and the cords of his neck stand out as if he is struggling against his own body or an imaginary garrotte.

Is he having some kind of fit or even a heart attack? I feel his pulse. His wrist is tense, rigid and spasmed, but at least his pulse is strong. His bulging eyes are staring out at a point far beyond this world.

I go to the nightstand and wet a cloth, then dab his forehead, which seems to have no effect. He's descended to a deeper level.

I've failed.

He cries out, "I know her name, Polly, it's Lavinia!" Then he sinks back into a reverie.

Lavinia. The name on the picture frame. The picture frame that's hidden beneath my bed at home.

Now I know for certain who the girl is, or who he wants her to be.

The question is, what do I do with that knowledge?

CHAPTER 42

There's nothing more I'd like tonight than to miss my appointment with Waltz. But I have to go.

Waltz, however, is not in his office when I knock, although I can see that the light is on. It's late so I suppose that he is eating supper or taking the air. Rather than stand in the hallway, I take the liberty of going inside and closing the door gently behind me.

Without his huge presence, the office feels hollow. The great grandfather clock counts the seconds in the corner and the flickering electric light sparks up dust motes. I advance across the carpet and take a seat.

To my surprise, on the desk between the papers is a glass, drained, which still gives off a faint whiff of brandy.

My eyes rove further over his desk. It's strewn with papers. For a man with such an orderly mind, he appears to be in some disarray. Sitting there, waiting, listening to the clock, I find myself attempting to decode the upside-down lettering on some of those closest to me.

Most of them appear to be bills or letters from creditors.

Some are final demands. There is one other file, however, red leather bound with twine that intrigues me.

It's unmarked.

Dare I take a closer look?

Suspicion overcomes me and, checking the door over my shoulder, I stand and edge round to Waltz's side of the desk. The twine is tied in a knot but my nimble fingers manage to unpick it in seconds, spreading the string neatly on either side of the leather. Then, running my hands over the glossy, heavy surface, I open it.

I hear the doorknob turn.

I slam the folder shut and roughly scramble the string together, not having time to re-tie the knot. I sit down heavily, bolt upright in the chair, my hands in my lap and my gaze snapped down.

The door opens and I glance up, as if disinterested, to see Waltz enter.

He's surprised to see me, in fact, I've never seen such an unguarded look on his face. He's pale and exhausted, his hair is dishevelled. The disarmed expression doesn't last long, however. He takes in the desk and then looks back at me. As he does, his face assumes its more normal look of authority.

"Hardacre, this is a surprise. I would not normally expect to find you inside my office."

"Forgive me, Sir, I thought it better to come in than to arouse suspicion among the other staff by loitering outside."

"Indeed, sensible girl." He heads behind the desk, his eyes cataloguing the papers on it. He gives the glass and the red folder a sidelong glance. Taking the folder, he places it in a cabinet behind his desk. He positions his bulky back between me and it, but I hear the tiniest of clicks as he turns the key.

Then he sits behind the desk, moves the glass to one side as if it were of no consequence, and stares at me.

G.H. LUSBY

"I suspect that you have something to report. Are you quite well, my girl? You seem a little distressed."

"I'm afraid our patient has taken a turn for the worse, Sir. He seemed quite agitated all day and in the last few hours has entered an odd state. He's stiff as a board and not responsive to any questions. I don't think he's asleep. It might be the medicine."

He rubs his hands together anxiously. "And did he talk much before he slipped into this state? Tell me everything, Polly, it is most important."

I dare to tell Waltz about Weighton's suspicions of the doctors. "Have you been to see him, Sir? Spoken to him?"

"Poor, deluded man. I have indeed visited him, to check on his condition, but have held no productive conversations with him. The medicine has meant that he has been thoroughly at peace each time I have visited him."

I mention the fantasy about the town over the moor and say that I've drawn Mr Weighton on in his delusions.

Waltz smiles. "Good. Blackmoor seems to be the dark fulcrum of his fantasies. What else have you learned? You must tell me. His very life depends on you. Search your memories of the last few days – what is the one thing that may hold the key to bringing him back?"

I fall silent. I know, but I won't say.

"Alas," says Waltz, "the man is condemned to a life in an asylum, strapped down for his safety, never to walk outside as a free man again. We have failed him, Polly." Waltz places his head in his hands.

I give in.

"His wife, Sir. I believe he feels in some way responsible for the death of his wife. He said as much previously when I found him sleepwalking in the gardens. I think that his guilt might be the cause of all this, Sir. I think he has created this imaginary girl in some way so that he has another chance to save his wife, or someone very like her."

I think back to that night in the garden and something else Weighton said. "*Why did you do it?*" I think about his words, "*She took herself away from me.*"

"I think his wife ended her own life."

"Are you sure? And Mr Edgeland thinks it was his fault?"

Edgeland? I pause, not sure what I've just heard.

"It's the only thing that I can think of, Sir."

He sits back in his chair, smiling, and I see that hope has returned to him, and that hope sends a chill through me. It's threaded with something hard and evil.

"My father, Sir. You'll be able to get him his position back at the school?"

Waltz laughs. "Well, I don't think I exactly said that, Hardacre. The governors did make a decision already, you know. We can't turn over the education of the town to a drunkard. I'm sure, though, that he can find some alternate work in the town. Something that can accommodate his intemperance."

"But you promised, Dr Waltz! You said you'd use your influence."

He flashes a glare at me. "Don't be impertinent, girl. Don't forget your place. You have done well for tonight but don't let it go to your head. You are dismissed. We do not need any further help from you in this matter. Off you go."

So that's it, then. It's over.

Mr Weighton is to be left to Waltz and Strangler.

Or is it Mr Edgeland?

CHAPTER 43

I feel a wave of weariness. In the dragging walk home, a hard kernel of suspicion gnaws at me. I question everything.

I begin to wonder if I've been infected by Mr Weighton's... Mr Edgeland's madness.

Brook Street is quiet, with only a few farm hands staggering their way back from the Rose and Crown. I wonder if my father is still there, but, as I enter our little house, I see him sitting by the fire. He looks up with sad, bleary eyes.

Samuel is still up, giddy with tiredness. He totters towards me chanting, "Poll-ee, Poll-ee." His face is dirty.

"Has he eaten, Dad?"

My father looks sheepish and mutters something not being sure.

I sigh and pick up Samuel, going to the pantry to find what's left of the bread. I hack off a bit of the crust and scrape some dripping across it and give it to Samuel, who promptly throws it on the dirty flags.

I can't take it. I feel rage surge up through the floor, up my legs and into my chest, where it explodes. "You've been at the pub again, haven't you, Dad? Did you think to ask Nelly if she'd fed him? The little lad is half starving while you go and get soused! It's disgusting, your own son. Look at him, little skinny wretch. I'll bet you've had your fill, though, haven't you? How much of our money did you spend tonight? How much of *my* money, seeing as I'm the only one who brings a penny into the house?"

He crumples in the face of my anger, his cheeks going pale, his watery gaze dropping to his feet as if he is the child and I'm the parent.

"Look at me, Dad. Be a man and look at your daughter. You have to stop this. You have to get right again. I can't do all this alone. You're deserting us. You're deserting me!"

My rage breaks into sobs.

"It's today, Pol. It's the day," he says quietly.

"What bloody day, Dad?" I shout at him through my tears.

"It's the anniversary of her death, Poll."

I can't stop the words coming from my mouth. It's like being tied to a runaway horse. "I don't care, Dad. Mum is dead and all the drinking in the world isn't going to bring her back to us. You need to stop right now and look after what's left. We are all that's left of her. You are pissing away her memory!"

He goes quiet, reaches for the bottle, and then stops himself, fists clenched, jaw clenched.

I realise what I've said.

He can't bring himself to face me. Every muscle in him is tensed and his eyes bore holes in the floor.

When I see there will be no response from him, I pick up Samuel and the crust of bread, my heart collapsing inside me, and carry him upstairs. Once I settle him, I steel myself to go back down again. All the fight is gone from me and what's left is guilt. I've twisted a knife in my own grieving father's heart.

I wonder if I'd have done that two weeks ago, before all this started?

I creep downstairs.

He is still there, as I left him, the bottle where it was, his gaze where it was.

"I'm so sorry, Dad. I've been so busy."

For a while, he says nothing, then, finally, "No. I'm sorry. And I'm worried about you, Pol."

"There's no reason, Dad. Just work, that's all."

I settle down by the stove and stare into its last crackling ribbons.

"You don't seem yourself, my girl. I know I'm not the best father in the world but at least let me have some concern for my daughter. You do such a job looking after us. Keeping us together."

He looks into the fire, and we sit there, both staring at the dying coals as they shift and settle.

"You've been wrapped up in something, Pol," he says, "something's bothering you, beyond my incompetence as a father."

I object, but he raises his hand. "What you said was true, girl. But there's something else. Tell me."

I chew my lip. "I'm afraid I've done something wrong," I say. "There is a poor man at the hotel who I've been tasked with looking after. He's sick and I'm worried I've been making the situation worse for him. He needs proper medical attention and I don't know why Dr Waltz won't let him. It is almost as if he is being detained there against his will."

My father scowls. "What's a chambermaid doing looking after a sick man on her own?"

"I don't know, Dad. I think it's because..."

"Well?"

"I think it's because Waltz has power over me. Because of our situation."

"Because of me." He stares into the fire, his eyes glistening.

"He is on the board for the school. He said..."

My dad waves a hand at me, and then runs it over his eyes. He swallows hard. "Who is he? This sick man."

"Just a poor bereaved widower. I fear he's losing his mind. I don't know why they keep him there and don't get him proper medical attention."

"Has this man done anything inappropriate, Pol?"

I laugh. "No, Dad, there's nothing like that. But the strange thing is he's there under an assumed name. He's known as Mr Weighton, but I found out tonight his real name is Edgeland."

He looks up sharply. "Edgeland? John Edgeland?"

"How did you know?"

"Well, the papers are full of him. The heir to Jacob Edgeland, the great industrialist. He's one of the richest men in England. He's been missing these two weeks. He didn't tell anyone where he was going. It looks like he's been hiding up here, then."

I am stunned. Things start to make more sense. My mind churns over this new news.

"So what are you going to do about this, Pol?"

"I am really worried, Dad. I don't trust Dr Waltz. He's going to have Mr Edgeland committed, I think. He's been consulting a doctor from Highroads."

"Who?"

"Dr Strangler?"

My father scowls. "I wasn't there long, thank God," he says, "but I was there long enough to know not to get on the wrong side of *that* man." He ponders. "What is it that Seneca says? 'All cruelty springs from weakness.' I reckon that Waltz is weak, from what you say. Cragside has not been doing well these last few years. But Strangler isn't cruel. He's beyond

that. All he cares about is money. He can conjure up any justification in the world for the right price. I've seen him drag
men who could have recovered to the surgeon and smile
while he did it. You must tread carefully, Pol."

I nod, then stand and place the bottle in his hand.

"I'm sorry, Dad. I miss her too."

He takes the bottle and swigs and I leave him to the
embers.

CHAPTER 44

Oh, God. I think I'm finally starting to understand.

I thought I was a nursemaid, but I've been an inquisitor.

I've delivered this man, and his deepest secret, to Waltz and Strangler.

What have I done?

I slip out of my dress and get under the sheets, budging Samuel across the mattress to gain space. I try to snuggle into him but he's all sweaty elbows and knees. I turn over, dragging the sheets with me, wrapping myself tight. I lie on my back and close my eyes but all I can think about is this man with a secret name, lying there rigid and locked in some awful nightmare.

My mind keeps turning back time, scrolling over the day, then the week, thumbing over the details, relentless in its quest for some kind of meaning. Three images keep returning to me.

The red leather folder.

The silver picture frame

The red medicine.

I see his desperate face, softened by the sight of his imaginary damsel, his Lavinia. His slipping sanity, his grief.

I am a fiend in a chambermaid's uniform. All through this I have manipulated him, walked him down this road to the end.

And what is that end? Will it be what I saw when I went to see my father in Highroads? The men who stank like animals in their suffering, contorted from within. Shouting at their cell doors, waiting for the night, and the visit from the doctor to take them to a room somewhere deep in the building where a few taps of the hammer will take away their pain and everything else?

I have tried to be good. I have tried to do what's right, and for what?

My goodness has been twisted, abused and taken advantage of.

No more.

The key to this is inside the folder, in Waltz's office. I'm certain of it. Within that cabinet, behind lock and key, is that leather folder, and inside is something, some document that holds the truth.

I don't know what finally spurs me.

Maybe it's the knowledge that a life of guilt is no life at all.

I will be good. But it will be on my terms.

At some time after midnight, I climb out of bed and dress again. Ready to return to the hydro.

CHAPTER 45

I creep downstairs, past my still sleeping father, head lolled on his chest in his chair, the bottle still next to him.

He looks so peaceful. I envy his oblivion.

I open the door and step into the night. The cool dark air washes over me.

Then, beyond discovery, I set out, walking quickly, crunching up the deserted lane, past the dead houses under the cold moon, up through Whitmoor, and beyond, climbing the road that leads to Cragside.

Its dark shadow blots out the stars on the horizon. Silhouetted turrets and high gables crane into the vast dome of the sky. How vast and merciless the universe is. Can there be a God in that dispassionate sky? There's no intelligence in the cold light of those stars. Nothing that would give a fig about one solitary girl walking to her doom.

The bells of St Anne's ring out two, both chimes seeming to echo my footsteps up the road. I pull my shawl tight against the night.

I know the way well enough and am no stranger to nights

at Cragside, but this is different. I have dark intentions. In the crystal cool night, it's clear to me now. Waltz means harm to that poor man I've helped to cripple with that foul medicine. Now I, his torturer, am the only one who can save him.

Up the driveway I go, keeping to the grass verge to muffle my footsteps.

The building towers ahead now. I know that my best hope to get in unspotted is the servants' entrance to the rear of the building. It's unlikely to be locked, even at this late hour. There's a light on in the front lobby but I stick to the shadows, skirting around the pools of light beaming out across the driveway and lawn. I see the night manager in there. I glance up at the window I know to be Waltz's office. It's dark. He is likely retired for the night.

Around the back of the hotel, I see the servants' entrance. I hurry to it and try the doorknob. It's open, thank God. Then I stop and peer down the side of the building. There's a light in one of the garden rooms on the lower ground floor. I know it's his.

I creep down the side of the lawn and a shadow crosses the pool of light that spills from the room. I watch as the shape takes the form of a man. It draws curtains of shadow. It has to be Waltz.

What's he doing in there?

I hurry back to the servants' entrance.

I doubt any of the other staff will be up and about at this time, so I turn the knob and ease the door open.

Inside is a faint guttering light, a flickering candle set on the table. Its single bead of flame has become a constellation, glittering off the brass pans that hang above the fireplace and the stoves. It lights one small face in that cavernous room.

Maureen. She's asleep.

She must have pulled the short straw for the night shift. Poor girl must be exhausted, she's curled up beneath the bells, in a chair, a fleck of drool sparkling in the corner of her loose mouth.

I step past her, my boots giving the faintest of squeaks, but she doesn't stir.

My objective is the key cupboard, just behind her. Her head is slumped back and she gives little breathy snores as I brush past. The cupboard is mounted on the wall and has a tiny key in its lock. I reach out and give it a delicate turn. There is the slightest click and it swings open.

I check Maureen, but she has heard nothing.

Then I squint into the dark rack of keys, trying to find what I need. There are two, the one for Mr Edgeland's room on the lower ground floor, and that of Waltz's office.

I find the first easily, but there is no spare for Waltz's. Of course, he's not going to let just anyone go in there unsupervised. Still, I slide the one for the bedroom off the hook and stow it in my skirt pocket.

Maureen stirs, smacking her lips. She looks so young and innocent in the candlelight. My cares make me feel suddenly ancient. For some reason, I feel an impulse to place a kiss on her forehead, but, of course, I don't.

Instead, I sneak out from behind her and across the kitchen to the door which stands half open. Darkness folds around me so I hold out my hand to trace my way along the wall.

Then I'm out, and safe.

I wonder what to do. Do I try for Waltz's office while I'm confident he's occupied?

No. I need to know what he's doing in Mr Edgeland's room. For better or worse.

I gather myself and head in that direction.

I move along the hallway, trusting to memory and my trailing fingers to guide me in the right direction. I reach the bottom of the stairs and creep up them towards a paler shade of darkness. Then, tiptoeing out of sight of the night manager, tipped back in his chair across the lobby, I find the steps down again to the guest quarters below.

I stumble slightly, my feet slipping on the polished wood, but finally reach the bottom. I move quickly to Edgeland's room.

There's light leaching through the crack at the door's base, flickering and faint as Waltz moves the lamp around the room within. I press my ear to the cold wood. There's muttering inside but it's faint. Then I see a patch of light, the tiniest lozenge of brightness, scurrying across my pinafore like a firefly.

It's coming from the keyhole.

Crouching, I press my eye to it and squint through its workings, into the room beyond.

My viewpoint is narrow, but I see Waltz, sleeves rolled over meaty forearms, the leather binder in his hands, pacing the floor, staring at Edgeland, who lies, much as I left him, on the bed. I can't see his face.

Waltz is flushed and angry. "My dear chap. All you have to do is sign. You will feel better. That's all there is to it."

"No!" Edgeland's voice is strangled, desperate.

"Just sign. Here's a pen, old boy. Make it all better."

Another person is in the room. He takes off his coat and hangs it on the bedstead, obscuring my view of Edgeland.

"SIGN!"

There's a cracking noise, the sound of a blow being landed. Edgeland cries out.

"Simply sign. Here's a pen, John. I can call you John, can't I?" says Waltz.

"It was not me. It was not my fault!"

"Then I'm afraid we don't have any choice," says Waltz, his eyes narrowing. "We don't want to hurt you, Mr Edgeland. We are trying to help you." Then he looks at the door, biting his lip. I ease back lest he somehow sees my eye at the keyhole.

Then he gives a signal, his eyes raise to a portion of the room that I can't see from my vantage point, and a shadow crosses the keyhole. Dr Strangler approaches the bed. I hear another terrible wet crack and a howl of pain, then another, and another.

Waltz turns on Edgeland. "We judge that you are guilty of the most heinous of crimes, that of murder, not of some enemy, or stranger, but of one closest to you. Your wife, Isabella. Do you confess? Do you confess? Will you not sign the paper before you and end all this?" At this, he takes the red folder from beneath his arm and, opening it, presents it to the man lying on the bed. "Will you not meet your God with a clear conscience and a glad heart?"

I thought the gentleman's wife was Lavinia. I don't understand.

Then Waltz goes to a leather bag and fumbles, pulling something out. I recognise at once. It's a hammer. The same heavy surgical hammer he uses to test patients' reflexes. The man on the bed wriggles and screams. It's a wet, gurgling cry. Waltz hands the hammer to Strangler. There's a terrible crack and a scream.

"Confess!" booms Waltz. "Confess! Murderer!"

I hear another crack and then there is silence. I can't see what's happening

Then Edgeland gives a final single terrible cry for help that nearly makes my heart stop. It's a name, but it's not that of his wife.

It's mine.

And, fighting back hot tears, I whisper his.

CHAPTER 46

I rock back on my heels, my insides like water.

What can I do? I'm a skinny girl against two desperate men.

I shift, trying to stay silent, and look again.

I can't do anything, except watch in horror.

Mopping his brow, Waltz turns to Strangler and says in a low voice, "We're done. It may be time to move him to Highroads."

"There are more eyes there, more chance of being discovered."

"I have a business, Strangler! I can't have all this noise and disturbance. We may be in an isolated part of the hotel, but the sound does carry and I can't afford for guests to complain or get suspicious. It would be the end of us. At least at Highroads, they're used to screams in the night. Can't we smuggle him in, not register him?"

Strangler wipes his hands on a cloth, studying the bloodstains as he does so. "He'll be here soon. I'll go and get help. We can't manage him as we are. I'll need a couple of trusted orderlies. It will mean paying them off."

"I don't think money is going to be an issue anymore," says Waltz with a grim smile.

They start to move towards the door.

I fall back from the keyhole and look around somewhere to hide.

My only chance is to get to the pile of discarded laundry in the corner before they open the door.

I sprint to it and fling a musty, damp sheet over myself, feeling like a small child hiding from its mother. I'm sure I will be seen instantly. I hold my breath and try to still my trembling.

The door opens and I hear the two men emerge, the door close and the key turned in the lock behind them. Then I hear their footsteps going down the corridor, away from me then up the stairs.

I draw back the sheet and peek out. They've gone.

I get up and rush to the door.

Delving into my pocket, I find the key and, with two hands to still my shaking, unlock the door and peek in.

Mr Edgeland is lying on the bed, confused and agitated, wrists and ankles strapped to the bedstead. His eyes roll wild in his skull. On seeing me enter, he cringes away, then opens his mouth in shock.

"Polly!"

I motion to him to be quiet and close the door silently behind me.

"I called for you. How did you find me? You came to Blackmoor to save me?"

Then, thinking for a second, a look of horror comes over him. "No. Oh, no. Now I understand."

His feet begin to scrabble at the bedclothes as if he is trying to propel himself away from me, but his ankles are held tight.

"Don't be ridiculous, Mr Edgeland," I hiss. "I'm trying to

rescue you. They'll be back in a minute and we've got to get you out of here. God knows how, though."

He looks confused and lets me fumble with the bindings at his wrist which are tied good and tight. Eventually, I manage to get one undone. As I do, he reaches out and embraces me with his free arm, pressing his weeping face against my chest.

"There's no time for that!" I say, pushing him away and going to the other side of the bed. "They mean to take you away from here and then there'll be no hope at all."

The second binding is so tight it takes all my strength to unpick, but eventually I do it.

I keep an ear out for the sound of returning footsteps outside and move on to his ankles.

He sits up, cradling his broken fingers.

"We've got to go," I say. Then I spot his trunk under his bed.

I haul it out and fling open the lid.

"Get dressed," I say, pulling out a pair of trousers and a shirt. "We'll have to go through the patio doors. Once we're in the darkness, we'll be safer. If they catch us, who knows what they'll do? I'll bet they're not beyond murder."

Compliant, he lets me help him dress. I'm more used to undressing my drunken father than trying to stuff a grown man into clothes, but I do my best without hurting his swollen fingers. Eventually, he looks half decent.

Pulling back the curtain, I try the patio doors. They are locked, of course.

I look around for something to jemmy them open with. The only other option is going out the door but that will risk running straight into Waltz and Strangler.

There's an almighty crash.

Edgeland has kicked the doors open and they swing, splintered and broken. The night air floods in. "Let's go," he says.

We run, pelting across the lawn, around the side of the hotel to the main driveway.

We can't risk being seen on the main drive, especially if Strangler is out in his carriage, so we keep to the dark shadows of the trees, tripping over roots and helping each other up when we stumble.

Finally, we reach the gateway, silvered by moonlight. Once we are through that boundary, I think, with no logic, that we are safe. No alarm seems to have been raised by the noise of our escape. All seems peaceful.

I head down the road, exhilarated.

He grabs my arm, stopping me.

"No. No. We have to go back."

He stands there, looking back at the hotel, a look of intense concentration on his face. I can't tell if he is still confused anymore or if that awful medicine is wearing off.

He is a million miles away from me.

CHAPTER 47

I call and, like an angel, she comes.

I wrest myself with what little strength I have from the ligaments and vines of steel that pierce me. As I do so, the platform swings on greasy cogs and chains.

I twist and writhe to tear out the metal barbs from one of my arms and watch in wonder as the puckered wounds heal to tight-lipped scars. I look up at my arms, chained at the wrists, the threaded vascular cabling, the white skin bruised with black and yellowing stains. What poison is pumping through me now? Can I even trust this vision of Polly before me?

She grabs me and gives me a good shake.

That feels real enough. Then she tries to untie the binding at my wrists.

I garble something grateful at her, my words are like cotton balls in my mouth, my tongue thick. The scene shifts and the vaulted dungeon melts again into the familiar bedroom at the hydro. Polly is frightened, leaning over me, fumbling at the knots. I can see tears on her face, and smell her breath coming in panicked gusts.

I remember the doctors. Their questions. The hammer.

As if summoned, pain flares in my broken fingers.

"No. Oh, no. Now I understand."

I am lying in my nightshirt on top of the covers. The room is warm and smells of men and sweat. I have been here all along, and yet...

And yet behind the twisting briars of the wallpaper, something is moving. Swirling patterns, twisting ghosts of ammonites that vanish when I turn to look at them. The scene begins to melt again.

It's not Polly, it's Lavinia, clawing up the bedclothes towards me, mouth open, hacked tongue root fluttering in a silent scream.

I push and pedal away from her, but my ankles are chained to the platform.

"Don't be ridiculous, Mr Edgeland," she hisses, "I'm trying to rescue you. They'll be back in a minute and we've got to get you out of here. God knows how, though."

She unpicks the knot and my arm is free. I hold her to me, feeling her warmth, her rib cage and the softness of her breast against my face. She pushes me away and while she unties the other knot, I assemble my thoughts.

They wanted something from me. They made me sign something before they left. What was it?

She tells me to dress, and I realise that this girl, this brave girl, has untied me. I sit up and there is a flash of pain in my hand. The fingers are split and twisted, swelling like rotten fruit. I let her help me pull on some clothes, not caring about my modesty as she tugs the bloodied nightshirt off me.

Above me, the gears and cogs, dripping with bloody spikes, whine and rotate, hungry still.

Once I'm dressed, with boots pulled onto my sockless feet, I try to stand and to my surprise find that I can; it makes me feel stronger.

The shapes behind the briars are becoming more distinct.

I squint at them and there, within the walls, figures begin to appear.

Suspended within each of the walls are dozens of bodies, early Blackmoor experiments doubtless, encased in bronze and gilt, splayed, intertwined with wires, valves and machinery, their pale faces made up of scars and burns to look like nothing so much as the royals from a deck of cards, Jacks, Kings and Queens, white faces, burnt red and black skin, angular scar tissue filigreed with the mechanism. Worst of all, these tableaus are still alive, moving in slow, repetitive, almost dancelike patterns. With horror, I realise that while their movements are determined by the machinery within them, the only parts of them that are free, independent and truly alive are their eyes, which bulge and look from side to side with panicked irregularity, and then all at once fix on me with a look of desperate hope and pleading.

Polly tries the patio doors but they are locked, of course. She turns to look around the room and the eyes of the experiments follow her.

I have to get away from the nightmares around me. I have to get to the fresh air.

Summoning all my anger, I kick at the doors, nearly knocking myself off balance, and smash them open where they swing loose.

"Let's go," I say.

WE RUN INTO THE NIGHT AND THE AIR CLEARS MY HEAD, but not my memory.

Keeping to the shadows, to the trees, we head for safety, glancing behind to look for any sign of pursuit.

A swell of exhaustion drains the iron from my limbs, and more than once, Polly has to support me, grabbing me under the arms as I slump. I stub my toes on rocks and roots.

Perhaps it's the lingering drug or the moon behind me but the world takes on a dream texture, a gauzy unreality that makes me, for chilling moments, wonder whether I am still actually restrained in that terrible room.

The shadows crawl across the lawn and in my state, I imagine they are rents in the earth, perforations into some black void beneath the tenuous skin we walk on. I know if I stumble I could fall into that abyss and never be seen again.

So I must keep to the light, stay in the moonlight, on its narrow silvery paths, for my safety, to get to my destination, wherever that is.

And next to me is Polly, ready to catch me when I fall, and I her.

Then, as we approach the gates, I have a moment of clarity. I stop.

The fragments of memory and nightmare start to slot together and a clear picture forms in my mind.

"What is it, Sir? We've got to go. Now, before they find out you're gone."

"Polly, I can't."

She grabs me by the lapels, shaking me. "We have to go now! They're going to take you to the asylum."

I gently reach up and prise her hands from me, holding her wrists as best I can.

"You don't understand, Polly," I say, "they made me sign something."

"The confession?"

"It was no confession," I say, "it was a legal contract. I have to destroy it."

"Why? What is it?"

I look at her, more sure of this than anything I've felt or thought in months. "It's everything."

CHAPTER 48

H e's not for persuading.
I plead, I beg, but it's no use.
"I can't let them have it, Polly."
"What is it?"

He looks confused, and passes a hand across his face. "Something important enough to drug me and drive me half insane for. Something they're willing to have me locked up for. We must get it back."

He seems coherent enough, but his eyes roll and his jaw bunches the way it did all those days I was caring for him. If I hadn't seen Waltz and Strangler with my own eyes, I'd think he was still suffering from delusions.

It's no use. The longer we stand here arguing, the more chance we have of them seeing us. God knows what they're capable of.

"How, then?"

He rubs his stubbled jaw. "I don't know, I don't know…"

"Waltz's office," I say. "That's where he'll keep that folder, the one with the document in it. If it's anywhere, it'll be there."

"Then let's go."

He takes my hand with his unbroken one and we set off back through the shadows, back towards the hydro.

As we run through the grounds, in the wrong direction, to my mind, I hear the sound of a horse.

"Behind the tree," I say, pulling Mr Edgeland out of sight.

There, trotting down the driveway, is Strangler. We duck down and let him pass. As he passes through the gateway, he breaks the horse into a gallop.

Edgeland's breath has gone strange. In the faint light, I can see his eyes are wild.

"Take deep breaths, Sir," I say. I touch my palm to his forehead. God, he's burning up. It's that awful stuff wearing off.

"Come on," I say and pull him to his feet. He weaves, then steadies himself.

We set off again. Above us, I can see Waltz's office. It's dark.

Where is he?

I decide to gain entry in the same way as before, through the servants' entrance. We keep an eye out for sounds of upset; clinging to shadows, keeping out of the moonlight. At the doorway, I peer inside through the windows and see that Maureen is gone, but the candle remains. I beckon Edgeland to follow as I open the door and step in.

Closing the door quietly behind us, we pad across the stone flags, our passing making the candle flutter and flare. I see my face reflect, bulge and distort in the bronze pans that hang like armour above the dead fireplace.

We are just about to head up the stairs when there is a smash and a scream behind us.

I turn to see Maureen, her eyes wide and jaw wider, standing over shards of china.

"Polly?" she says, eyes popping.

"Shhh!" I say, nodding at Mr Edgeland standing beside me.

She stifles a cry as she sees him for the first time, and then we watch as a parade of conflicting thoughts and suspicions make their way across her innocent face. Finally, they settle on a conclusion and she assumes a look of shocked amusement.

"Polly Hardacre, you flighty thing!" she whispers, as if my companion can't hear.

"Enough! You stay quiet, Maureen, if you know what's good for you."

"I knew it!" she whispers, clapping her hands together.

"Any word of this to the other girls and I'll rip your hair out," I say.

Edgeland steps forward into the light and she gives a little curtsey, her gaze swinging between us two like she's at a tennis match. She's flushing to her roots.

He takes out a coin from his pocket and slides it across the kitchen table towards her. "Sorry for the shock, young lady. I hope we can rely on your... discretion?"

I have to give it to him. He's still half scrambled from that medicine, but he still manages to come across as fairly suave.

Maureen gawps at the coin, then pockets it lightning quick and gives another quick curtsey and giggles.

We leave her to it, stepping into the dark stairwell up to the lobby.

He takes my hand again in the dark and we climb, wincing at every creak.

We emerge into the ground-floor lobby, across from Waltz's office.

The night manager isn't at his post. I reckon he's either answering a call of nature or is off doing his rounds.

I creep across the corridor and reach that familiar oak door. If the office is locked, all is in vain.

It's not.

The handle turns easily. I open the door and, checking around me, slip inside. Mr Edgeland follows.

The moon has risen above the windowsill and a faint silvery light shines in, across the mahogany desk. I glide across the floor, almost in a dream. I wonder in detached amazement at how I've allowed myself to come this far. I reach the desk and my fingers flutter across the papers there, searching for the feel of leather, for that mysterious folder. There's nothing.

Then I remember the cabinet. I go to it and pull at the door. It's locked. There's no key.

I curse under my breath. Of course it's locked.

Has he even been back with the signed document yet?

Where is he?

Where would he put the key? I send my mind back to the afternoon, trying to see again the image of him. I see his bulk turned against me, the click of the lock and then a motion, a shuffling. He pocketed it. All this is for nothing.

Then I hear the door knob turn and I freeze.

The door opens and a pool of orange light bleeds into the room.

CHAPTER 49

I grab Mr Edgeland and fly to the coat closet in the corner of the room. It's the only place I can think of.

We bundle inside and I gently close the door behind us, taking care to leave it open just a crack. We squat there in the dark, faces brushed by the rough tweed of Waltz's Inverness coat, smelling of tobacco and mothballs.

A figure enters the study and I duck back out of the light, bumping into Mr Edgeland, who falls against the back of the closet.

I hear creaking as heavy footsteps cross the room.

I chance a peek out and see Waltz. He is carrying an oil lamp which flickers faintly and bobs like a will-o'-the-wisp as he holds it before him. He is still stripped to his shirt sleeves. He is carrying the red leather folder under his arm, the string trailing behind him like the tail of a kite.

He sits at his desk with a sigh, throws the folder across it carelessly, and places his head in his hands. The folder spins and skids into the paper, sending it flying, swooping and looping down like leaves to the floor.

He takes a deep drag of air through hairy, wheezing

nostrils and wipes his face with his fingers, dragging them across his jowls, leaving red marks.

I dare to open the closet door a little further to see more clearly, trusting the darkness to keep me hidden.

He is shuddering and gasping, and I realise that he's crying with great half-stifled lurching sobs as if he doesn't quite know how. I sink back down, just keeping him in sight, wondering what on earth is going on.

Then I realise.

He must have discovered Mr Edgeland's escape!

Waltz sits back with a creak in his leather chair and opens a drawer in his mahogany desk. He takes out something wrapped in oilcloth, and then carefully unfolds it, as if unwrapping a dead bird.

It's a pistol.

He wipes the gunmetal with the oilcloth and checks its chambers before clicking it back into place. He seems calm now. He places the oilcloth on his left shoulder and puts the barrel of the gun to his right temple.

I put my fist in my mouth to stop crying out.

Should I give up our presence to save this man or let him take his own life? I half open the door, and then he takes the gun down, oblivious to me, and places it before him. I sink back into my hiding place.

Behind me, Mr Edgeland is craning for a better view, he puts his hand on my shoulder and leans forward. I can feel his breath on my ear.

Waltz takes up the gun again and places the barrel under his chin, then, hand shaking, changing his mind again, puts it in his open mouth and bites down on the metal. He tenses his thumb on the trigger, tears streaming down his face.

I squeeze Mr Edgeland's hand and shut my eyes.

But no shot comes.

Instead, I hear Waltz open the drawer again and put the gun away. Then, with a cough and a sniff, he stands.

He opens the folder and reads the document over, then closes it again and wraps the string around it. Then he rolls down his sleeves and fastens them with cufflinks from his pockets, smoothing back his great grey mane of hair. He steps out from behind his desk and begins to walk toward the closet.

I realise he's going to get himself a coat.

We cringe back from the gap in the door and crawl back into the depths of the closet. There is no way he won't see us down here.

Then a knock comes at the study door.

"Come," shouts Waltz.

The door opens and I hear a muffled voice.

"Of course, please send him in," says Waltz.

I crawl back to the gap and see Waltz rush to pick up the papers from the floor, stack them on the desk, compose himself, straighten his tie and stand, erect and still, in the middle of his study. The door opens and a shadow falls across him.

"Good evening, Sir, I trust you had a pleasant journey. I wasn't expecting you until the morning." Waltz is ingratiating, jovial, terrified.

A new man enters. I think at first it must be Strangler, but there is no way he could have made it even as far as Highroads in the time he has gone. It's someone else, in travelling clothes, carrying a valise and a top hat.

I shuffle forwards to get a better view.

"Have things gone according to plan?" says the man in a light, oily tone.

"We have the signature on the agreement. It took some persuasion, but we have it. Both documents. Witnessed by myself and Dr Strangler with the appropriate wording. It only remains for you to sign the second document."

Waltz slides the folder over to the man. He opens the folder and scans the document, his gloved finger above, but not touching, the paper. Then he turns it and does the same to a second paper.

"Do you have a pen?" he says.

Waltz takes a pen from an inkwell on his side of the desk and hands it to the man. He is sweating.

The man quickly signs with a flourish and hands the pen back.

"That is excellent." The man places his top hat on the desk and takes a seat. "Forgive me, Dr Waltz. It has been a long journey. I wish I could have taken the train to Whitmoor but alas, the timetable did not allow it. It's been a long drive from Bradford."

"Of course, of course. Can I offer you some refreshment, a brandy?"

The man waves him away. "What of Mr Edgeland, is he pliant? Are you ready to execute the final stage of the plan?"

"Mr Edgeland has been co-operative, although I fear he is not a well man. Dr Strangler is right now on his way with some orderlies to escort our guest to the hospital for treatment. Let's hope he recovers... eventually."

"Poor young man," says the stranger. "May I see him before he goes? I would like to."

Waltz hesitates, "I... unfortunately, there has been a little complication."

There's no answer.

Waltz swallows. "Mr Edgeland has temporarily escaped."

Silence. Then the gentleman stands. "Do you have men looking for him?"

Waltz rubs his head, terrified. "No one knows. There's nothing I can do until Strangler gets here."

"You, Waltz. I don't know you. Strangler I trust, he's done valuable work for us in the past. But you... you I don't know. How long has he been gone?"

"I don't know. No more than half an hour, I'm sure."

Behind me, Mr Edgeland crawls forwards and leans over to look through the crack in the doorway. He peers at the figure in his travelling coat, his back still turned to us.

"Doctor," the man sounds like he is holding back a storm, biting the words out in solid chunks, "I suggest you take action now, or not only will our arrangement be cancelled, I will see to it that this place is bought and burned to the ground, and you are found dead in a ditch before the month is out."

Edgeland's hand tightens on my shoulder, a terrible realisation spreading across his face.

Waltz growls through clenched teeth, "I promise you, we *will* find him, Mr Mire."

CHAPTER 50

I crane my neck past Polly, feeling her hair brush my cheek, and catch a view through the crack. Waltz is there, blustering before another man in a travelling coat, with a greasy black beard.

It is Herbert Mire, my father's lawyer.

For a moment, I doubt my senses. There is still enough of that vile medicine in my bloodstream to trigger another delusion, I'm sure, and it is no stretch for it to conjure Mire here and implicate him in some plot against me. In some respects, that seems the more obvious explanation for his sudden appearance.

Except Polly can also see him.

And the truth shines through the fog. Now it all makes sense.

The scale of the conspiracy to defraud me of my inheritance is clear. Did he approach Dr Strangler before his encounter with me at the pub in Holborn? Did spies follow me from my father's bedside? Or was the alarm raised by my self-injury later that night?

Should I also, then, look to Bell as one of Mire's spies?

Did he alert Mire to my distress and did this prompt Mire to influence the Doctor before our meeting at my house?

Whatever the events that set this plot in motion, it's clear that Mire has been the architect of it, that he intends my father's empire for himself.

And why not? I admit he's probably a more competent man than I am. He is as devoid of any moral compunction as my father was. Perhaps he's the son my father never had. Maybe I should gladly cede my birthright to him.

Perhaps he thought I'd abandon him on taking up the Edgeland mantle? Hire a new broom. Perhaps he's done all this out of some warped sense of duty to my own father's memory, sensing that his tuition of me was proving fruitless.

And under Mire, what will become of the firm? It will continue to bleed the world to fill the coffers of the family, a useless accumulation of wealth. A spider will be replaced by another spider, spinning lies and promises like webs. And for what? Gain and greed.

I can't allow it. I have a chance to change that legacy. Do something with it.

If my delusions have taught me one thing it is that something must be done to redress the balance, to stop the machine.

I will not submit.

But what can I do?

I watch the two men, in sudden stark horror at my position. Here I am, nursing a broken hand, crouching in a closet with a poor girl who has been made the instrument of deception.

Waltz, flustered and frightened, snarls at Mire, "I promise you, we *will* find him, Mr Mire."

Sometimes, the direct approach is the only way. I am heir to the Edgeland empire, and I've had enough of hiding.

I stand, ignoring Polly's clawing hands at my coat. I push open the closet door and step into the light.

"It appears you have found him," I say.

Both men turn, agog.

Mire's face warps into any number of practised masks designed to appease, charm, intimidate, shifting between one and the next. Then he must realise the futility of further deception and settles his face into its natural expression, that of utter contempt.

"John, you're up and about, how marvellous."

Waltz has fallen back and is gripping the desk behind him.

Polly steps out behind me.

Waltz gasps, then roars, "You little bitch!"

God bless her, the girl sticks out her chin, holds herself up and stares him down. "Doctor," she says, ladling the word with sarcasm.

Mire moves to place himself between us and the door. "Well, John, what are you going to do now? You've already signed across the ownership and management of the firm to me, acknowledging your lack of fitness for the task. Will you not seek the support of these good doctors in treating you for your illness?"

The room shifts a little under my feet. The medicine is still in me, making the walls swim a little. I glance at the heavy portraits on the walls and see the faces move, shifting, turning like snail shells. It's as if the founding investors are moving closer for a better look, leaning in from their windows.

"If that treatment involves them drugging me and driving me half mad, if it involves them threatening this girl, and breaking my fingers to extract my signature, then I'll politely decline, Herbert."

He smiles. "So what is it you want, then? You have been

clear that you despise everything your father and I worked for. I won't stand by and watch you piss your father's legacy away. He might have thought that you were redeemable over time but I'm not sure I have the patience and faith to find out. You've fallen too far from the tree, my boy. Time to kick you into the long grass."

I wobble a little. God, it's hot in here.

"Hand over the contract and perhaps we'll find a way to bury all this. There is still the chance of a position for you, Mire. If you turn it over to me now."

Mire's eyes flash. "A chance of a position? For me? You cosseted little brat! I was running this business for most of your life. Do you think your father, senile and weak as he was, could grasp what he'd created? Oh, he was a fine mill owner to be sure and had the hunger for the game, but what he started I grew to a point it was quite beyond him. You, him, no one can contemplate the scale of this firm now. It is everywhere and I am everywhere. I sleep four hours every night. I work every minute I'm awake. This firm is mine, even without the contract you willingly signed. I deserve every penny this business earns. I've already paid for it with sweat and blood."

"It's time for a change," I say. "I'm letting you go. You no longer have a position."

At this, he laughs, throwing his head back. "You have no say in that, you have no say in anything. You've signed to that effect."

I feel sick. The room is pitching and it's all I can do to stay vertical.

"What about this girl's testimony?" I say, and all eyes turn to Polly. "What about when she testifies that you kept me here against my will, fed me drugs, tortured me and tried to drive me insane?"

Polly, suddenly pinned by their gaze, gives a curt little nod. Her eyes are hard and determined. She is my anchor.

"Who is going to believe some silly chambermaid, when there are eminent doctors to deny her story?" says Mire, smirking. "Besides, I'm sure Dr Strangler has more than one available room up at his asylum. I hear that some of the treatments there can be quite brutal, simple and permanent."

I've heard enough. I advance on him, my good fist clenched, wanting to smash that snide face of his.

I hear a click behind me.

Looking back, I see Waltz has his pistol out, cocked and pointed at Polly's head. She's shaking, trying to be brave.

"I think, Mr Edgeland," Waltz says, "we've had quite enough heroics for one night. It may be better if you both come with us and await the return of the good Dr Strangler."

CHAPTER 51

"Not in here," says Waltz, nodding Mire towards the door, "the bathhouse is empty and quiet. We won't have an audience. We can keep them there until Strangler and his men arrive."

Mire nods and smiles at me. "John, come quietly, won't you? You don't want this girl to get hurt."

I raise my hands and back away from Waltz. Polly shuffles over to me and we go, my arm around her, out of the study with Mire and Waltz following.

"Put your damned hands down," hisses Waltz at me as we step into the light of the lobby. I chance a look back at him, but he has stowed the pistol in his pocket.

The night manager's desk is unattended. I stay quiet and lead the way out of the main entrance and into the night.

"If you run, I'll put a bullet in you," says Waltz quietly, shoving me in the direction of the bathhouse.

"It's not all over for you, Waltz," I say. "If you let us go now, I can invest, be a silent partner in the hydro. You'll never have any concerns for its solvency again."

"Be quiet, John," says Mire, "you have already invested,

didn't you know? That was the second document I just signed."

Polly is shivering, and not from the cold. Her face is bleached white, her eyes frightened. I have brought her to this end. This poor girl has risked so much to save me. I think about what Strangler and his men will do to her at his hospital. I wonder who will care.

Ahead, the bathhouse is dark. The trees shake and dance. It's still some hours from dawn.

Waltz strides ahead, jingling the keys in his hand. Reaching the door, he checks around and unlocks it.

"Damn," he says, "I should have brought a lantern."

The door opens and he steps inside, there is a sputter and a flare as he lights a match, sending light crawling across the walls, illuminating his jowled face in chiaroscuro.

"In," says Mire, putting his palm between my shoulder blades and pushing.

I turn and slap his hand away. He raises a finger before my face like a school teacher admonishing a child. Then, with a deliberately slow movement, he presses the end of his finger to my nose, crushing it against the cartilage till again I slap it away.

He smiles, safe in the knowledge that Waltz has his pistol.

"In," he says again.

We comply and step into darkness.

Waltz leads us through the vaulted corridor, our footsteps echoing off the marble arches. The match dies and Waltz strikes another. I wonder, as he does, if this is my moment to attack. His hand is off the gun. I brace myself ready but then the match flares and his hand returns to his pocket.

Besides, Mire is right behind me, and I am still weak from the medicine. I'm not sure I could take both of them.

"Is there somewhere we can lock them?" says Mire.

"There is," says Waltz, "this room down here should be

fine. There's no way they can be heard back at the hotel."

We arrive at a heavy door, which he unlocks and pushes open.

He turns to me. "You'll be quite safe here, Mr Edgeland, until Dr Strangler returns. I suggest you both make your-selves comfortable and don't cause any more fuss. You must see that it's futile."

Then he grabs my sleeve and shoves me in, throwing Polly in behind me. Before I can turn to confront him, the door slams shut and the lock clicks.

We are in darkness.

I sense Polly next to me, hear her breath, feel her warmth.

"Are you alright?" I say.

"Well, not really," she replies. "I can't see a thing... wait."

The moon must have emerged from behind a cloud because suddenly there is a light above us. There is an arched window in the ceiling and through it, a faint silvery trickle of light streams down, gently hinting at our surroundings as our eyes adjust to the dark.

We are in one of the treatment rooms. Pipes are running along the walls.

I pass a hand over my face. My legs are weak.

"It's the pressure chamber room," I say.

"There's no other way out," says Polly, "and no one will be coming here until long after we're gone in the morning."

The door to the room is locked and the window is too high.

I step across the fretted moonlit floor to the tank and run my hand across its steel carapace, feeling the cold knobs of the rivets against my palm.

I wonder when I will finally be free of hallucinations.

"Looks like we are stuck, then," I say, sinking onto the floor with my back against the tank. Polly comes over and sits beside me.

"How is your hand?" she says.

"Utterly goosed," I say, "but it's bearable as long as I don't knock it. It's probably the least of our problems now."

She doesn't say anything for a while. Then she asks in a quiet voice, "What do you think they'll do to me?"

"Best not to think about it, Polly, but it doesn't look good. We'll have to rush them or something when they return."

God, I'm tired. I feel like I could sleep for days.

"But they're bringing orderlies from the hospital. I've seen them at work before, Sir. My dad was in there for a while after my mum died. They deal with lunatics every day, I don't think you and I will be any kind of problem. Chances are they'll have restraints ready and waiting for us if we try to escape."

She begins to sob. "I just wanted to look after my family, Sir. I'm sorry for everything I did."

"But Polly, you saved me. If it wasn't for you, I'd be on my way there now."

"No. No. If it wasn't for me, you'd be home in London or wherever. It's all my fault."

I ask why.

"They made me drug you. They said it was for your own good. All the time I was caring for you, they were trying to drive you mad, to get you to sign. I just made everything worse. I've been a liar. I fed you that medicine before you were confined to the room. I tricked you into staying here. If it wasn't for me, you could have taken the train back home and none of this would have happened. The worst of it is I knew, I knew in my bones they were up to no good with you, but all I could see was the money, and the pride I had that I, stupid, useless Polly Hardacre, had been lifted up to do something different. I'd been trusted with something that meant I was better than the rest of the girls."

"Did you know their plan?"

She shakes her head, sniffing.

"Then you're innocent of everything apart from trying to help a man in distress, Polly. I don't think any the less of you. How could I?"

I hug her, feeling her sobs against my shoulder.

Then, realising how close we've become, we separate and sit back against the tank again, listening to our breath in the darkness.

Eventually, she turns to me again. "Sir. If you don't mind me asking, what was it like all those days you were in my care? Do you remember any of it?"

I shudder. "Some," I say, "a lot of it is like a dream. I remember a girl, obsessing about her. Did that come out?"

She laughs. "Oh, yes. It certainly did."

"And I remember a long nightmare about Blackmoor, you know, the town over the moor. Very strange it was too. I must have seemed half mad."

"Not half," she says with a grim laugh.

"I wonder what it was all about," I say.

"You know, the girl had a name."

"Did she? I forget."

"Lavinia."

I stop short. That name. Not the one I was expecting to hear. I remember screaming for Isabella when they were hurting me in the room. Remember seeing her standing next to me, bleeding. But Lavinia? What was that?"

Then I remember.

Oh, God, my poor girl.

"One night at the theatre, I saw her on stage, it was *Titus Andonicus*, not my usual thing. Isabella was playing Lavinia and towards the end of her first speech, I swear she gave a smile.

"She lit up the theatre and I knew I was in love.

"I went back every night that week, sitting in the front

row, and on the third night, she saw me, recognised me from the previous night and looked curious. It's an odd thing to be recognised from the stage, it's as if a barrier between two worlds has fallen away.

"The night after that, I sat in the same place and she saw me again and when it came time for her to finish her speech, she spoke directly to me, our eyes joined and the whole of London was lit up with fireworks.

"It wasn't an infatuation, you understand, Polly, it was more like recognition, as if we had known each other before, or there was a bond between us which existed which neither of us could understand.

"I went round to the stage door with a posy, like any other adoring devotee, aware of how pathetic I was. When she came out, she gave me a look as if she had been expecting me and we simply walked and talked together like a married couple. I can't explain it. There was no courtship, you understand, we simply became man and wife instantly. The actual wedding itself was a formality.

"There was something about her, a blithe lack of concern for anything remotely practical. It was a wonder she survived in the world. She earned a pittance at the theatre, and truth be told wasn't even that great an actress. She'd been raised in the East End by an honest, hard-working mother, but had a talent for mimicry and accents. There was something vague and nebulous about her personality which allowed it to be filled with other characters. So she took to the stage.

"It was in India when she lost our child. She was never the same again. The poor girl just wanted to see her mother, who she had deserted out of love for me. But in my selfish pride, I wouldn't let us come back home.

"Then finally, one night, I found her in the tub. My shaving razor lay in a puddle on the floor next to the bath, stained with blood. I remember her hair floated around her like the petals of a flower. Her wrists were cut open.

"I shouted for help, for the khansama, but there was nothing that could be done. She slipped away in my arms and I watched the light that had lit up that London theatre die. All I could think was that it was me that had snuffed it out."

Polly takes my good hand and squeezes it.

"I've everything anyone could ever want in the world," I say, "things that people like Mire and Waltz are prepared to lie and even kill for. I suppose I should just get on with my life and stop whining about it. I've never had a day's hunger in my life. Not like you."

"But at least I've got a family that loves me, Sir."

"I can do so much with what I've been given. I can see that now. I can do things that would never, ever occur to the crows, to Mire, to my father. I can do good, Polly. I can do some good with this life. I just need to be able to live it."

"Well, you'd better crack on and get living then, Sir, because we've got an hour or so before they come for us and then it'll be all up."

"Call me John, please, Polly. I think we're beyond formality now."

"John, then," she smiles.

Then she stops and drops my hand.

"What's the matter?" I say.

She looks like she's been slapped.

"I've got an idea," she whispers.

"What?"

"About how to get away."

"Well, then," I say, "we'd better hear it."

"And if it doesn't work... if we die, well, it might be a better way to go."

CHAPTER 52

"W hat do you know about this chamber?" I say.

"Well," he says, "I believe it's a hyperbaric pressure chamber. These pipes pump pressured air into it. It's supposed to do something beneficial to the lungs but all it did for me was to make me faint."

"But it's sealed, and strong, yes?"

He nods, not understanding.

"These pipes," I say, "aren't just pressured air." I run to the rows of pipes running along the wall, my hand follows a thinner one and it reaches a gas tap. "There is a boiler in the bathhouse that's heated every day. It supplies the heat for the Calidarium and the sauna and lights the gas lamps in here. It's old, Mr Edgeland. They've replaced most of the old gas lamps in the hotel, but these..."

He joins me and runs his hand over the gas tap.

"About three years ago, there was an explosion at one of the houses on Brook Street," I say. "My dad said it was because someone had left the gas on, or there'd been a leak in one of the old lead pipes. He said there was no way he'd let anyone put gas in our house, which is a laugh because there's no way we could ever afford something like that. He said it's like having a bomb in your house."

"You think if we fill this room with gas, we can trigger some kind of explosion?" he says.

"If they come before dawn, they'll need lights, won't they?"

"And if we lock ourselves in the pressure chamber..."

"Exactly."

I can see in the gloom that he's smiling. "Polly, you are a remarkable individual. Why have they got you making up beds?"

"Just short-sightedness on their part, Mr Edgeland," I say. I fiddle with the gas tap and turn it on. There is a faint hiss and the familiar pungent smell of coal gas wafts across our faces.

"Cover your face," I say.

But Mr Edgeland is stepping back, following the pipes with his eyes. Then he picks something up from a table.

"Stand back," he tells me. I press my sleeve across my mouth and nose and watch as he goes back to the wall, carrying what looks to be one of the wooden clogs they make guests wear in here. He raises his arm and smashes it down on the pipes.

There's a great clang, then another, then another as he beats the pipes with the clog.

"Try the chair," I say.

He lifts it by the legs and swings it with all his might at the artery of pipes. There is an almighty crash and cold water starts spraying across the room.

"Wrong pipe!" I shout at him.

"No, it isn't," he says, covering his face with his sleeve.

Sure enough, we are swamped by a wave of coal gas.

I grab his sleeve and pull him to the pressure chamber. He

spins the wheel and opens the door. We clamber inside and swing the door shut behind us.

It's pitch black inside, but I can feel there is a wooden bench running around the perimeter of the tank. It's cramped but comfortable.

"We can't seal it from inside," he says, his voice echoing off the steel walls. "We'll have to hope the door is enough to stop the gas from coming in, otherwise we'll be poisoned."

There are some vestiges of the gas in the room, but it doesn't seem to be getting any worse.

"I think we're safe," I say.

We look at each other, both thinking the same thing. This is not, by any sane definition, safe.

"What if they don't bring light with them?" he says.

"Then we're no worse off than we were before." I check the porthole in the door. "Besides, it's still a couple of hours till dawn, and it's dark in the bathhouse. If they don't smell it first and are warned off. What do we do now?"

"I suppose we just sit and wait."

And so we sit on opposite sides of the tank on the benches, listening to the muffled sound of the water swilling across the floor outside.

"Do you think we'll have enough air?" I say.

"I think that'll come in through a separate pipe, through this grille," he says. "I can't smell gas. I think it's clean."

"I wish I knew what time it was."

We try to make ourselves comfortable. Somehow sleep catches up with me and I feel myself bobbing off on its waves, but something in me is tethered to the waking world, and as soon as I feel myself straining at its rope, it jerks me awake with a little tug.

I wonder what Mr Edgeland is thinking, sitting over there in the darkness.

"How is your hand?" I say, more to make conversation than anything.

He doesn't answer, and I wonder if he has slipped back into a dream himself. I hear his soft breathing in the darkness.

I realise that if I am to die now, it won't be all bad. I've tried to do the right thing, to have a good heart.

Outside, the noise of the water has stopped and I wonder if it has passed the level of the pipe. I don't want to stand to look out of the porthole in case I wake Mr Edgeland. If the water isn't leaking out of the room, I reason, the gas might not either.

I nod off again, and when I snap awake, I see that some time must have passed. The light at the little round window is paler. Dawn is coming.

Oh, God, I hope they get here soon, otherwise, this might all be for nothing.

I stand and Mr Edgeland, visible now, stirs, wiping his eyes. It's stuffy in here.

Wiping away the condensation, I can see the chamber clearly in the weak light.

Suddenly I hear something. I look at the door to the room and think I see the doorknob turn.

I throw myself at Mr Edgeland, burying my head in his shoulder as, at the same time, he realises what's happening and pushes us both to the ground, curling himself around me to protect me.

Nothing happens.

Then the world ends.

CHAPTER 53

I come to, wondering how long I've been in bed. Then I realise that the weight of Samuel against me isn't Samuel at all. It's Mr Edgeland's arm.

There is a howling gale in my ears.

We are covered in bits of glass. Some shards are sticking into him, their punctures marked with little pools of blood.

Outside, a thousand miles away, I hear masonry fall.

I open my eyes, grit makes me blink, and tears stream. There's dust in the air, settling on us, settling across the shards of glass, soaking up the blood.

I try to sit and in moving wake Mr Edgeland, who groans, then cries out. He is hurt. I push myself up on one elbow.

The door to the pressure chamber has blown open, bent slightly like a roughly opened can of food. There is more light outside the chamber, more than could have come in from the little window alone. There's another muffled crash above the ringing in my ears and the light brightens. The ceiling must be falling in.

I check Mr Edgeland, he is coming to, looking down at

G.H. LUSBY

his bloodied arms. I help him up and he says something, but I can't hear. I am deaf.

I struggle to my feet, the steel chamber is whole but battered, and through the warped gap in the doorway I can see the room beyond has been blasted and blacked, the bricks knocked through on one wall into the Calidarium beyond.

Dust floats in the air, coating everything with a creamy fog. I help Mr Edgeland up and I try to pluck out some of the more prominent bits of glass. He doesn't seem badly hurt, but, like me, he's dazed.

He gestures that we should try to leave.

We pull on the door but it is bent and stuck on its hinges. As we heave it back, bricks slide off the roof of the pressure chamber and clatter to the floor. One more yank and the door opens and we can look properly at the devastation beyond.

The walls have blown through on two sides, into the corridor, and the vaulted space of the Calidarium. The roof has caved in around the window and looks unstable. The grey dawn reaches in with arms of gauze. It catches on the dust and illuminates a waterlogged pool of rubble.

The pipes are blasted apart and water sprays in angry jets.

We climb across the rubble and then sink to our knees in cold water, wading through the filth in the direction of what used to be the door. It is completely gone, only a splintered hinge in the collapsed door frame. Then I see it.

There is a body there, half submerged in the water, clothes floating around it. Its limbs are loose and broken, like a thrown doll. The face is a mask of mangled, burnt flesh. The arm that sticks out of the rags is missing its hand.

A great cold fist of terror closes around my heart and lungs and squeezes the breath out of me.

I can't tell who it is. Perhaps one of the orderlies from Highroads.

312

We edge past it, trying not to look.

As we do, it moves and an agonised groan comes from somewhere inside its tangled body. Then it lies still again.

We clamber over a pile of collapsed brickwork and into the dark of the corridor. There is a fire somewhere in the bathhouse up ahead. It sends nightmarish flashes and flickers and fills the air with smoke. The building around us feels like it's settling, deciding on whether to collapse or not.

"We have to get out!" I shout at Edgeland, and he looks at me dumbly, then nods. He is as deaf as I am.

We struggle on, tripping over debris, supporting each other.

My foot touches something soft. I scream, it's another corpse. This one is unmistakable, it's Strangler. He has been blown in two, a terrible absence under the cavity of his rib cage. God knows where his legs are, perhaps under the rubble somewhere. What's left lies there still and covered in dust. His glasses are smashed, but somehow miraculously pinned to his face. There is a rent in his thin-haired scalp. I can see the white bone of his skull in the firelight and something soft beyond.

My hearing is starting to return. I hear the building groan and shift around us.

Edgeland grips my hand and we step gingerly over what's left of Strangler and pick our way along the corridor.

The groaning becomes a crash and a wall behind us collapses, sending up clouds of dust. We run, falling over ourselves, aiming for the pale shape of the doorway at the end of the corridor.

But it's too late, the walls are folding and falling around us, and a wooden beam crashes down behind, narrowly missing me. I'm hit on the shoulder by a tile, then another, and then a great torrent of masonry starts to avalanche down upon us.

Throwing our arms above our heads, we run, pell-mell towards the daylight.

I know that I'm not going to make it. Mr Edgeland is half carrying me. Debris hits us.

Rubble pours down either side and we make one final pelt for the doorway, bursting through it in a cloud of dust as the walls collapse either side and onto us. We lie, covered in dust and bricks, bruised and bleeding.

Then there are hands on me, lifting off the rubble, hoisting a beam off my legs, brushing the dust from my face. I feel strong arms under my shoulders and, with great heave, they drag me out from under the crushing pile.

"Oh, God, thank God, Polly, I've found you," comes a familiar voice.

I look up, blinking, into the dawn light and, in a daze, see that I've been pulled to safety.

By my dad.

CHAPTER 54

I press my face into Dad's chest and feel his arms around me.

Then he lets me go. "Help me, Pol. He's half buried."

Mr Edgeland's hand extends from the rubble. He is covered in dust, tiles and bricks. Together, my father and I pick the worst of it off him and haul him onto the lawn. Only when he is clear and stirring, wiping the dust from his face, do I get a chance to see what has become of the bathhouse.

Half the building has collapsed, and the other half is on fire. Great ribs of stone, the archways and buttresses from the Calidarium, stand stark and picked clean against the blue dawn. Flames lick the ruins and a pall of dust extends out over the lawns.

The fire has carried into the hotel itself and has caught in the south wing. The alarm has been raised, doubtless by the massive explosion, and guests are busy congregating on the lawn in front of the hotel in dressing gowns and nightclothes as staff run around, trying to organise some kind of effort to save the building.

"What are you doing here?" I ask Dad.

He looks at me with clear eyes. "I woke and found you gone, Pol. After our chat last night, I had a horrible feeling you'd come back here, so I came to look for you. I couldn't stand to lose you as well, my love."

I look around, panicking. "Where's Samuel?"

"He's with Nelly, don't you fret."

"Oh, Dad. They were going to take us both away, lock us up, we had to do something."

My dad looks around at the destruction, at the collapsed bathhouse and the flaming hotel. "I reckon you did something, Pol," he grins. "I'd hate to get on the wrong side of you."

Despite the pain, I manage a smile.

"There'll be plenty of time for you to tell me the tale later."

Mr Edgeland has managed to sit up, and then attempts to get to his feet. I take one arm and my dad takes the other and we heave him up, his legs buckling like a newborn deer.

"Mr Edgeland, this is my father, Edmund Hardacre," I say.

He looks up, face bruised, eyes bleary and manages a watery smile, then he extends his unbroken hand and shakes my dad's. "Your daughter is a remarkable woman, Sir. If it wasn't for her, we'd both be dead."

"Aye, she's a good girl, Sir. But she has a vindictive streak, as you'll have noticed. You've been in the wars a bit, haven't you? We can't offer you much, but you're welcome to come back to our cottage and recover yourself until your people come for you. Now, it might be good to make ourselves scarce and avoid too much questioning."

Edgeland removes our hands and attempts to balance on his own two feet, then he takes in the ruin around us.

"Over there!"

He hobbles through the dust and smoke to a twisted pile

of rags on the ground. He stands over it, silhouetted against the flames, then kicks it gently as if to stir it to life. It's still.

I make to walk over to see but he holds up a warning hand.

"Stay there. It's Mire. You don't want to see this, Polly, or you, Sir."

He returns, shaking his head. "Thank God. It's over," he says.

I hear shouts from behind us.

The main body of the hotel is on fire. Guests and staff are retreating to the safety of the tree line. The fire wagon from the village has finally arrived, but the volunteers are overwhelmed and there's nothing a few buckets of water can do to stop the blaze.

Fire eats into the bones of the buildings and huge cliffs of black smoke rise.

"We should go and help," I say. "We need to make sure everyone got out."

"I'm not sure anyone's going back into there now," says my dad, "but you're right, we should go see if anyone needs care. Jesus, what a mess. Look at these bloody idiots, they're going to be in trouble if it falls. Come on!"

We set off, hobbling down the path towards the front of the hotel, and as we do, we see another figure standing watching the blaze. Although his back is to us, I recognise his bulk immediately.

I hiss at Mr Edgeland, "Waltz!"

Dr Waltz's hair has been burned off, right down to the scalp, which is raw and bloody. His clothes too are badly burned, but he seems calm enough, standing watching his life's work go up in an inferno.

We approach with caution, Edgeland leading, followed closely by my father.

He hears our footsteps and turns.

God, his face. He is badly burned, swollen, red and wet. His eyes are so puffed, it looks like he's wearing a charred mask. One of his ears is gone completely.

He looks at us, mute, and watches as we walk around him, giving him as wide a berth as possible. He is still, dumb, and confused.

Then, as we hurry on our way, we hear his voice, charred and weak.

"You've destroyed me," he croaks.

My fury goes up, Lord knows where I get the energy from, but I'm seething. Everything that we've had to endure over the last few weeks, all this death and suffering. All this comes from this man's weakness. "No, Sir. You did this, you did it and there's no getting away from that!"

I stride towards him, fists balled, chin out. "Are you happy now, Doctor? You'd put this man and me in an asylum, or have us killed, and for what? For this pile of rubble? Go to hell!"

Waltz bellows back, "You did this."

He raises his arm. He points the pistol directly at me.

He squeezes the trigger. I shut my eyes and brace myself.

There is a crack as the gun fires. Then I feel an impact, a punch to the chest that knocks me off my feet.

The world somersaults and then goes black.

CHAPTER 55

When I wake, I realise only seconds have passed. I am lying on my back, looking at the clouds of smoke foaming across the sky. The grass is soft under my head. There is a crushing weight across my chest. I look up and see Mr Edgeland lying on top of me. He is still and lifeless.

Panicking, I scramble up, my breath coming in little gasps.

Waltz stands over us both, still holding the gun.

My dad is approaching him, hands outspread, talking calmly. "Now, Doctor, there's still a chance for you, don't you do anything else you're going to regret, Sir. You've spent your whole life trying to heal people. Don't end it like this. You put that gun down, Sir."

Waltz looks at me and back at my father then seems to make his mind up.

"Dad!" I scream.

Waltz raises the gun, but instead of pointing its barrel at my father, he sticks it under his chin and pulls the trigger.

There is another crack, and simultaneously he falls

straight down like a severed marionette, legs buckling and splaying beneath his bulk. He lands somehow still sitting up, slumped and loose, head lolling. It's cracked open through the top like a boiled egg, spilling grey yolk. There is no blood that I can see.

Then it comes, streaming out through his mouth and nose as he starts to drain off.

I manage to sit up, shift Mr Edgeland off my chest, and roll him over.

He has been shot in the arm. Blood soaks his shirt and through into his jacket. He is unconscious, but, thank God, he has a pulse.

My dad helps me get free of him and we do our best to stanch his wound, pressing it down. I tear off a strip of my dress and we make a tourniquet, patching him up as best we can. He wakes, crying out in pain, his face contorting, in the same way I saw through the keyhole as he was tortured.

"It's alright, Mr Edgeland," I say. "I think the bullet didn't lodge in you. Rest a moment."

He looks up at me. "Are you hurt?" he says.

"No. No, you saved me, Sir. Thank you." Quite unlike me, I feel tears of gratitude spring in my eyes and I turn into a blubbering mess.

He reaches out and touches my hand. I can't say what, but something passes between us.

"Will you please stop calling me Mr Edgeland, Polly," he whispers, "and you can forget about getting any kind of tip after the rotten holiday I've had."

There is a mighty crash behind us and the central wing of the hotel collapses. There is a cheer from the crowd, who now seem resigned to watching the spectacle rather than doing anything to stop the blaze. Most of the town seems to have come out to watch the show. Children are laughing and running around on the lawn. The local bobby, Sergeant

Cummings, looks completely at sea and has resorted to trying to hold the crowd back, shouting at them to stay out of the range of the burning timbers. They completely ignore him. Whitmoor hasn't had a show like this in years.

"Should we go and help?" Edgeland says.

There don't look to be many casualties, apart from a couple of the older guests who are being cared for by Hubbard and her girls. Sooner or later, though, someone is going to find these bodies up here, and there'll be some explaining to be done.

"I think they're fine," I say. "Besides, you were supposed to have left here a couple of weeks ago. I think we can do without the questions. Come on, Dad," I say, "we need to get away while we can." Then I stop short.

"What is it?" says my dad.

"Maureen," I say, "she saw us." Then I consider for a moment. "I think it'll be fine. After all, who'd believe the story of a silly chambermaid?"

"Wait," says Edgeland, mastering his pain a little and staggering to his feet. He lurches over to Waltz's still sitting corpse and delves into the dead man's inside pocket. He pulls out a crumpled, bloodstained piece of paper.

"Open it, Polly," he says. "I can't."

I take it from him and unscrew it, flattening it out as best I can. Tight lines of script march across the page. At the bottom are four signatures, one of which is J. Edgeland, signed in a desperate, spidery scrawl.

My dad reads it over.

"I'm no lawyer, Mr Edgeland, but I reckon this is your agreement to sign over the ownership of all your interests to a trust, managed and owned by one Herbert Mire, who I'm guessing is that deceased gent lying up there at the bathhouse."

Edgeland nods. "There's another sheet."

My dad opens the second page and again skims over it. "And this cedes ownership of the Cragside Hydropathic Establishment to the trust and guarantees certain payments to Doctors Waltz and Strangler. Quite large payments, by the looks of it." He hands the paper back. "I think you've had a very lucky escape, Mr Edgeland. I never realised having a fortune could be so dangerous. I think if you'd gone with Strangler, you'd have ended up having a nasty accident before too long."

The sun is up, spreading a burnished light through the smoke across the moor. Men are working in rows, beating back the flames before they catch the heather.

The north wing of the hotel collapses, sending panicked screams up from the crowd. Everyone scampers another twenty feet or so away from the fire.

Mr Edgeland takes the papers, screws them up and throws them. They are carried on a breeze and land in a pile of burning timber. The flames catch and the papers curl and fragment, sparks spiralling up like fireflies into the morning air.

CHAPTER 56

And so, yet again, I find myself being nursed back to health, for a few weeks at least.

In the aftermath of the events at Cragside, I try to maintain my anonymity. I stay at first at the Hardacres' little cottage, a poor place that it is. They open their house to me and I fear I take up far too much room in it. The doctor is certainly bemused when he visits and finds a stranger there who pays with such large notes.

Most afternoons, I sit in front of their little stove, dozing, letting the poison I've been fed leave my blood, letting the wound in my shoulder slowly knit. It is a painful process and the former is by far the hardest.

I still have nightmares, and am plunged into the depths of the horrors I experienced. Every time I wake, I expect to find myself tied to the bed in the hydro, and see my persecutors standing over me. I see the face of that mutilated girl when I blink, imagine her standing across the room from me, her mouth open in horror, her severed tongue exposed.

Sometimes I doubt my reality, thinking that I am in a

dream inside a drugged nightmare. It's only the presence of the stuff of normal life around me, the drying washing, the bustle of the family, that grounds my fancy and stops me from being dragged down by it.

I crave the medicine, becoming irritable and cold in its absence. I pine for liquor to fill the void. I am guilt-ridden for any distress I have caused these good people. Great waves of emotion creep up on me, almost knocking me over with their ferocity.

I find memories of my Isabella surfacing at the strangest moments. I've kept them down for too long and they refuse to be contained anymore. I am rocked by tears some days and don't try to hide them, feeling their hot salt flush me out. Other times I reflect, staring at the stove in the early hours while the Hardacres sleep, letting my feelings finally unfurl like a tightly bound flag given air, discovering its colours for the first time.

Mr Hardacre is also trying to rid himself of demons. He is similarly brittle. Together we make a fine pair, exhausted and emotional but sanguine about our futures. We spend long hours talking and I learn about his former life as a schoolmaster, a respected man in the community brought low. He had sought to tamp down his grief with spirits and in letting them do their work, they took him down with it. He tells me that the love of his family is the silver ladder he needs to climb back, that he is already looking back down with new clarity at how far he has come.

We agree after a few days that life without the nullifying shade of our private medications is terrifying in its brightness. That the only way forward is to face the sun, blinking and naked, and walk forward out of the shadow into the hard light.

I watch Polly with her little brother, Samuel, a quiet,

sensitive boy who reminds me of myself. There is a softness beneath her brusque manner with him. The child knows that he is secure and loved, even in the face of a hard Yorkshire ticking off. Mr Hardacre, too, reads to him, plays the fool. Over time, I too find myself reading to the boy, playing silly guessing games that I'd previously have found inane but now find comfort. The boy, in payment, raises smiles in all of us that help with our healing. I am glad to use my money to feed him properly for the first time in his life and watch colour bloom in his pale cheeks, and flesh grows on his thin bones as the days go on.

Poor Polly. Yet again, she is forced to be a nursemaid. As I recover, I become more helpful, and Mr Hardacre, I sense, puts a lot more effort into the house in atonement for years of neglect. She is bruised and cut but has bright new steel within her. She is a constant marvel to me. How can such a slight frame contain such bravery, such goodness of heart? She deserves better than this meagre life.

I briefly consider asking for her hand, but I've already caged and killed one poor girl. I can't let that happen again. Not yet.

My final confession to Waltz, however extracted, was from the heart.

I'm grateful to him for that.

I determine, though, that I will do my best to help her in some way, once I return to the world.

THAT DAY COMES EARLIER THAN I HOPE.

One morning, there is a knock at the door. I'm on my own in the cottage and open it to find a man with a thick grey moustache in a travelling coat.

"Mr Edgeland, isn't it?"

I hesitate for a moment and then realise the game is up. I reach out and shake his hand, feeling suddenly very self-conscious in my shirt sleeves.

"My name is Parker," says the man. "I've been engaged by your family. I've been trying to find you. I'm very sorry to have to disturb you here, but there are a lot of people wondering and worrying about your well-being, Sir."

"I'm surprised it's taken this long to find me," I say.

"Well," and for a moment the man looks slightly embarrassed, "I've only been on the case for a week. I think before that, they assumed you'd gone off on a flit for a few weeks, you know, to get away after your father's... well, you know."

"I do. I understand, Mr Parker. I have been staying with this family since the Cragside Hydro burned down. I'm sure you've heard about that."

Parker nods. "Indeed, I thought for a nasty couple of days that you'd been lost in the fire, Sir. It was a bit of a job to track you down. Are you quite well, Sir? People have been very concerned."

I smile. "I'm sure they have. I think it's time I moved back into a hotel for a few days. As you can see, I was injured in the fire." I point to the bandages wrapping my arm.

Parker raises an eyebrow. "Yes, Sir. It was talking to the doctor that led me here. He'd treated a stranger with what he'd thought was a gunshot wound."

"Not at all. It was a bit of falling masonry."

"Of course, Sir."

"Parker, you are welcome to send a telegram to my people that I'm perfectly well and will be returning in a few weeks. In the meantime, I'll take lodgings in a hotel in town. I think I've imposed on these good people for long enough."

And with that, I close the door on his face. I slump back against it, feeling the world crashing in on me.

So I move into the Crescent Hotel. I take the suite and send for a tailor from Bradford to make me up some new suits. Parker is the first of several visitors I have over the following weeks. There is a succession of family members and employees who make the journey north, not able to wait for me to come to them. All of a sudden, I am the most popular man in Whitmoor and I'm sure I become quite the talk of the town, holding court in the Crescent.

I send most of my visitors packing back to London as soon as they arrive. I am determined that I'm not going to be drawn into the web my father has spun for me.

Instead, I begin to draw up my plans.

I innocently ask about Mire, whether he can join me, but it appears that Mr Mire has also gone missing. Not been seen for weeks. When people look closer at his dealings, it tran- spires that he had been embezzling the firm for years, decades perhaps. I assume that he's fled the country with his ill-gotten gains. I decline the pleas from the family to hire detectives to hunt him down. There is too much other work to do.

They send his lieutenant, a fresh-faced young man called Housman, who has an eager mind and some vestiges of conscience still left in him. I spend hours with him in the hotel suite, cultivating his better nature, leaching a fuller understanding of my father's legacy and its tentacular extent. Together, we forge a plan to do some good in the world.

It won't be easy, we both acknowledge that. There are many, many fingers in the family pie. It will take some time to prise them out, but it can be done. Then the real work of dismantling the whole bloody enterprise can start. There are better uses for the vast capital the Edgeland empire has accrued. We won't make many friends in the process, and we will doubtless get fleeced regularly, but we agree that it will be a small price to pay.

ONE OF THE MORE SURPRISING THINGS THAT COME TO light as Housman and I chart the labyrinth of interests is that I turn out to own Blackmoor! My father and Mire had pressured the previous owner, Mr Stone, to sell the mill there the day before my father's death.

On a whim, I take a carriage around the bulk of the moor to visit the town and see Mr Stone. On my descent into the town, I feel a familiar tension wrench my shoulders and neck. I wonder how much the town will meet the image of my nightmares.

It is quite pleasant to find that, rather than being the grim hell on earth I expect it to be, the place is relatively clean, well run and progressive in its approach. Mr Stone has been kept on as a minority shareholder and manager of the mill and is pleased to show me around, particularly as he discovers I am not cut from the same cloth as my father. I see the work he has tried to do, bettering the lives of his workers, and building a hospital and a church.

The place is entirely different to the version in my imagination. I'm particularly relieved to find that the streets are not named after fallen angels at all but after his children.

"Cynics might say I'm just trying to keep the workers pliant, but I think I've got a higher purpose than that, Sir," he says as he proudly shows me around the park he has planted. "Most of these families have come down from the Dales, they've been living on nothing but potatoes and porridge when they could even get that. Here at least they have regulated working hours, hot food, and leisure time at the weekend. It's more than most of them have ever dreamed of."

I nod. "And education? For their children?"

"We were just finishing building the school when your father bought me out. He put a stop to that, unfortunately. It's my biggest regret, Mr Edgeland."

He shows me the half-built school house, a sad shell.

An idea begins to form.

CHAPTER 57

The day finally comes when it's time for Mr Edgeland to take his leave of us, and return to his life. Autumn has come to Whitmoor and there's a chill in the air. Leaves rasp across the pavement as I take my last walk over to the Crescent Hotel to see him.

There is no business for him today, he has made sure that Housman and his other attendants have gone on ahead with their instructions. He said he wanted time to pack and think before heading back to London.

But wants to see me.

Since he moved into the hotel, we've seen much less of him. Samuel in particular has missed his silly songs, but I've told the boy that Mr Edgeland has serious business to take care of now, grown-up things. I've pretended to my dad that I'm not that fussed about his absence, but in my heart, I've missed him too.

Mind you, it's good to have a bit of room back.

I go straight up to his door and knock. He opens it immediately, as if he's been waiting.

"Hello, Pol, come in, come in."

I shuffle in and he pulls a chair up for me. This feels very formal. I don't know how to behave around him anymore. When he was in our cottage, he was one of the family. Now he's suited and strange, full of ledgers and plans. But there's hope and excitement in his eyes, a world away from that lost man I met at the hydro.

He paces up and down, then, scratching his head, sits opposite me.

"I've wondered for a while how to ask you this, Pol, without it seeming presumptuous, but I want to do something to help your father... and you."

I bristle a little with injured pride and then remember that we are in sore need of help. Now the hydro is gone, reduced to blackened bones, there's no work for me, and my dad, for all his newfound sobriety, is still doing what work he can at Hag Farm and that's not nearly enough. Once our rich benefactor is gone, we'll be hungry again.

"You don't have to, you know."

"Codswallop," he says. "I wouldn't be here without you both, especially you, and you're not going to be a bloody martyr. You'll get what you're given and smile, and like it."

I have to laugh. "You've been spending too much time with Yorkshire folk, Mr Edgeland."

He grins back, and things thaw again between us. He leans forward and says, "You know I sold Blackmoor back to Mr Stone, at less than my father paid him for it?"

"I'd heard, he must be very happy about that."

"You can't imagine. I do retain a significant share in it, but what good is a mill without a workforce, and what good is an uneducated workforce? They've got a school they're building over there, a decent one, it was a condition of my sale that they go through with it. I'd like your father to be Headmaster. Do you think he'd be interested?"

My heart turns over. "Oh, God, you'd do that for him? Oh, John, that's wonderful."

"You'll need to move over there, but there's a good-sized house with the position that's standing idle. It has a lovely garden with apple trees. Sounds like a good place for little Samuel to run around. He'll have his work cut out for him, mind. Lessons to write, other teachers to hire. A budget to manage. What do you think?"

I clasp his hands. It's not in my nature to be grateful, but this is more than I could ever have wished for.

"He will need other teachers, Polly. Do you think..."

"Yes. I'd love to."

I don't know what I thought when I came over here. Part of me had some faint hope, and dread, that he'd ask me to marry him. I know that's not the life for me.

Still, along with the excitement and joy of this offer, there is a part of me sinking inside. This is goodbye, then.

"There's one more thing... John," I say.

I don't know why I've held this back for so long. I reach into the pocket of my skirt and pull out the picture frame.

"I... took this from your room. I thought you would want it back. I should have done it before, I'm sorry."

He pales, takes the frame from me and stares into the velvet blank where the picture should be. Then he takes a juddering breath and places it, face down, on the desk. For a second, I see the drawn, haunted man from the hydro. Then the cloud passes, he looks at me and smiles, whole again.

He is all packed, what little remains, in a new shiny black leather trunk. A porter wheels it on a trolley up to the train station and we walk ahead, arm in arm. I get glances from all around as we saunter up Station Road. I don't care what any of them think now. It's petty nonsense, the lot of it.

"Has your stay been everything you were hoping for?" I ask, my eyebrow arched.

"Oh, much better. I didn't know the cures here at Whit-moor were so thorough," he says. "I can't say I'll be recom-mending it, though."

We arrive at the station and wait on the platform. There are a few other travellers, mainly tourists and gentlemen farmers heading for Bradford. We distance ourselves from them, enjoying our few remaining moments together.

He has gone shy again, rubbing his chin. "I can't tell you, Polly, how much I... how much you have done for me. I wish there was some way... You know how I..."

I reach up, wrapping my arms around his neck. Pressing my mouth to his cheek, I whisper, "We both know that's not going to work. You've got a new life, and so do I."

He holds me tight. "I will come back, Pol. I can't say goodbye like this. I'll come back in the spring, once my affairs are set in order. I'll come and see you in your new house on the other side of the moor. If I may?"

I pat his cheek. "Any time, you are always welcome."

The train arrives and the passengers disembark. He gives me another kiss, on the cheek, and drags his trunk behind him up into the first-class carriage.

Then, too soon, it lets out a blast of steam and begins to chug away.

I watch his face, young and hopeful, as the great metal creature crawls down the track until steam and smoke cover him and he disappears into the distance, pulled away from me by the machine.

Then, all I have left is my faith in him, and that, for now, is enough.

ACKNOWLEDGMENTS

No book is the product of one person and this is no exception. Hydro was written over several years, stopping and starting, re-writing and re-arranging. It started as a short story for the Leeds Savages writing group and then, over time, grew organically as it burrowed into my mind. At some point in the rewrites, I got sober.

I'd like to thank Gavin Sinden and Pete Etherington for enduring early drafts and giving me feedback.

Thank you to Natalie Peatfield for being a lighthouse and truth-seeker in both writing and life, and for her incisive notes.

Thank you to Cecily Blench from The History Quill for insightful editing and for helping me, and the Victorians in the book, rediscover Lavinia and Titus Andronicus. Thanks to Alisha from E-Book Launch Cover designs for nailing exactly what I wanted.

Most of all thank you to my wife Emma for her love and support, for putting up with me crawling out of bed at five-thirty every morning and for always being my first and most important reader.

ABOUT THE AUTHOR

G.H. Lusby got lost in Bradford Industrial Museum as a child. The horror of the machines stayed with him. He lives in the shadow of Ilkley Moor and when he's not writing, working or washing up, spends his time wandering among the heather, the grouse and the ancient stones.

Hydro is his first novel.

Printed in Great Britain
by Amazon

39919214R00199